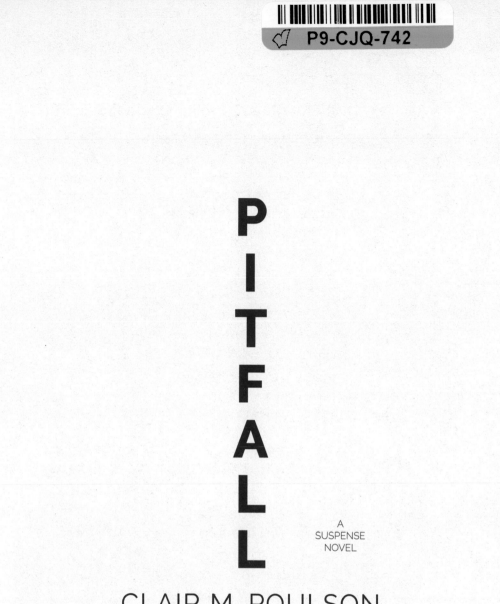

PITFALL

A
SUSPENSE
NOVEL

CLAIR M. POULSON

OTHER BOOKS AND AUDIO BOOKS
BY CLAIR M. POULSON:

I'll Find You
Relentless
Lost and Found
Conflict of Interest
Runaway
Cover Up
Mirror Image
Blind Side
Evidence
Don't Cry Wolf
Dead Wrong
Deadline
Vengeance
Hunted
Switchback
Accidental Private Eye
Framed
Checking Out
In Plain Sight
Falling
Murder at TopHouse
Portrait of Lies
Silent Sting
Outlawered
Deadly Inheritance
The Search
Suspect
Short Investigations
Watch Your Back
Fool's Deadly Gold

PITFALL

A
SUSPENSE
NOVEL

CLAIR M. POULSON

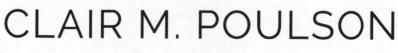

Covenant Communications, Inc.

Cover images: *Low Key Portrait of Evil Looking Man* © Dundanim, Shutterstock.com; *A Man Running at Sunset Followed by a Curious Crow* © Ollieevansphoto, Shutterstock.com; *Field Burning* © Mocker_labs, Shutterstock.com

Cover design by Kimberly Kay © 2020 by Covenant Communications, Inc.

Published by Covenant Communications, Inc.
American Fork, Utah

Printed in the United States of America
First Printing: February 2020

26 25 24 23 22 21 20   10 9 8 7 6 5 4 3 2 1

978-1-52441-124-4

To all those people who, like me, love the many
animals of the Blue Rock Ranch.

CHAPTER ONE

PITFALL: A HIDDEN OR UNSUSPECTED DANGER OR DIFFICULTY

SPARKY GRAVES WAS A LITTLE bit self-conscious about his name. *Sparky* was not a nickname. It was his actual given name. He'd like to have had a conversation with his mother or father about his name, but he couldn't. They had died in a horrendous car crash just a few weeks before his second birthday. His adoptive parents told him that—ironically—he would have died in that same crash if his parents had buckled him into his car seat.

They had both died instantly, he'd been told, while he presumably lay unconscious in tall, dry grass over a hundred feet away. There was a child's car seat in the backseat of the crumpled vehicle, but it appeared Sparky had not been in it. When they eventually found him, the police theorized that Sparky, unrestrained in the back seat, had flown out of the car when a back door came open.

The driver of the first vehicle that came on the scene of the winding, dirt backroad where the accident happened had called 911 and reported two dead people in the car. They didn't know when the accident had happened or if there had been other passengers. It wasn't until the bodies of the couple had been removed from the crumpled vehicle that an officer noticed the child's car seat tangled up in the wreckage. Panicked, the officers searched the vehicle for a child, but to their relief, they didn't find one. Being prudent officers, they searched the area around the car, thinking that maybe the baby, if there was one, had been thrown out. They then searched nearly a hundred feet from the wreckage in every direction.

Finally, satisfied that there was no baby or child to be found, that whichever child the car seat was for must have been with someone else—family or a babysitter perhaps—they completed the investigation. Measurements were made, photos taken, skid marks recorded. A careful calculation was made using the information they had gathered, and the speed of the car when it left the road on a gentle but bumpy curve was established at something near one hundred miles per hour. It had rolled an estimated ten times before finally stopping in a shallow depression filled with long grass and brush.

An empty bourbon bottle and several empty beer cans were found in the car and strewn along the road. Once a wrecker had removed the car, the scene was cleaned up, and the officers headed for their desks to write the reports.

No one could ever figure out where the couple—identified as Walt and Karma Piler—was headed when they met their violent deaths. Nor did they know why they were in rural Kansas driving on a backroad. Their license plates were from Connecticut, and the deceased persons' driver's licenses also gave a Connecticut address. Officers worked into the night attempting to locate next of kin but met with no success.

Officers in Connecticut went to the address printed on the driver's licenses. The house was empty, the back door hanging open. There was not even any furniture in it. Neighbors knew the couple but said they had left several weeks ago, that a large truck had been loaded with their belongings and had driven away. Not one person could say where the couple was moving to. They were described as unfriendly and discouraging of friendly overtures from neighbors. They had lived in the house for about a year, but no one knew where the husband worked or even what kind of work he did. They did say that he drank a lot, and they worried for his wife and little son. From time to time, they heard loud arguments coming from inside the house.

The young wife, neighbors told police, stayed at home and cared for their blond-haired baby boy and a large yellow cat that the boy seemed to love. She was not as unfriendly as her husband when he was not around, and when asked by a neighbor why they named the little boy Sparky, she'd said, "We were going to name him Walt, like his father, but the first time I looked at him in the hospital, it seemed like his eyes sparkled. So we decided to call him Sparky."

They also told the police that the woman never seemed to let the baby out of her sight, and none of them had ever been asked to babysit him. When that information was relayed to the police in Kansas, they charged back to the accident scene, having decided that there may have been a child in the car after all.

The road where the accident occurred was one that had very little use. But when the officers arrived there well after dark on that clear, moonlit summer night, there was an old Chevy pickup parked beside the road. Three teenage boys had shot a rabbit a short way from the accident scene.

One of the youth had heard what sounded like a baby crying up ahead somewhere, then a loud, anguished yowl. They had run up the road toward the sounds, all three of them carrying their rifles and flashlights. They admitted that they were scared. But the crying was so intense that they dared not leave the area without first investigating.

Following the sounds, they had come upon an implausible scene. A young child wearing nothing but a diaper, with cuts and bruises all over his little body, was sitting up in the dry grass, crying as loud as any of those three had ever heard. Beside the child was a large yellow cat. That was the source of the intense yowling.

When they approached, shining their flashlights, the cat stood facing them with its hair standing on end and green eyes glowing angrily from the lights they shined. It hissed and spit and they backed off.

One of the boys had pulled a cell phone from his pocket, but before he had time to make the call, they heard sirens in the distance.

The police officers, like the teenagers, were astounded at what they saw when they arrived. It was as if the large yellow cat was watching over the little orphan boy, protecting him from dangers real or perceived. It took the cops a while to get the cat to move aside so they could pick the distraught child up. An ambulance that had followed them to the scene soon sped for the nearest hospital with the little boy. The cat ran off into the grass and brush. No amount of calling by the officers brought it back. Upon their earlier inspection of the car, they had found an almost empty sack of dry cat food beneath a crumpled seat. The cat, now on its own in unfamiliar territory, had indeed been protecting the child.

It took a couple of days before a search by officers in Connecticut finally found a birth certificate that appeared to be that of the little boy, Sparky Piler, whose parents' names matched the names found with the dead couple.

The hospital kept the boy for two days for observation, but other than a number of minor cuts and bruises, he seemed perfectly healthy. The Kansas Department for Children and Families was called in and took guardianship of the child, placing him in a foster home while police continued to search for any living relatives. None were found. No address or any record of the couple could be found anywhere in Kansas or the surrounding states. Even moving companies in Connecticut seemed to know nothing of the Pilers' move.

The little boy cried a lot and continually asked for his mother and was often heard calling, "Kitty, Kitty." He was not quite two, but he knew a lot of words. Of course, he was not able to shed any light on where his parents were going or anything about them. Nor could he tell them anything about the cat, even though it was obvious that he missed it. All he could recall was riding in a car for a long time.

Eventually, little Sparky Piler accepted his foster parents, Donald and Sydney Graves. And within a couple of years, they adopted him and began to raise him as their own son. But it was a rocky road for Sparky. The older Graves son never fully accepted him. The brother, just two years older, was jealous of him, and behind their parents' back, he made life quite miserable for Sparky. That caused Sparky to be a moody, shy, and withdrawn child. He was courteous and kind to others, but in school, because of his shyness, he made very few friends, despite studying hard and doing quite well in his classes.

As he grew older and the years passed, tensions with Kal, the older brother, increased but never in the presence of their parents. Kal was sly and he was a good actor when it fitted his designs. One day when Sparky came home from school, Kal had arrived home first. Sparky was certain that neither of his parents were home, for their cars were gone. But he could hear someone in his parents' bedroom. His younger siblings always arrived a few minutes after the older kids, so he knew it wasn't them.

Sparky walked quietly to his parents' room. The door was open, and when he glanced in, he saw Kal rifling through one of the drawers in a desk in their room. He knew, and so did Kal, that his parents kept some money in there, mostly hundred- and fifty-dollar bills. He opened his mouth to tell Kal to put it back, but just then he heard his mother's car pull up outside.

Kal had several large bills in his hand. He turned to leave the room and saw Sparky standing there, watching him. The dark look of hatred that crossed Kal's face was one Sparky saw often but which his parents never witnessed nor believed existed. Kal raised his empty fist and pointed it threateningly at Sparky.

"Kal, Sparky, are you boys home?" their mother called the moment she stepped through the front door.

Kal looked at the money in his hand and then at Sparky. Suddenly he thrust the money at Sparky's feet and shouted, "In your room, Mom. I just caught Sparky stealing money from your desk."

"I did not!" Sparky cried in outrage as his mother came running. Kal stepped back, leaving the money at Sparky's feet.

"See Mom, there it is. He dropped it when he heard you come in the door."

Sparky's mother's hands flew to cover her mouth. And for a moment, she stared at the two boys. Kal repeated what he claimed to have seen. After a moment of indecision, disappointment filled her eyes. "Sparky, I can't believe you would do such a thing. Dad and I trusted you," she said.

"Mom, it was Kal. I caught him and then he threw it at me when you came in the house," Sparky objected, knowing that his protest was in vain. His parents always believed Kal.

For a brief moment, his mother again looked unsure, but then she made up her mind and said, "Sparky, go to your room. Your dad and I will decide what punishment to give you when he gets home."

Kal slipped past them and out of the room.

"Mom," Sparky started, "you gotta believe me. Kal always blames me. And you and Dad always believe him."

"Go to your room," she said. But once again, Sparky thought he saw a moment of doubt in her eyes.

Defeated again, Sparky left, knowing that any doubts his mother had would be quickly erased by his father. But he didn't go to his room. He went to Kal's. Kal was two years older than Sparky, but he was a lot shorter and lighter built. Sparky was especially strong for his age. In a fair fight, he could beat Kal any day of the week. He stepped into Kal's room and closed the door. Kal sneered from where he was already lounging on his bed.

"I'm done with you doing this to me, Kal," Sparky said as he approached the bed. He stopped and stood defensively, with his hands on his hips, and then glared at Kal. "You're going to admit to Mom that it's you who was stealing, not me."

"Who's going to make me?" Kal said as he swung his legs off the bed.

"I am," Sparky said as he brought his hands in front of him, his fists bunched.

"And you think Mom and Dad will let you do that? Ain't gonna happen, little brother. Now get out of here."

Sparky had absorbed several years of bullying, and it all came out at once in that supercharged moment. He threw a punch at Kal so fast that his older brother didn't have time to duck. But a moment later, Kal was on his feet. "I'll kill you for that," he said as blood ran from his nose.

Sparky shook his head. "No, you won't." And he hit Kal again. Kal barreled into him then, both fists swinging—neither one connecting. The next punch by Sparky put Kal to the floor. Kal did not stay down. He came up again, but this time he held a switchblade knife he'd pulled from a pocket in his pants.

"Boys," the voice of their father thundered. Kal dropped the knife at Sparky's feet just like he had done with the money, and he stepped back, wiping blood from his nose and his mouth.

"What is going on here?" their father demanded as he rushed into the room.

"Sparky was going to kill me," Kal said, "because I caught him with money he'd taken from your desk. He punched me, and then he pulled that knife on me. He was just about to stab me when you shouted. I can't take it anymore, Dad. You've got to do something about Sparky. I keep telling you and Mom that."

"Dad, it's not like he says," Sparky protested angrily.

"No, it never is," Donald Graves said sarcastically. "Kal, go clean up. Sparky, you come with me."

Sparky quietly followed his father, fuming inside at the injustice of it all. He couldn't understand why his father always, without hesitation, took Kal's side. He was told to wait in his room while his parents discussed what had happened. A few minutes later, both parents came to his room. "Sparky, your mother and I have made a decision. You have gone too far this time. We cannot allow you to push your weight around. You are causing trouble much too often. We should go to the police, but we have decided to give you one last chance. If you accuse Kal of anything after today or even so much as touch him, we will have you arrested," his father said.

"We love you, Sparky," his mother said, failing to meet his eyes. "But this can't continue. You will come with us and apologize to Kal and then you are to stay in your room for the rest of the night."

"Also, Sparky," his dad said, "you will not be getting paid for your work at the shop for the next six months."

Sparky's mind was racing. Kal had done him dirt one too many times, and this was by far the worst. He did as his parents told him to and said he was sorry to Kal. Kal, always the con artist, said, "I accept your apology."

In the middle of the night, Sparky's door opened, waking him from a troubled sleep. Kal had the knife again. He held the knife in front of him as he said softly, "Don't you ever cross me again or I'll use this on you, or better yet, on Johnny or Courtney."

Sparky feared that Kal would do just that. He was not about to let Kal hurt his little brother and sister. He loved them and knew that they were victims of Kal's as well. "Have it your way, Kal. I'll do as you say," he said as his mind raced about how he could best keep the younger kids safe.

"You'd better, or I'll kill you, Sparky." Kal slipped from the room. When he was gone, Sparky got out of bed and began to do what he felt he had to do.

The next day, at age fifteen, Sparky did not come home from school. His parents contacted the police and reported him missing the following morning but made no mention of the trouble that had occurred between their sons. The cops were unable to find him. It was as if he had vanished into thin air. No one had any idea what had become of the handsome, husky, blond-haired boy named *Sparky Graves*.

CHAPTER TWO

ALTHOUGH HE MADE NO EFFORT to contact his family and tell them where he was, Sparky Graves knew where he was. What he didn't know was where he was going. Sparky did not hate his adoptive parents. He loved them—his mother more than his father, for his father was not a tender-natured man. It was Kal who persecuted Sparky mercilessly. He also managed to stir the two younger children up against him.

Sparky wasn't sure at first why his sister, ten-year-old Courtney, and his other brother, eight-year-old Johnny, always sided with Kal. They had both been born after his adoption, and he had loved and doted on them both while Kal pretty much ignored them. After seeing some of the mean things that Kal did to them when he thought no one was watching, Sparky realized the truth; it seemed that Kal had turned the two younger children against Sparky by using threats, intimidation, and fear.

Threats were part of his psychopathic nature. He had threatened several times to kill Sparky if he told his parents what was really going on, and Sparky had believed it. So when he left that day after school, he told himself he was doing it to cause less strife in the Graves's home, to maybe allow his younger siblings to find a measure of peace, and to protect his own life. His hope was that Kal would not be harder on Courtney and Johnny after he was gone. But staying certainly wasn't helping them.

It was not an impulsive move on Sparky's part. He had thought long and hard about it over the past several days. Serious thought came after a particularly bad incident. Kal had lied to their parents about a ding in the family car that the seventeen-year-old claimed Sparky, at fifteen, had caused. That had been less than a week before Kal had attempted to steal money from them, then blamed that on Sparky too.

When Sparky denied driving the car that day, his brother appealed to the two younger children, who Sparky was certain Kal had already threatened to get them to back him up. They both said that Sparky had been driving it, but Sparky had noted that neither of them looked at their parents when they told the lies, nor would they look at Sparky. Sparky tried not to hold it against his parents for believing their biological children over him, but it did hurt. He had told the truth. They had lied. And he was told that he would not be able to use the restricted driver's license he'd obtained shortly after his fifteenth birthday until further notice.

Not only did it hurt him, it also hurt his parents, especially his mother. She told him that they hated placing restrictions on him but felt that he would never learn unless they did. She had been kind when telling him how she felt, but his father, on the other hand, had sounded angry and his face had turned red, his eyes blazing. Not realizing the extremely deceptive nature of their oldest son and the mean streak he somehow managed to hide from them, they could never figure out why Sparky lied to them or why he seemed to act out so much.

His teachers at school had told his mother many times that even though he was shy, Sparky was a model student who never acted out. She'd asked Sparky why he behaved at school but not at home. As usual, she did not accept his explanation that Kal lied about him. But she told him that she knew he would do better and suggested he be especially kind to Kal.

At this point, Sparky simply did not want to see his family go through more strife, but he knew it would happen if he stayed. He couldn't change his older brother. But after the latest incident over the money, Sparky realized the time had come for him to leave. He didn't believe that his father would ever take his word over that of Kal's and that he would make sure that his mother didn't either.

So, unbeknownst to his family, Sparky had packed a large duffle bag with several changes of clothes, his toothbrush, a bar of soap, a couple of bath towels, a flashlight, and all the cash he had at home, which was just a little over three hundred dollars. He also packed a stash of candy bars, energy bars, and some other edibles that he had squirreled away just in case this day ever came. In his pockets were his restricted driver's license and a copy of his birth certificate—the amended one the court had ordered to be made when he was adopted. He had snuck the bag out of the house late the night of Kal's most recent threat. He'd hidden it in a nearby park, deep in some shrubbery, where it was unlikely to be spotted before he made his getaway.

After school was out, he went directly to the park and hid himself in that same shrubbery, making sure no one saw him crawl in. There he waited until several hours after dark. He was aware of cars driving by the park, and peeking out from time to time, he identified some of them as police cars. He was certain they were looking for him, but he had no intention of being found. He'd also seen his parents' cars go by, first his mother's and later his father's with Kal seated beside him. It made his heart ache and his stomach upset. He even cried, heartsick over leaving his family, but he felt like what he was doing was the best for his family as well as for himself.

He was determined to make a clean break and had very carefully planned each move he was to make. In the dark of night and with a heavy heart, he finally left his hiding place and, carrying his duffle bag, worked his way toward the freeway. At a truck stop there, he looked over the vehicles, wondering if there was a way he could catch a ride without anyone seeing him. At this point, he didn't care where he went. He would worry about that later. Right now he needed a ride that would take him far away from Goodland, Kansas, and his psychopathic brother.

Sparky watched from the side of the small convenience store as a large truck pulled in and parked. It was carrying a load of big pipes, open ends tempting him. It wouldn't be comfortable, but he was certain that he could crawl into one of them and be both secure and hidden from anyone who might look for him. He made up his mind, picked up his duffle bag, and waited until the driver had entered the store. Then, looking about and seeing no one, he hurried over to the back of the truck, threw his bag into one of the pipes on the bottom of the load and quickly scrambled inside.

Sparky had seen other trucks like this one parked here several times over the past few days when he would go into the convenience store to purchase candy and other items. He had no idea where the trucks, including the one he was now stowed away on, were going, but it didn't matter. This truck would carry him far from the only home he had ever known. After about a half hour, he heard the driver enter the cab of the semi and shut the door. A minute later, the big rig roared to life.

Sparky crawled over halfway into the pipe, but he could still see out. As the truck entered the freeway heading west, Goodland faded behind him. He settled in as best he could, uncomfortable though it was, and began what he hoped was a long and uneventful journey. For the next day and a half, he made his home in the pipe on the back of the truck, only slipping out quickly to relieve himself and get a drink of water each time the truck stopped. Using change and currency he carried in his bag, he purchased bottles of water and more candy, chips, and nuts from vending machines.

Sparky soon came to recognize the driver each time he saw him, so he always made sure he scampered back into his pipe when he saw the man getting ready to leave. He was a little shorter than Sparky with a large stomach and a long moustache. On one occasion, Sparky managed to shed his natural shyness and get his courage up while he was outside of the pipe. He approached the driver and struck up a conversation. The driver showed no sign of recognition, so Sparky said, "I've noticed a lot of trucks like yours on the freeway. There must be a big pipeline project somewhere."

The driver told him it was a very big project in an area outside of Las Vegas, Nevada. Sparky visited a bit longer, trying to act normal, like he was just passing the time while he waited for someone in the restroom. After a little bit, he politely wished the driver a safe journey and then sauntered away, eventually slipping back into the pipe when he was sure he wasn't being observed. When the driver stopped in rest stops two nights running and apparently slept in the truck, Sparky took more time away from the discomfort and cramped space in the pipe.

He replenished his supply of water and food each time. He even bought a couple of sandwiches from inside a large truck stop at one point. No one seemed to pay any attention to him, so he felt relatively secure. But he was careful not to let himself be seen again by the driver of the truck he was stowed away on. That would raise the man's suspicions. The most he got from other folks he encountered was an occasional nod of the head or a polite hello.

Sparky did not want to ride clear to the pipeline construction site in Nevada. He had picked up a map at one of the first stops his truck had made and consulted it sometimes when the truck pulled to a stop.

When he reached a location called Salina, Utah, not far from a much larger town the map identified as Richfield, he decided now would be a good time to leave the uncomfortable pipe he'd lived in and strike out on foot. There was simply no way he'd take a chance on ending up in the hot desert around Las Vegas.

His mind made up, he grabbed his duffle bag and once again climbed down. A moment later, he sauntered toward a restroom and went inside. There he washed up the best he could, brushed his teeth, combed his blond hair, which was getting much too greasy, and changed clothes in one of the stalls. He even got a little to eat after leaving the restroom. He patiently waited until the truck he'd been riding in pulled away and then he hiked back toward the freeway.

A couple of cars passed him. One, driven by a pretty girl, slowed, and he thought she was going to stop, but instead, she suddenly sped up and drove on. He didn't blame her; she had no way of knowing that he wasn't a threat to her. He kept walking. More cars passed and entered the freeway. Just before the westbound on-ramp, an elderly fellow in a battered Dodge pickup truck pulled up beside him and shouted through the open passenger window, "Need a ride, young feller? I don't know which way you're going, but I'm heading west if you want to join me."

Perfect. "Sure, thanks," he said to the old man.

"There's room in the back for your duffle bag," the fellow said with a friendly grin.

"Okay, I'll put it back there."

"So where you off to, young man?" the old fellow asked after Sparky had stashed his duffel bag in the back of the truck next to several bags of grain and some blocks of salt and had climbed into the cluttered cab.

"Just looking for a job somewhere," Sparky said. "Doesn't matter where."

The old fellow looked over at him before letting out the clutch. "How old are you?" he asked.

"Eighteen," Sparky lied. At six foot, he did look a lot older than his fifteen, almost sixteen years. He figured he could get away with the lie, trying not to dwell on the pitfall it placed in his way if someone were to ask for identification.

"Where do you hail from?" the man asked, seeming to accept what he said about his age.

Sparky had anticipated this question and he had a ready answer. He was from western Kansas, so he'd decided to say he was from Kansas City, right near the Missouri border in the far eastern edge of the state. It was hundreds of miles from his home in Goodland. He feared that he might need to use his birth certificate sometime, but when he did, he was prepared to say he was born in Goodland but grew up in Kansas City, hoping no one would look closely at his birthdate and discover his deception. So that was the answer he gave the old fellow.

"What kind of work you looking for?" the old man asked. Before Sparky could answer, the fellow reached a callused and arthritic hand across the seat and said, "Sorry, you probably want to know who I am. Name's Alfred Briggs. What's yours?"

"I'm Sparky Graves," he said. "Thanks for the ride, Mr. Briggs."

"Glad to help a young feller out," Alfred said. "But it's okay if you call me Alfred. So again, what kind of work you looking for?"

"I'll do anything," Sparky said, and he meant it. He was not lazy and had always done more than his share of the chores at home and of the work at his father's vehicle repair shop, often doing his brother's work just to avoid a fight.

"Anything at all?" Briggs asked as he let the clutch out, pulled onto the road, and headed for the nearby onramp.

"Yes, anything," Sparky said.

"Ever do any farm work?" Briggs asked, glancing briefly at Sparky as he shifted into a higher gear.

"Not much," Sparky said. None, in fact. He didn't think it could be too hard, and he could learn quickly.

"I'd be willing to provide room and board and a few bucks here and there if you're interested. I could sure use some help on that place of mine," Alfred said. "I'd love to have you help me, unless of course you're headed to somewhere farther west."

Sparky's heart raced. He tried not to look too excited, but he was ready to jump at the chance. It would give his parents time to forget about him while allowing him to save a few dollars before moving farther west. "Gee, Mr. Briggs—" he began slowly.

"It's Alfred, Sparky," the old man broke in with a smile.

"Sorry, Alfred, but like I said, I haven't had much experience. But I'm a fast learner," he said.

"Does that mean you will stay with me for a while?"

"Sure, why not?" Sparky said, unable to keep his grin to himself. "I'd like that. But what would your wife think about me being there?"

"I lost Mama to a stroke almost a year ago. We never did have any kids. It was just the two of us and a whole bunch of animals we both love, and she did more than her share of the work. It's been hard for me to keep up since the good Lord took her from me."

Sparky looked over at him and was embarrassed when he saw a trickle of tears course its way down a tanned, weathered cheek. "I'm sorry to hear that," he said. "So sure, if you'll just tell me what to do, I'll do my best."

"I do believe you will," Alfred said as he wiped at his tears with the back of one gnarled hand. "I would be most grateful."

The two rode in silence for a few miles. Sparky kept glancing over at the old man, but he seemed lost in his thoughts. He figured he was probably thinking about his late wife. When Alfred finally spoke again, it confirmed what he'd suspected. "Me and Mama, we have worked this farm of ours out near Monroe for nearly sixty years. We never got rich, but we made a good living." Alfred was silent for a moment. When he spoke again, it was with a weary tone to his voice. "Getting old is not easy, Sparky. We both slowed down. The farm shows it. Fences are falling apart. Sheds need repair. Weeds are waist high around the house and

the barn and the sheds. Sure could use some sprucing up around the old place."
He held his right hand toward Sparky. "As you can see, the arthritis has made my
hands hard to use. I can barely grip a shovel or a pitchfork anymore."

"I'll be glad to help," Sparky said, feeling a sudden euphoria come over
him. He couldn't believe his good fortune. To be somewhere rural with animals
around appealed to him. He'd always wanted to be around animals, but it had
never happened. There had been times when he'd dreamed of having a large
yellow cat, and he even thought he could remember one.

He'd asked his mother about it one day, and the answer had surprised him.
"They say there was a cat with you when you were thrown from the car and
that it didn't want to let anyone near you. I even heard you had an arm around
it. The cops finally managed to scare it away from you so they could pick you
up. Nobody ever knew what happened to that cat."

The old man's farm was not as small as Sparky had imagined. In fact, to him
it seemed wonderfully large, but it was very run-down. There was no doubt a
lot of work needed to be done, but he didn't mind. He was anxious to get to
work, to try to forget about his parents, his siblings, and the troubled life he'd
left behind.

"Well, here we are," Alfred said as he smiled at Sparky and stopped the old
truck outside his granary.

"Hey, this is cool," Sparky said. "It's so green here with all these trees and
bushes. I love pine trees." He waved an arm at the tall trees.

"Those are spruce," Alfred clarified. "But they're related to pines. The
broadleaf trees are poplars. There's an orchard with a variety of fruit trees behind
the house. Farther out on the farm are a lot of cottonwood trees. Down on the
creek there are way too many Russian olives. They're a terrible tree, a weed really.
Thorny things that are impossible to control. The horses like to eat the Russian
olives. The cows, sheep, and goats nibble at them too. But I wish I could just get
rid of them. Occasionally an animal gets a thorn in its mouth, and that's a serious
problem. Thank goodness it doesn't happen very often."

The two of them got out of the truck. "First thing we gotta do is unload
the sacks of grain and blocks of salt I have in the back," Alfred said.

"You tell me where they go, and I'll carry them," Sparky offered. Alfred
seemed more than glad to let him help. He was surprised, however, at how
hard the old fellow worked with his gnarled hands and obvious advanced age.
It only took a few minutes until the grain was stored and the blocks of salt were
stacked at the side of the granary. "We'll be taking the salt out to the animals
today. I let them run out and I shouldn't do that. They need their salt. All but

the goats, that is. They get a special supplement. I keep my goats separate from all the other animals except some llamas. I actually have llamas with both the sheep and the goats."

"How many animals do you have?" Sparky asked.

"Oh, I dunno," Alfred said. "I've let the cow herd dwindle cause it was getting too hard to handle them. I probably have only about twenty cows left and one bull. That's beef cattle I'm talking about. I also have a milk cow. She will be having a calf real soon. Anyway, I also have around a hundred head of ewes and bucks." Sparky must have looked puzzled, because Alfred said, "Sheep. And like I told you, I have some goats, meat goats. There are about forty or fifty nannies and a couple of nice billy goats."

"You mentioned horses," Sparky said as the two of them wandered back to a fence with fields extending a long way beyond it.

"Yeah, I have a couple of nice geldings, but they're getting old. I also have a nice young mare that I bought from a neighbor just before Mama died," Alfred said. Sparky thought it was strange that Alfred referred to his wife as Mama since he'd already told him they never had any children.

"I call the mare *Ginger*. She's a nice sorrel." The old fellow chuckled. "There must be thousands of sorrel mares named Ginger. She's supposed to be broke really good, but I've only ridden her a couple times. It's too hard for me to get up on a horse anymore." He shook his head sadly. "I get around okay though. I have a pretty nice four-wheeler. I do most of my chasing of animals on it nowadays. When we haul the salt out today, we'll have it in a little trailer I can tow behind the four-wheeler."

"I look forward to helping," Sparky said as a large yellow cat streaked by, reminding him of the one he thought was buried somewhere deep in his memory. He felt a sudden urge to call out to the cat, but he didn't.

"That there cat is one of several that are around. They help keep the mice down. That one is quite tame. Mama loved the old fellow. Since her passing, I guess it feels neglected. "I feel fortunate having found you, Sparky. There is a lot of work you can help me with. I guess God's looking out for me after all. Maybe I'll park the truck over by the garage and then we'll hook the trailer to my four-wheeler and get it loaded. You can ride Mama's four-wheeler if you like. It's in the shed, but I haven't started it since Mama got sick."

Sparky's head was spinning. He knew about four-wheelers, but he had no idea what a sorrel was or a gelding. He had to figure that out. He wished he had a computer or even a cell phone. Then he could Google the words or ask Siri. He'd just have to hope he could figure things out by watching and listening closely to his elderly benefactor. Maybe, if he worked hard, he'd eventually feel comfortable enough to ask Alfred questions like that. At this point, he didn't want the guy to think he didn't know anything about farm animals for fear he might not want to keep him around. And already he was loving this place. It felt like home—not the home he'd left, but the home he'd often dreamed about. The tension that was always with him back in Goodland was already fading. He was excited about starting a new life here.

"It sounds like you have a lot of animals," Sparky said.

"Oh, not really. Some of the other farmers in the area have a lot more than I do. I used to have more."

Just then a black-and-white dog approached. He barked a couple of times but settled down at the old fellow's command. Then he sniffed at Sparky, who petted him. The dog seemed to like it, so he dropped to his knees and petted some more. The dog licked his face, making Sparky laugh. He'd never had a dog. He began to experience something he'd never felt before except in that foggy memory of a yellow cat. He wasn't sure what it was, but he sure felt fond of this animal.

The dog suddenly surged to his feet and began to run around, jumping and barking. Then he ran back to Sparky and once again jumped up and licked his face. Sparky began to rub the dog's head and stroke his back. The dog acted like he couldn't get enough. Suddenly, Alfred said quite loudly, "That's enough, Sparky. Settle down now."

Sparky jerked his hand back. "I'm sorry," he said.

Old Alfred Briggs began to laugh. "I'm so sorry. I didn't mean you, Sparky. I meant the dog. You both are named Sparky." He slapped his leg and then began to laugh some more. Sparky found himself laughing right along with him.

Finally, their laughter subsided, and Sparky said, "What a great dog. I love him already, and I don't mind if he gets so excited."

"Well, as long as it doesn't bother you, I guess it's okay. He is a great dog. And he's valuable. Young but well trained. He helps me herd the cows and the sheep. But I have to watch him around the llamas."

Sparky knew what a llama was. At least he knew what they looked like. "Will the dog hurt the llamas?" he asked.

That made Alfred laugh again. "No," he said. "It's just the opposite. Llamas and their smaller cousins, alpacas, protect the sheep and goats from dogs and coyotes. They will kill to protect the herds. I've got my llamas pretty well trained to know that Sparky is an exception, but I still keep a close eye out when he's in the pastures with me."

"I think it's cool how many different animals you have. I hope I can get to know them," he said. "Is that strange? I mean, I want the animals to feel like they can trust me."

"I have a feeling you and the animals will get along just fine," Alfred said. "Now, tell me, Sparky, what's your given name?"

"Sparky is my only name," Sparky answered.

"You mean it's not just a nickname?"

"Nope, it's my real name."

The old fellow rubbed his chin with a gnarled hand for a moment. "Sometimes I just call my dog *Dog*. So I guess it's okay if you and he have the same name. You can call him Dog or you can call him Sparky. Or if you want him to come, you can just whistle." The dog had wandered off, but as a demonstration, Alfred whistled and Sparky the dog came running right to him. He jumped around Alfred for a moment, and then he again came to Sparky who petted him and talked to him.

After a minute or two, Alfred said, "Sparky, why don't we go gas up Mama's four wheeler? Then we can get on them, deliver the salt where it's needed, and then take a ride around the place. I'd like you to get familiar with it."

"I've never driven a four-wheeler," Sparky said, embarrassed.

"It's easy. I'll give you a crash course and away we'll go. You've driven cars, haven't you?" Alfred asked. "You have a driver's license, don't you?"

"Yes," Sparky said as he thought about the restricted license in his pocket. He hoped he wasn't setting himself up for a fall with all his lies. But he didn't know what to do about it. So he just shoved it from his mind. He was not going to let worries dampen his spirits.

For the next hour, they rode across what Alfred called his "little farm," occasionally setting a block of salt in old tire rims Alfred used specifically for the salt. Sparky loved every minute of the time as they drove around. It had taken him no time at all to feel comfortable driving the four-wheeler. Frankly, he was having a fantastic time. They stopped several times in addition to setting out the salt, and each time they did, the animals, whatever kind they were near, would come trotting to Alfred, and with his gnarled hands, he would pet and scratch and talk to them. Sparky was soon doing the same. And he loved it.

The final stop on their tour was at the pigpens. "Pigs can be pets too," Alfred told him. "I like to fuss with the young pigs, but I always have to watch out for the sows, the mother pigs. They can take offense to having their little ones messed with."

"What do they do, attack?" Sparky asked.

"They can and will if they're riled. But the really dangerous animal here is the boar. That's the daddy pig," Alfred clarified. "Right now he's in his own pen. It's right over there."

Sparky noted the strong but short fence as he admired the huge brown animal. "Can't he jump out?"

Alfred chuckled. "No, he can't jump. Pigs aren't jumpers. They're more like tanks. They just charge and slash."

"Did you say they charge and *slash*?" Sparky asked.

Alfred chuckled. "Not the sows, but look closely at this boar. He has tusks. Do you see them sticking out of the sides of his mouth? They're very sharp. A hog like old Sherman here could slice a man's gut open faster than you can even imagine."

"Sherman?" Sparky said.

"Yeah, like a Sherman tank."

Soon enough, they left the pigs and continued on their way. As the afternoon passed, Sparky hoped there was not a pitfall awaiting him. His life was suddenly too good to be true. *I could live here forever*, he thought. He couldn't stop smiling. For the first time in his life, he felt like he was where he truly belonged. Over the next week, he worked until his back ached and his hands were blistered, but he was happy. Alfred became very fond of him, and he made sure that Sparky knew how much he was appreciated. Sparky couldn't imagine anything could destroy or even dampen his newfound contentment.

CHAPTER THREE

KAL GRAVES WAS BOTH GLAD and angry that his much-detested little brother was gone. He was happy not to ever have to see his face or hear his voice. Trouble was, it left him having to do work he'd always been able to pawn off on Sparky.

He turned more of his attention to his younger brother and sister. Courtney was ten and small for her age. Johnny was as big as their sister but two years younger than her. Kal had long since instilled fear in the two of them. He was able to force them to do things he'd been told to do, things he used to make Sparky do. They knew better than to complain to their dad or mom. He kept reminding them of what he'd do if they ever said a word. He always took delight in the way they both trembled and even bawled when he gave his warnings. Yes, they would do as he said. If they didn't, he would do as he threatened.

At his father's mechanic shop, it wasn't so easy. The little kids had no chores there and seldom came in. He'd always been able to make Sparky do the more complicated stuff so he wouldn't have to bother to learn how to do it. His father, who spent most of his time in his office, always thought Kal was doing the work while Sparky was loafing.

The garage had several bays, and Donald employed other men. Kal tried to manipulate them like he had Sparky, but it wasn't working so well. As a result, he botched a couple of jobs. However, he did lie and tell his dad that he only did things the way the other guys told him. His dad needed those other men, so he never reprimanded them. Still, Kal spent much of his time trying to figure out how to get out of working in the garage and still get paid. Perhaps he should look for another job, something easier, like flipping burgers.

Nine days after Sparky had vanished, Kal had managed to skip school, which was not uncommon for him, and apply for a job at a local burger joint. They said they would have a position for him in a couple of weeks. So with a chip firmly in place on his shoulder, he waited until school would be out and then headed for his dad's garage to break the news to him. He had what he believed was a great way to justify his leaving mechanic work.

When he got to the garage, he noticed his mother's car parked out front. She hardly ever came to the shop. What was she doing here? He'd wanted to break the news to his father alone and then let him help break it to his mother. But he guessed he'd have to talk to both of them, because he wanted to get it over with. He approached the door to his dad's office but froze when he heard his mother say, "Don, I need to talk to you about Kal. There's something going on with him that has me worried."

"He's okay, Sydney. I think he misses his brother and it's eating at him."

"No, it's not that," Sydney said. "I've been feeling tension in the younger children the past few days, more tension than when Sparky was still home."

"Of course. That's only natural. They miss Sparky," Donald said. "He was usually quite good to them. It was only Kal he was so rotten to."

"Yes, and I also know that they've always taken Kal's side where there was a problem. I've been thinking about this a lot the past few days." She paused, and Kal could sense her hesitation. "I think Kal was taking advantage of Sparky and somehow making Courtney and Johnny back him up. I've wondered about that for a long time, but now I'm more convinced. I don't think Sparky was the troublemaker we may have thought he was. We need to do something."

"Oh come on, Sydney. We both know it was Kal that did the lion's share of the work both at home and here at the garage. Sparky was always trying to get out of doing things. Let's face it; he was just a lazy kid."

"According to whom?" Sydney asked, her voice raised a little. "According to Kal, that's who."

"And according to Courtney and Johnny," Donald reminded her.

Kal began to pace back and forth and clenched his jaw and his fists over what he was hearing from his mother. It got even worse when she said, "Donald, I've been watching Courtney and Johnny closely. I just told you that I think Kal somehow gets them to support him, but the more I think about it, the more I think that Kal is actually bullying them."

"Since when?" Kal's father demanded angrily. "He's never been a bully."

"I know you feel that way, but there were incidents at school. We brushed them off, since Kal felt bad about them, and we figured it was just normal boy stuff. But I told you before Sparky ran away that I felt like he was afraid of Kal."

"What? Are you kidding me? You know what a big guy Sparky is. And you also know that we had to punish him for beating Kal up on more than one occasion. If one of them had reason to fear, it would have been Kal." For a moment, not a word passed between his parents, but then his father said, "You're worrying for nothing. The only thing either of us should be worrying about right now is getting Sparky found and back home. Kal can't do all the work by himself. And when he is home again, we've got to make sure he does his share."

"Donald, be reasonable. We love both of those boys, but since Sparky's been gone, I've felt like I've seen a lot of anger in Kal that I hadn't noticed before. I got to thinking about the day we got a ding in my car. I really believe that if Sparky had done that, he would have told us so."

"But he didn't, so Kal had to tell us for him," Donald argued. "And Courtney and Johnny both said it had been Sparky driving the car that afternoon."

"I've been thinking about that, too, Don. I remember Kal saying, 'You guys tell them. You know it was Sparky who dented the car.' That was one of the times I wondered if Kal was controlling what they said."

"That's nonsense, Sydney! They both agreed with Kal because they knew it was Sparky who damaged the car."

"I think we were wrong. Think about it. Neither of the children would look either one of us in the eyes when they said it. They spoke with their heads down. And that wasn't the first time that happened, either. We've been blind to it, but I'm telling you, Kal bullies them, and we need to put a stop to it before it gets worse."

Kal was getting angrier by the minute, his clenched jaw aching. His mother was trying to mess everything up for him. He couldn't let her do that. His dad saw things his way, but for some reason, his mother apparently didn't trust him. He hated her!

His mother spoke again. "Don, I checked with the school this morning. Sparky was there the day the car was damaged until quite late. He only came home around the time I noticed the damage to the car. A teacher said he was in the library studying, and the librarian told me the same thing. He couldn't have taken the car that day. Kal must have been the one who damaged it. And that last day, the day he was trying to steal our money—what if Sparky was telling the truth? What if it was him who caught Kal stealing rather than the other way around?"

His father raised his voice. "You're getting things all wrong. I'm sure those folks at the school remembered the day the car was damaged wrong. And remember, the money was right there at Sparky's feet, right where he dropped it when you entered the room. You need to get over this and let it lie. I know how hard it has been on you the past few days, but it's not fair to blame Kal for things Sparky did."

Kal smiled at that. Yes, his dad was okay. But his smile was wiped away when his mother said, "I'm going to have a serious talk with the kids when they get home from school. I honestly believe that Kal is responsible for Sparky leaving. I suspect he threatened Sparky one too many times, and Sparky didn't want to fight with him anymore because he knew he would hurt Kal and we would punish him. Remember, we did tell him we'd have him arrested the next time something happened. Don, if Kal was responsible for making Sparky leave, we need to do something about it. Kal will only get worse when Sparky is found, and I worry for the other kids. We have got to put a stop to it now."

"Sydney, that's enough!" Donald shouted. "I don't want to hear another word about it. I think you're losing your mind. I know you're upset about Sparky vanishing like he did, but you can't let it affect your mind like this. Kal is a good young man, and I won't have you making trouble for him. Sparky's gone. Maybe he'll come back and maybe he won't. Don't blame Kal. Instead of coming to us with his troubles, whatever they were, Sparky took the coward's way out and ran away. At this point, I think maybe it's for the best."

"Donald Graves! I can't believe you actually said that," Sydney said angrily, her voice raised. "He is our son."

Kal had to hurry and duck out of sight as his mother rushed from the office, fuming. He knew what he had to do, and he had to do it before she put pressure on Johnny and Courtney and made them admit that she was right.

***

Bill Finch ended the phone call he'd just received from his ministering partner. He had promised Alfred Briggs that he would come visit him this week. He was very fond of the old fellow, and he had tried to be especially supportive of him since the passing of his wife. But his partner had just been unexpectedly called out of town for his work. He wouldn't be back for two or three weeks.

Bill had been trying to think of some way he could help Alfred. He was not a farmer himself, but he knew that Alfred worried that he wasn't getting everything done that needed to be done. Alfred was not active in the church, but he was a good man, an honest, hardworking fellow. Bill held out hope that someday he could convince him to come to church. He thought that maybe he could organize a group from the Elder's Quorum to spend a Saturday helping Alfred. He and his partner had talked about that just moments ago on the phone. His partner had told Bill that he should go visit Alfred even if he couldn't be there with him.

That was what Bill wanted to do, but he didn't want to go alone. He could ask his wife to go, but she had severe allergies to animals, and Alfred always had his dog in the house in the evenings, so that wouldn't work. Just then, his fifteen-year-old daughter, Kay Dell, walked in and inspiration struck.

"Kay Dell, I just got off the phone with my ministering partner, and he has to be out of state for a while. I feel like I need to make some visits this week, and I could use a partner to take his place," he said, grinning.

"Dad, I know what you're thinking. Look at me. I'm a girl," she said, throwing her arms in the air and pirouetting.

"And a right pretty girl at that," Bill said.

"But Dad, girls don't go with men to make visits. I go with Mom," she said with a frown. "Sorry."

"Actually, President Nelson didn't say that girls couldn't accompany their fathers if it would be good for the people he visits. And what I am thinking is a special circumstance," Bill said. "I only visit three families. And the one that we always visit last is Alfred Briggs so we can spend all the time with him that he wants us to. He is very lonely and likes our company. I feel especially strongly about visiting him this week."

Kay Dell suddenly brightened. "He's a farmer," she said. "I wonder if he would let me see some of his animals if I went with you. You know how much I love animals."

"Yes, and I know you'd like for us to have a dog. The other kids feel the same," Bill said. "But we can't because of your mother's allergies."

"Dad, if you promise you'll ask him if I can see his dog and maybe some of his other animals, I'll go with you," she said, suddenly very enthusiastic.

"I've been worried about the heavy load that Brother Briggs has on that farm since his wife died. She always helped out a lot. He has it all to himself now, and his arthritis is making it even harder," Bill told his daughter. "I was going to ask him if he would be okay having a group from the Elder's Quorum come on a Saturday and help him catch up on a few things."

"Dad, that's great, but I have a better idea. How about if I go to his farm sometimes to help him? That way I could also spend time with his dog and his other animals," Kay Dell said brightly. "Please, Dad, will you ask him if I could help him? I know how to work hard, and he doesn't even have to pay me."

Bill looked closely at Kay Dell. He could tell that she was quite serious, and suddenly, he felt like she might be the answer to his concern over the fellow being so badly overworked. "Kay Dell, I think that's a wonderful idea, but you can't let it affect your school work."

"I won't, Dad, I promise," she said.

"Okay, we'll talk to your mother about it, and if she agrees, then we'll ask Brother Briggs what he thinks. I can't imagine that he would refuse to let you help him. What a great idea, Kay Dell. So, you will go with me to visit him this week—even if you are a girl?" he asked with a twinkle in his eyes.

Her answer was a tender hug.

***

In the middle of the second week on the farm, Alfred Briggs and Sparky Graves, along with Sparky the Border collie, had just finished a tasty meal of fried potatoes, fried steak, sourdough biscuits and home-canned pears. There was not a lot of variety in Alfred's cooking from day to day, but Sparky loved it and didn't care if he ever ate anyplace else again—or *anything* else.

Sparky the dog had become as close to Sparky the boy as he was to Alfred. Only two or three times since that first day had Sparky heard the old man call the dog anything but *Boy* or *Dog*. Sparky called him by his name as well as the other titles. The dog answered to anything. Sparky suspected it was the sound of his and Alfred's voices that he responded to.

The furniture in the house was old but comfortable. Sparky had a bedroom to himself. It was a nice room, bigger than the one he'd had at home. It had a nice big closet that seemed pretty bare, containing only the few clothes he had escaped his home in Kansas with.

As Alfred and Sparky sat together watching national news on the TV, Alfred told Sparky that they would drive into Richfield one of these days for a few things he couldn't get in Monroe, and when they did, they would get Sparky some real leather boots, denim pants, strong work shirts, and whatever other clothing he needed.

None of that was of interest to young Sparky Graves. But suddenly, he heard his own name mentioned on the TV, and he and Alfred quit conversing to listen intently to what was being said.

There had been a murder in the small town of Goodland, Kansas, and the police were looking for the son of the murdered woman, a boy who had run away from home nearly two weeks earlier. The woman was identified as Sydney Graves, age forty, of Goodland. Sparky's whole body began to tremble and it was all he could do to suppress a scream of anguish.

What followed left Sparky literally trembling with shock. The police were looking for the son who had vanished. They reported that he had been seen arguing with his mother on the deck overlooking the backyard of their home by an older brother. The older brother, who Sparky already knew was Kal, told police that he saw his brother shove their mother over the railing. When she fell, her neck was broken and she died before the witness could summon help. Then the newscaster said the name of the fifteen-year-old who was now wanted for murder was Sparky Graves, who had apparently not gone as far away as the authorities had expected after he had disappeared. A photo of Sparky flashed onto the screen.

Sparky was stunned by what he'd just heard. He sat and stared at the TV even as he broke out in a sweat and his trembling grew worse. He began to feel faint and hoped he wouldn't pass out.

"That's you they're talking about," Alfred said in surprise, turning to look at Sparky with concern in his eyes. "That's your name and your picture, and Sparky, you don't look so good."

"I know," Sparky said, his voice broken. "But I promise you, I didn't kill my mother. I would never do that. I love my mother." Tears filled his eyes and he rubbed at them self-consciously.

"You think I don't know that, Sparky?" Alfred said kindly. "First, I've gotten to know you pretty well these past few days. That's not the kind of guy you are. And of course, we both know that you were right here on my farm when that occurred. Which means your brother was lying."

"He always lies," Sparky said as sadness over his mother's death overpowered his anger at his brother's blatant lie.

"Sparky, I am so happy to have you here. I don't want to lose you. I enjoy your company and am grateful for all the work you do," Alfred said as he clicked the TV off and faced Sparky. "But I think for both of our sakes, you need to be totally honest with me. Do you agree?"

Sparky lowered his eyes, swallowed, and said, "Yes, I do. I'm sorry I lied." His chin quivered. "I was afraid that if you knew I was a runaway, you would have turned me in. I can't go back to Goodland. Kal would kill me."

"I agree with that, Sparky. That's especially true after the lie your brother told the police."

"They will believe Kal, Alfred. Everyone always believes Kal. I think Mom wanted to believe me, but Dad wouldn't allow it. You don't know my dad, but he's not a loving person. I never felt like he ever loved me the way Mom did. Kal is his pet. Kal's the reason I had to leave home. And now I'm afraid I made a big mistake. I left and someone, probably Kal, has killed my mother." Tears filled Sparky's eyes.

"Sparky, look at me," Alfred said firmly. Sparky looked up. "Okay, let's get one thing straight right now. You *are not* responsible for her death. Whoever killed her is. And if you think that may have been your brother, then that is where responsibility lies, not with you."

"I still think she would have been okay if I'd stayed. All I had to do was whatever Kal told me to and not beat him up, which I always wanted to do when he lied and got me in trouble for something he'd done."

"I take it he bossed you around," Alfred said.

"Constantly, and even though he's smaller than me, he's two years older. Still, the few times I resisted his orders and fought him, I easily beat him. Then he would tell my parents I attacked him. They always believed him, and I'd get punished."

"So why did you leave?" Alfred asked softly.

"Because Kal told me he would kill me if I didn't do what he said, and he didn't mean he'd beat me up, and we both knew that, because he couldn't, but he always had a knife and he'd pulled it on me before. He would have stabbed me or found some other way just like he must have done with Mom."

"Okay, Sparky, I want to hear all about your life before you met me. Do you have siblings besides Kal?"

"Yes, Courtney and Johnny. She's ten and he's eight." He choked up at the thought of the two of them. This must be horrible for them. He pulled himself together and went on. "They lied for Kal all the time. But they are good kids. I usually got along really well with them, but I'm sure they turned against me because he either bribed them or threatened them. It's more likely he threatened them."

"Okay, you can tell me more later, but first, tell me how old you are."

"I'm fifteen, like it said on the news. Kal is seventeen," Sparky said, his body trembling. "And as you know, I am not from Kansas City. I'm from Goodland. It was near there that my birth parents were killed, and only me and a yellow cat somehow survived."

"A cat, huh? What happened to the cat after that?" Alfred asked.

"I don't know. I guess he ran off. Your cat reminds me of him, I think. I mean, I was so young that I don't remember the accident at all, but somehow I seem to remember the cat. It's weird."

"It was probably your pet. So you don't have a driver's license; is that right?" Alfred asked.

"I do," Sparky said, pulling it from his pocket and showing it to Alfred. "As you can see, it's a provisional license. I would have gotten my regular license in a few months. But now that will never happen."

"Do you also have a birth certificate, or is that in your home in Goodland?"

"I have it in my room. I brought it with me."

"That's good. I'd like to see it."

Sparky went to the room, retrieved it, then handed it to Alfred who looked it over and handed it back. "So you were born in Goodland?"

"No, I was born in Connecticut. No one knows why my birth parents and I were in Kansas. When I was adopted, the judge ordered that a new certificate be made. My last name was then changed to Graves. But they kept my first name. And my birth place was changed to Goodland."

"All right, Sparky, tell me about your home life, if you will."

For the next hour, that's exactly what he did. Alfred listened carefully, occasionally asking a question to clarify something. From time to time, Alfred dropped into deep thought and looked very troubled. He even got up and paced the floor for several minutes. Sparky watched him and worried, not at all sure what Alfred would do.

Finally, Alfred sat down again, rubbed his eyes with a gnarled hand, and said, "I'm sorry that you had to go through so much because of your brother. I'm glad, though, that you're with me now. I will do everything I can to make sure that you're safe here. I could get in trouble if anyone finds out who you really are, and that's what I've been worrying about. You're underage, and by law, I suppose I should report that you're here. But under the circumstances, I feel like I should take that risk in order to keep you safe. I could vouch for you on the timing, but then it's just my word against Kal's. We have no way of knowing if that would be enough."

"Thank you, Alfred. But I don't want to get you in trouble. I can just leave, and you can pretend you never knew me."

Alfred shook his head. "No, I can't do that. I feel like God led you to me, and now I have to take whatever risk I must to keep you safe."

For a moment, Sparky watched Alfred's face. Finally he said, "I don't know how to tell you how thankful I am that you found me like you did. I promise, I will do everything I can to help you with this farm of yours."

He had to rub tears from his eyes, embarrassed that his wonderful new friend saw them. He had never been so happy in his life as he was here with Alfred. And he had never been as sad as he was over the terrible news of his mother's murder.

CHAPTER FOUR

THE NEXT MORNING SPARKY AND Alfred were eating a breakfast of fried eggs, homegrown bacon, home-bottled grape juice, and sourdough biscuits with peach jam that had been bottled by Alfred's wife. They had already been outside doing the chores, as they did each morning at the crack of dawn. Sparky had worked up a hearty appetite. And yet, his stomach churned at the thought of being accused of killing his own mother and of his beloved little siblings being left at the mercy of a dangerous brother.

He ate slowly, hoping that Alfred wouldn't notice his loss of appetite. But he did notice and said, "I'm sorry if this doesn't taste good to you. I'll bet your mother was a wonderful cook."

Sparky tried to shake off the sadness and concern at the drastic turn his life had taken. "She was, but so are you. This is so good," Sparky said as he ate.

"Yes, it is, my boy," Alfred said as he looked fondly at Sparky. "I'm so sorry for what you are going through. And I thank you for helping me fix breakfast, even though I'm sure your heart is breaking."

"It's only fair," Sparky said. "But I am worried about Johnny and Courtney. And I am afraid that I'm going to be a problem to you. Perhaps I should just turn myself in even though I didn't do anything wrong."

"Sparky," Alfred said as he set his fork down and looked sternly at him. "You have done nothing wrong. And don't worry about me. We'll figure this out somehow."

"I don't see how," Sparky responded. "I should never have left home. I only made things worse."

"You did what you felt you had to do, and I have a feeling that you honestly didn't have any other reasonable choices. Now go on and try to eat. You need the energy."

"I'll try," Sparky said and picked up his fork.

"I know you will and we will both enjoy it even if it isn't your mother's cooking," Alfred said as a cloud passed over his weathered face. "But it won't be the same after we run out of Mama's canned fruit, juice, and jam."

"Gee, I never thought of that," Sparky said as he tried to shove his gloomy thoughts aside.

"I have. I've thought about it a lot. I don't look forward to the day we have to eat store-bought fruit and vegetables, but I know that day's coming," Alfred said sadly. "That's one thing Mama always did herself. I'd pick the fruit, and we'd harvest the garden vegetables together, but Mama always did the canning by herself. She would never let me help, so I don't know how to do it. Oh, just listen to me Sparky. There's no need to fret over something we can do nothing about when there are things more pressing. If you are going to work here, you need some good strong farming clothes and footgear."

"I have some money that I brought with me," Sparky said. "And though I can't get it now, I do have several thousand dollars in a savings account in Goodland. But that's lost to me. If I somehow tried to get it, the police would figure out where I am. Anyway, I can buy some if we can go to a store somewhere with what I brought with me."

"You save your money, Sparky. And don't worry about what you've lost. I'll buy the clothes, but I don't think it would be smart to take you into town," the old fellow said. "We saw the newscast about the police looking for you. And if we saw it, you can bet that a lot of other folks in the area saw it as well."

"Ooh," Sparky moaned. "You're right. Somebody might recognize me. And I sure don't want to get arrested and sent back to Goodland or get you in trouble."

"Nor do I want you to, and I'll take my chances. You are worth it to me. So, I'll go to Richfield this morning. I'll just need to have all of your sizes, including those for shoes, pants, shirts, underclothes, and a hat," he said.

"I'll write you a list, but I'll give you money for it," Sparky said.

"No, you won't," Alfred said firmly. "I told you that besides room and board, I'd pay you a small wage for your work. So here's the deal; I'll buy the clothes as part of your salary. And I won't take any argument about it." He gave Sparky a stern look, but then he smiled.

"Okay, if you insist," Sparky said. "Thank you. While you're gone, I'll try to fix up that piece of fence we were looking at yesterday. I think I know what to do now."

Alfred gave him some further instructions as they walked outside, then stopped for a moment at his old truck and said, "I think I'll drive my Silverado today. I need to replace the brake pads on the old Dodge before I drive it much more."

"Silverado? That's a Chevy pickup. I've worked on them before in Dad's garage."

"Sure is," Alfred said. "I bought it just before Mama died. I wanted something more comfortable for her, but she didn't get to ride in it much, and I only drive it once every few weeks now."

"Where is it?" Sparky asked, looking around the yard. "I haven't seen it."

"I guess you've never been in my garage," he said as they passed the Dodge and walked over to a sturdy frame building that looked like it would only hold one vehicle. He'd wondered what it was but had never asked and he had never snooped, despite his curiosity. "It's in here." Alfred slid the garage door up and revealed a shiny blue truck. "This truck has so many bells and whistles on it that it intimidates me. Since you've worked on ones like this before, you will probably understand all the things this truck does."

Alfred pulled a set of keys from his pocket but then shoved them back in. "I just thought of something, Sparky. I get visitors around here from time to time, and I don't want you to have to run and hide when someone comes. The clothes and hats I'm going to get will help disguise you, but I think we need to do something with your hair."

Sparky wasn't sure what to say, but finally he muttered, "You mean you want me to dye it?"

"No, I don't think we need to be that extreme," the old fellow said with a smile. "Well, actually you might think what I'm going to suggest is extreme. I know you probably like that hair of yours as long as it is."

"It's not that long," Sparky said as he ran his fingers through it. His hair was over his ears and fell around his collar. He liked it like that, but he had a feeling he knew what was coming.

Alfred took off his hat and patted the short, thin, gray hair on his head. "My hair is too thin to look very good in a butch. But your hair is thick. You'd look okay, and you'll be surprised at how much cooler it is. Plus, it's a whole lot easier to take care of. What do you say? Do you want a butch cut?"

Sparky shrugged his shoulders. He liked his hair, but he wasn't going to impress anyone here on the farm. And he really never had worried much about impressing the girls. "Sure, that would be fine. But aren't we taking a chance going to a barber? He might recognize me from the news."

Alfred chuckled. "Nothing to worry about there. I'll be your barber."

"You?" Sparky asked, surprised.

"Sure, who do you think cuts mine?"

"You do it yourself?"

"Sure do. Mama always cut my hair until she got sick. I wore it longer than this, a lot longer. Mama used to cut it just the way she liked it, and that was always fine by me. I mean, she was the only one I ever cared to impress. But when she got sick and couldn't do it any longer I decided to try to do it myself." Alfred chuckled. "I didn't do so well, so I just clipped it all off. It made Mama laugh. So it was okay."

"I think you look fine," Sparky said.

"Thanks. How about if we do this right now, then I'll drive into Richfield and you can fix that fence."

A short ten minutes later, Alfred handed a mirror to Sparky. "Okay, what do you think?"

Sparky looked for a moment, thinking that he looked a whole lot different. And he actually liked it. But he kidded with Alfred and said, "I don't know if the girls will like it. Maybe we should put it back on."

Alfred chuckled. "Well, my boy, I think that would be kind of hard. Maybe next time you can cut mine."

"Sure, if you trust me," Sparky said.

"Sparky, I trust you. Believe me, you have earned my trust."

"I mean trust me to cut your hair."

"I trust you to cut my hair. What could you mess up? Anyway, I sure don't need to impress the ladies. The only lady I ever wanted to look good for from the very first day I laid eyes on her was Mama," Alfred said.

"Can I ask you a question?" Sparky said.

"Of course."

"This one is kind of personal. I don't want to make you feel bad or anything."

"Ask away. I have thick skin."

"You said that you and your wife never had children," Sparky began.

"That's right. We thought about adopting at one time, but we never did. We both came to regret that later in our lives, but by then, it was too late," Alfred said.

"My question is this. Why do you call her *Mama*? I mean, well, you know, my dad sometimes called my mother *Mom*. But if you never had children . . ." Sparky let the question dangle in the air.

"She often called me Papa, too. It's probably strange, but our animals were our family. I mean . . ." He paused.

"I understand. And I think it's kind of nice."

"I'm glad you understand," Alfred said. "There is one more thing before I go to town. Let's clean up here first, and then I'll get to that."

"I'll clean up after you leave. After all, it's my mess," Sparky said.

"If you don't mind, I'll let you do that. I'll be right back."

Alfred left the room and Sparky grabbed a broom. But he'd barely begun to sweep up his blond hair before Alfred returned, an iPhone in his hand.

"I bought this here phone for Mama a few months before she died. Do you know how to use one?" He handed it to Sparky.

"This is an iPhone 8." Sparky looked up at his aged friend. "I had one like this until the day Kal dinged up my mother's car and then blamed me for it. As part of my punishment, my dad took my phone away. It was always like that. Kal would do something, blame me, scare Courtney and Johnny into lying for him, and then my parents would take it out on me. It was Dad mostly. I think Mom suspected what Kal was really like. But Dad, he always sided with Kal no matter what and my mother didn't dare oppose him."

"I'm sorry about that," Alfred said. "But I am glad you know how to use the phone."

"Sure, and it does a lot of stuff."

"I want you to have it," Alfred said. "I'll buy one for me today, and you can teach me how to use it."

"This will be nice to have," Sparky said. "It does a lot of things that computers are used for. I could download some apps that have the news. It would be good to be able to keep track of what's happening on my mother's murder."

Sparky tried to turn the phone on, but it was dead. "It needs to be charged. Do you know where the charger is?"

"I think so," Alfred said as he headed out of the living room. He returned in a moment with the charger. Sparky put the broom aside and plugged the phone into an outlet above the kitchen counter. Then he turned it on and said, "I'll need one other thing to get into this. It's password protected."

"That's easy. We didn't want anything hard to remember. Mama used four ones."

***

Kal and his father were sitting in their living room with an officer from the Goodland Police Department. Donald had sent Courtney and Johnny to their rooms to play as he didn't want them to have to hear their conversation with the police officer. The officer, Sgt. Abel Bone, said, "I'm sorry to bother you two, but we have got to find Sparky. So far, we don't have any leads. We haven't been able to find anyone but you, Kal, who has seen him since the day he left school, the day he vanished. Are you sure it was him that pushed your mother? Could it have been someone else, an intruder perhaps?"

Kal's face flushed with anger. "It was Sparky. I know my own brother. So don't go trying to say I don't know who I saw."

"Sorry, Kal. Just making sure. So tell me, where were you when this happened?"

"I was in my room."

Donald broke in. "Kal's room is on the second floor, Sergeant, close to the balcony."

"Okay, thanks. We'll go look at that later."

"You guys have already looked," Kal said, having a hard time keeping his anger under control.

"It's routine, Kal," Sergeant Bone said. "We have to be thorough. So, you were in your room. Then what happened?"

"Like I said before, I thought I heard someone walk by my door. I had my headphones on, listening to music, so I couldn't hear too well. I didn't think anything of it. But I assumed it was my mother because Dad was at work and Courtney and Johnny were over playing on the neighbors' lawn with their dog. She's the only one it could have been.

"I took my headphones off and a minute later I heard more footsteps. They were going the same direction Mom had gone, onto the balcony. I stepped into the hallway because I was curious. That was when I heard Sparky's voice. He was swearing at Mom, but other than his swearing, I couldn't tell what else he was saying. I headed to the balcony. I was afraid Sparky might hurt Mom. She started crying, and then suddenly, she screamed. I got to the balcony just in time to see Sparky shove her really hard, so hard she went right over."

"What did Sparky do then? Did he see you?" the sergeant asked.

"Yeah, he saw me. He ran past me, shoving me so hard I fell," Kal said.

For a moment, Donald looked like he would cry. "I miss my wife so much. She was the world to me," he said, his voice breaking with emotion. "Sparky is really strong." Bitterness came to his voice. He stood and paced for a moment, rubbing his eyes. Then he again faced the officer. "Kal's lucky that Sparky didn't push him over the balcony too."

"I thought for a second that he might try it, but all he did was look down at me and say, 'You didn't see nothing, Kal. You ever say you did, and I'll do the same thing to you.'"

"Meaning that he would kill you?" the sergeant asked.

"Yeah, he was always telling me he'd kill me if I didn't do like he said. He was big. He loved to beat on me," Kal lied.

"Then what?" Bone pressed as Donald took his seat again.

"Sparky ran down the stairs. Where he went from there I have no idea. I was more concerned for my mother. It took me a second to get up. I banged my head pretty hard when he shoved me. So by the time I got to the stairs, I heard the front door slam."

"You don't know if he left on foot after that or if he might have had a car?"

"I'm not sure," Kal said. "I think I told you guys before that he left on foot. But I've been thinking about that. I remember now hearing a car take off. So he had probably stolen a car."

"Did you see a car?"

"No, like I said, I was worried about Mom. So I ran downstairs and out the back door to see if I could help her. But there was nothing I could do. She was dead." Kal forced a tear and looked down. He rubbed his eyes and with a choking voice said, "So I called 911 and waited with her body until you guys came."

"I see," Sergeant Bone said. "Tell me what Sparky was wearing."

"What he always wears. He had on a pair of tan pants and a T-shirt. It was the same clothes he wore to school the day he took off. I suppose he had his sneakers on, but I didn't notice that," he said. "Oh yeah, I just remembered something else. His pants and shirt were covered with dry mud. And when he ran past me, I could smell him. It was bad. I'm sure he hadn't had a bath or a shower since he left."

"Is there anything else you may have remembered?" Sergeant Bone asked.

"Nope, that's it. But if I remember something else I'll tell you. You've got to catch him, Officer. He can't get away with doing this to my mother." He faked another tear and choked back a sob as he said with downcast eyes, "She was a wonderful mother. I loved her so much. I don't know what we'll ever do without her."

"We'll get him," the officer said firmly. Then he turned to Donald. "I'll need to speak with the other children. One at a time, please."

"What do you need to talk to them for?" Kal asked, suddenly not acting so sad anymore, but feeling apprehensive.

"I just need to be thorough," Sergeant Bone said. "I'll be very gentle with them and won't take too long."

Kal jumped to his feet. "I'll get them," he said. "Should I send Courtney first?"

"That will be fine," the officer said. "Send her in. But I will need for you to be in another room while I speak with her."

"Why?" Kal demanded.

"For the same reasons they couldn't be here while I spoke with you."

"What about Dad. He can't stay either, can he?" Kal asked.

"Actually, he will need to stay," the officer said rather strongly, looking at Kal with questioning eyes.

Kal's manipulations were not working so well at the moment, so he decided to leave good enough alone. The last thing he needed was to alienate the officer. That wouldn't help him at all. So he left the room. When he got to the room where Courtney and Johnny were waiting, he stepped in and quietly shut the door. Then with balled fists and a fierce scowl on his face, he faced his young siblings.

They cowered as he said, "Sergeant Bone wants to talk to each of you one at a time. Courtney, you go first. When he is through with you, then you come back, and I'll send Johnny. Now, both of you remember this: You didn't see anything when Mom was killed. You didn't hear anything. You were playing on the neighbors' lawn with their dog. If either of you says something you shouldn't . . ." He gave them a warning look. "*You both know what I mean.* Courtney, you and I have talked about this. And while you are with Dad and Sergeant Bone, I'll talk to Johnny about it. If either one of you tell him anything other than what I told you to, I'll know, and so help me I'll break your fingers! And you will tell Dad that you got them caught in a door." Courtney whimpered, but Kal wasn't finished yet. "Little sister, when you get back, I'll expect you to tell me what the policeman asked and you'd better tell me exactly what you said to him. Do you understand?"

"Yes," she said in a broken voice.

"And what will happen if you disobey me?" Kal asked.

"You'll break my fingers in the door," she whispered.

"That or worse. Okay, go now, but don't be bawling and whimpering in front of Dad or the cop."

Courtney left. Johnny cowered in the corner, and Kal advanced on him. "Who killed Mom?" he asked menacingly.

"Sparky did?" Johnny asked, his answer sounding like a question as he trembled with fear.

"Don't ask me, you little brat. *Tell* me. Who killed our mother?"

"Sparky," Johnny said without meeting his brother's vicious glare.

"That's better. But why did he do that?"

"Be-be-because he hate-hated her."

"That's right, but when you talk to Sergeant Bone, what will you say?"

"You told me to say that I don't know who killed her."

"That's right. You tell him you don't know. If you tell him that I told you it was Sparky, what will happen to you?" Kal asked, his eyes boring into his brother's.

"You'll break my fingers?" Johnny said, a question, not a straight answer.

"Yes, I will do that, and if I have to, I'll make you disappear, just like Sparky did. Do you understand?" Kal asked, hatred and malice filling his eyes.

"You will kill me like you did Mom?" he asked, his voice breaking badly.

"I . . . did . . . not . . . kill . . . Mom! Sparky did! Johnny, you better get that straight in that stupid head of yours."

Kal had gone through this same dialogue with Courtney earlier. He believed he had both kids terrified enough that they would never tell the officer or anyone else what they thought happened to their mother. He kept harassing Johnny until Courtney came back. Johnny shot like a frightened rabbit from the room, his eyes meeting Kal's one last time as he left. Kal smiled. He knew how to control his brat siblings.

Kal then said, "Courtney, sit down. Okay, tell me everything that cop asked you and everything you said."

Kal didn't have to fake the look he gave his sister; it came naturally to him. The faking had to be done with his father and the cops. They had to believe he was devastated by the death of his mother and that he had actually seen Sparky push her off the balcony to her death.

Courtney spoke slowly and softly, fighting the urge to cry. "He asked me where I was when Mom died."

"What did you tell him?" he demanded.

"That I was at the neighbors' playing with their dog."

"Where at the neighbors'?"

"On the lawn," Courtney murmured.

"What else did he ask?"

"He asked if I saw Sparky."

"What did you tell him?"

"That I didn't think so, but that I was playing and might have missed him," she said.

"Very good, Courtney. You'd better not be lying to me."

Her eyes went to her folded hands. "I'm not lying to you."

He turned his head and smiled. He could see that she did not want her fingers broken, one by one. He could imagine her almost feeling how bad that

would hurt. When Johnny returned, Kal asked, "Did you say what I told you
to?"

"Y-yes," he said. "The policeman said for you to go back and talk to him
some more."

"Oh, he did, did he? Well, I'd better not find out you two lied to me," he
said. The threats that he'd made hung like a dark cloud over both of them as
he exited the room.

Back with his father and Sergeant Bone, Kal asked, "How did that go?"

"They are terribly broken up over the death of their mother," Detective
Bone said. "It was hard to talk to them. But they don't know anything anyway."

Kal felt relief wash over him. His threats had worked. "Yeah, I know," he
said. "I feel so bad for them. I wish there was some way I could make them
feel better."

"You can, Kal," his father said. "They look up to you. Comfort them when
you can. I'll do the same. Between us, we'll help them as well as ourselves get
through this horrible thing that Sparky did to Mom, to all of us."

***

Johnny and Courtney clung tightly to each other after Kal left the room.
It was Courtney who finally broke the silence. "Johnny," she began, "I think Kal
killed Sparky. And I know he killed Mom. We both saw him push her. Do you
think he killed Sparky?"

"Yes, I do. Courtney, I'm scared. I think he wants to get rid of us too,"
he admitted.

"But we can never say that to anyone but each other, can we?" Courtney
said. "Promise me you won't ever tell what we saw him do to Mom and what
we think happened to Sparky."

"I promise," he said. "Do you promise too?"

"Yes, I promise, Johnny," she said.

***

Donald walked out to the police car with Sergeant Bone, his gait slow and
staggering. The officer said, "I'm not sure that those children of yours will feel
better even when we catch Sparky and lock him up."

"That's what I fear," Donald agreed, his voice so full of emotion that he
could hardly speak. "I honestly never saw this coming with Sparky. He did
cause trouble from time to time, and he lied a lot, but I simply did not picture

him being capable of such a terrible thing. It breaks my heart." Tears flowed freely as Sergeant Bone got in his car and drove off.

CHAPTER FIVE

Sparky had finished fixing the short section of fence and took note of what needed to be done later on another section of fence. He inspected what he'd done. Alfred would have probably done a neater job despite his arthritis, but the fence was strong, and Sparky guessed that was what mattered most. Alfred had not returned yet when he got back to the yard on the four-wheeler, so he looked around for something else to do. It didn't take him long to make a decision.

He hooked up the little trailer to the four-wheeler, grabbed a shovel, and went to work pulling and digging out weeds from around one of the outbuildings. Those he couldn't pull, he cut out with the shovel. He had the trailer full to overflowing and was just wondering what to do with them when Alfred pulled into the yard in his shiny blue Silverado.

"I take it you got the fence fixed and needed something else to do," Alfred said with a grin when he got out of the truck in front of the garage. "I appreciate it. Did you fix yourself some lunch?"

Sparky was hungry, but he hadn't considered stopping his work before his benefactor got home. "No," he said. "I just kept working."

"Well, you've got to have something to eat if you're going to work so hard. Help me take these packages into the house and you can eat while I sort through things," Alfred said.

As they began to load their arms with packages, Sparky said, "Hey, you got brake pads for the Dodge."

"Sure did. I was thinking maybe I'd try to change the brake pads this afternoon."

"I can do that for you. I've changed brake pads a lot of times. Of course Kal almost always told our dad that he'd done it, but I don't think he even knows how." Sparky was smiling as he said it. He honestly didn't care anymore that

Kal had treated him the way he had. He was happier being here with Alfred more than he ever thought was possible. If only he didn't have the sorrow over his mother's death haunting him, life would be as near perfect as it could be.

"How about we do it together," Alfred suggested. He shifted the bags in his arms and grabbed another one. Sparky also loaded his arms. "You seem to enjoy working," he added as the two of them walked toward the house.

"I do," Sparky said. "You know, Alfred, what I really like about this farm of yours is how many different things there are to do."

"Variety is the spice of life," Alfred said. "I think that's what makes farming so much fun."

Once in the house, Alfred headed to the kitchen to fix Sparky some lunch. "What would you like?"

"I'll eat anything. Just fix whatever you want and I'll eat with you."

"I had a hamburger in Richfield."

"I can wait until dinner then," Sparky said.

Alfred insisted, so Sparky relented and had a cheese sandwich. Then Alfred said, "Let me show you what I got for you."

Sparky chuckled to himself as Alfred pulled items out and showed them to him. He was excited, and Sparky realized that Alfred was happy to be doing something for someone other than himself. He was such a good and kind man. Sparky found himself thinking how much he would like to be like Alfred when he reached adulthood.

There were a lot of things in the sacks. There were two brand-new western shirts and a couple pairs of new Wrangler jeans. There was also a pair of plain leather cowboy boots, which Alfred explained were for when they rode horses. There were socks and underclothes, pajamas, toiletries, a blue ball cap, and a brown felt cowboy hat.

"Now, that's all the new stuff," Alfred said as he pulled out a couple of large bags that said *Deseret Industries* on them. "I figured we might want some used clothes so that if someone comes by, they won't wonder why all you wear is brand-new clothes. He then produced four used western-cut work shirts, three pairs of worn blue jeans, a pair of scuffed leather work boots, and a jacket. "Come winter we'll find you a good heavy work coat."

Finally, Alfred showed Sparky the new iPhone he'd bought. They spent several minutes with both phones. Sparky downloaded a couple of free news apps, and he then showed Alfred how they worked. One was for Fox News. Both of them were worried when they read a story about Sparky and how he was being searched for all across the country. It was reported that he should be considered very dangerous, that according to his father and brother, he had no conscience, and if he did not get his way, he would not hesitate to kill again.

"I can't believe my dad has fallen for all of Kal's lies," Sparky said. "I'm afraid my little brother and sister must be terribly scared. I'm sure Kal has threatened them." He knew from experience that they would never dare tell their father the truth.

"I've been worrying about that, Sparky, but I don't know what to do without endangering you. I have to think about it some more. Maybe I can think of something I can do to help both you and your little brother and sister. Let's go get some work done. I've found that the best way to forget one's trouble is to work up a healthy sweat," Alfred explained. "And that's what you need right now."

After helping Sparky as he started working on the brakes, Alfred said, "You sure do know what you're doing. I'll just sit back and watch if you don't mind. I can't believe a fifteen-year-old can replace brake shoes as fast as you're doing it."

After the brakes were repaired, they hauled a couple loads of weeds to the goats and then went in the house for supper.

They were just finishing washing the last of the supper dishes when there was a knock on the front door. Alfred gasped. "Oh my goodness. I forgot all about the home teachers. I mean *ministering brethren*, as they are called now. I knew they were coming tonight."

Sparky had no idea what home teachers or ministering guys were, but he assumed he was about to find out. Then he had a worrisome thought. "Alfred, should I go somewhere so they can't see me? I don't want to be recognized."

"These are good men. Even if they figured out who you are, I'm sure I could talk them into keeping our secret. But, to be on the safe side, I think I shouldn't call you *Sparky*. What should I call you?"

Sparky thought for a moment. "My birth father's name was Walt Piler. Call me Walt."

The knock on the door was slightly louder this time. "I don't know if I can remember that," Alfred said as he hurriedly dried his hands.

"Walt, Walt, Walt," Sparky said.

"Walt, Walt, Walt," Alfred repeated softly as he hurried to the door. Sparky was nervous. He stayed in the kitchen and wiped the table for the second time. "Good evening," Alfred said after he had opened the door. "Come on in."

Sparky the dog stayed with Sparky the boy in the kitchen. He scratched and petted the dog furiously, terribly anxious about meeting a couple of men. He heard a man's voice say, "How are you doing, Brother Briggs?"

"I'm doing just fine, Bill. I see you have a new partner tonight," Alfred responded. Then he called out, "Walt, come in here and meet these folks."

Reluctantly, Sparky the boy walked to the doorway to the living room. Sparky the dog was right beside him. He drew up short when he saw the ministering brethren. He knew Alfred had said men. And one of them was. He was probably in his mid-thirties. He was around five ten with light brown hair parted in the middle. The other one was as far from being a man as it was possible to be.

Sparky barely saw the man. His eyes rested on a teenage girl, and he couldn't tear them away. He'd never been very interested in girls. And he'd certainly never seen one as pretty as the girl who stood before him, staring at him with eyes as blue as the sky, a perfect smile revealing two cute dimples and perfect white teeth. She had the prettiest wavy blonde hair he'd ever seen. It hung far down her back. He judged her to be about five six. Being in her presence made him feel shy—in a nice sort of way.

He finally tore his eyes away from her and looked at Alfred who was saying, "Walt, I'd like you to meet Bill Finch. His regular church companion was not able to come, so he brought this pretty young lady."

"This is my daughter, Kay Dell," Bill said. "She agreed to come with me tonight."

"It's nice to meet you, Kay Dell," Alfred said. "I know if I ever went to church I'd know you. But regretfully I don't. Why don't we all sit down?"

As Sparky claimed the nearest available chair, he tried to remember what his mother taught him, and he mumbled something that resembled, "It's nice to meet you two."

The girl, Kay Dell, sat on a soft chair directly opposite Sparky. The men sat on the sofa and began to talk. Sparky, now very nervous, tried to listen, but his mind had been hijacked, and he didn't seem able to get it back. The dog left his side and trotted the few steps to Kay Dell, where he began to lavish her with canine affection, rubbing against her legs and licking her hands.

Kay Dell seemed to lose all interest in Sparky the boy as she began to pet the dog and speak soft words to him. Then she slid to the floor from her chair and literally took the Border collie in her arms and hugged him. "What's his name?" she asked, looking up at Alfred as the dog rubbed against her, as if asking for more affection.

"His name is Sparky, but I usually call him *Boy* or just *Dog*. He sure seems to like you, Kay Dell. He took to, ah, to Walt, the same way," Alfred said awkwardly.

"He's so cute," Kay Dell said adoringly. And then, to Sparky the boy's surprise, and probably to Sparky the dog's surprise as well, she leaned forward and kissed the dog twice just above his moist black nose. The dog took it well. He responded by lavishing a kiss of his own on her face with his tongue, causing her to giggle.

"Kay Dell loves animals," Bill said. "But we can't have a pet of any kind at our house. My wife is terribly allergic to them." He chuckled. "The sort of contact that Kay Dell is having with Sparky would have Elena choking for lack of breath and breaking out all over with hives. She feels bad depriving our children of even one cat or dog, especially Kay Dell. But it can't be helped."

"That would be just terrible," Alfred said. "Mama loved our animals, all of them, like children. So do I, for that matter. And I am fortunate enough to have found a young man to help me who also loves animals."

"Yes. The name was Walt?" Bill asked.

"That's right," Alfred answered. "Walt Piler."

"Well, I'll tell you, Walt, I'm awful glad you're here. My partner and I have been worrying about what we could do to help Brother Briggs. Neither one of us are farmers, and we don't know the first thing about farming."

Kay Dell was still petting the dog, but she was also listening rather intently, it seemed, to the men talk. "Where are you from, Walt?" she asked, her eyes catching his, almost taking his breath away.

"He's from—" Alfred began.

Afraid that Alfred might mention Goodland, where Sparky was wanted for murder, he broke in and said, "Connecticut."

"You are a long ways from home," Bill said. "How did you and Brother Briggs meet?"

Alfred, who had given Sparky a look of relief when he stopped him from revealing where he was from, spoke up quickly this time. "He was hitching a ride over by Salina a couple of weeks ago. I gave him a ride, and when he told me he was looking for work, I talked him into coming to work for me."

"That sounds very fortunate for both of you," Bill said. "How old are you, Walt?"

Sparky started to say *fifteen*, but he'd barely started the *f* sound when Alfred cut him off. "He's eighteen," he said.

"Out of school then," Bill said.

"Yes," Alfred said. "I'll tell you, he is truly a blessing to me."

"So you have been here for two weeks, Walt?" Bill asked.

His interrogation was beginning to feel oppressive to Sparky, but he answered truthfully. "Yes, about that long."

"How do your parents feel about you hitchhiking your way across the country?" Bill asked next.

"They don't know. They were killed in a car wreck." It wasn't a lie. He was thinking, of course, about his birth parents.

"I'm sorry, Walt," Kay Dell piped in, and Sparky turned his attention to her. To his surprise, her blue eyes were filled with tears. "You're an orphan. That must be awful."

He did not correct her statement. "I'm getting used to it. Alfred has made it a lot easier for me. I was lucky to get a job with him."

The pretty girl smiled at the elderly man and said, "Thanks for being so kind to Walt."

From there, the conversation turned to other matters. At one point, Bill Finch said, "Do you mind if I share a short message with you from our prophet?"

"That would be fine," Alfred said.

Sparky missed most of the message as he was busy trying to wrap his mind around the strange terms he was hearing. *Ministering brethren, Brother Briggs, the prophet.* It made no sense to him. He could see that he would have some serious questions for Alfred after they left.

Even though his mind was busy, his eyes kept being drawn to Kay Dell. Occasionally, she would catch him looking and smile that fantastic smile of hers. For the life of him, he couldn't imagine why he felt so drawn to this girl.

He was pulled back into the conversation when Bill said, "It worries me. There is so much violence in the world today, and a lot of it involves young people. Did you see on the news that a kid the same age as Kay Dell, just fifteen, pushed his mother off of a balcony, killing her? It was somewhere in Kansas. It just makes me sick. I can't imagine why anyone would do something like that, and especially a teenager. One of the news reports said that the family was very stable as far as any neighbors knew. They were stunned by what happened. They also said that the boy, from all appearances, was a very fine young man."

Sparky's stomach was doing somersaults. He was afraid his face was turning red, for it sure felt hot. He had the urge to flee. But he knew that would draw attention to himself. How he wished he could just vanish.

Alfred helped when he calmly said, "Walt and I saw that on the TV. It is horrible, but at the same time, it makes me grateful that there are good solid young people like Kay Dell and Walt. If it weren't for kids like these, I don't know what we would do these days."

"I saw a picture of him," Kay Dell said. She looked at Sparky. "He had hair about the color of yours and mine. Somehow, I always thought of people who did things like that having either dark hair or no hair at all. You know, shaved heads. Is that silly or what? I know nothing like that has anything to do with who is good or bad. I'm just glad my parents have taught us kids to be kind to others. And I'm really glad for the example they set for us."

Sparky thought about his parents. He knew they were good people, especially his mother, but despite that, they raised Kal, and he was just plain evil. Now their sweet mother was dead. He shuddered as he thought of her and had to pull back a threatening tear.

Bill spoke again. "Thank you, Kay Dell. We try hard, that's for sure. So part of what the prophet wants us to get from his message is that it is the responsibility of adults to teach young people how to live righteously and to set a good example for them."

Sparky was able to relax a little at that point. Bill and Kay Dell had not recognized him. Perhaps it would all work out. A moment later, Bill said, "I mentioned earlier that I've been worried about how we could help you. Kay Dell and I came up with an idea. My wife agreed that we should talk to you about it."

Just then there was a scratching at the door. Sparky knew that sound. It was Geronimo, the big yellow cat, wanting to come in. Alfred said, "Sparky, would you go let Geronimo in?"

Sparky the boy froze. Sparky the dog got to his feet and looked at Alfred and then at the door. Alfred said, "I've got to where I always talk to Sparky. It's been hard since Mama died." He chuckled, but Sparky the boy knew a forced chuckle when he heard one. "Walt, would you open the door?" he said, even as the dog trotted over to it and stood there whining. "I know, Sparky old boy. You can't open the door. Sorry I asked you to. Walt will help you."

The look on Kay Dell's face had Sparky thinking that she was probably wanting to ask, *What is going on here?* But she was obviously a very polite girl and she didn't say it. As soon as the big yellow cat came through the door, her attention was drawn to it. And in moments, she was on the floor again, petting, loving, and kissing Geronimo. Sparky the dog was pushing against her, trying to steal her attention back.

Sparky the boy, unfrozen, slipped to the floor and called the dog, who left Kay Dell and let the girl fuss over Geronimo.

"You were about to mention something you and Kay Dell and your wife talked about," Alfred said.

"That's right. Of course we didn't realize that you had hired a farmhand, but I still want to run a couple of ideas by you," he said. "We would be glad to get a group of men from the church together and come out on, say a Saturday, and see if we could help you catch up on some work."

Alfred shook his head. "I appreciate the offer, but with Walt here, we are getting caught up. No, that won't be necessary."

"Here's another idea. Kay Dell loves animals, as you can see. She would be willing to come out occasionally after school and help out for two or three hours. As soon as school's out she could come more if you needed her to. And she wouldn't accept pay. She would like to do it just so that she could be around your animals."

Alfred was nodding his head. Sparky was holding his breath, trying to keep his heartbeat down. Kay Dell looked up expectantly. "Please, Brother Briggs," she said quietly. "I'll work hard and I'll try not to mess anything up."

Alfred spoke then. "Wouldn't it make it hard for you at school? I mean, I've understood that school activities keep you young people very busy. I wouldn't want to cause it to affect your studies."

"Oh, it wouldn't. I would rather be out here than anything I could be doing after school. I promise I'll keep my grades up if you let me come," she said, her eyes pleading.

"What do you think, Sparky?" Alfred said, slipping up once again. The dog looked up from where he was sitting beside the young man who had once again frozen. He thumped his tail. "See there, he agrees, Kay Dell. How about you, Geronimo?" The cat looked over at Alfred who was clearly trying again to cover the error he had made. Geronimo hunched his back and purred. "It looks to me like he agrees too."

Sparky was starting to relax. He was amazed at how easily his elderly friend smoothed out his mistakes. Alfred then asked, "Do you agree with the animals, Walt?"

He'd be an idiot not to. Kay Dell was pretty and seemed really nice. He said as nonchalantly as he could manage, "Sounds okay to me."

Kay Dell beamed.

"I vote yes as well," Alfred said with a huge smile. "So it seems that all four of us in this household agree. "When would you like to come, young lady?"

"We've also talked about this with her mother," Bill Finch said. "We were thinking Wednesdays or Fridays. And if you needed her, she could come on Saturdays occasionally too. We have family activities on Monday evenings. She has mutual on Tuesdays and a piano lesson every Thursday. If that doesn't work, we'll see if we can work something else out."

Alfred chuckled. "Me and Walt, we don't have anywhere else to be. That would be great, but I would like to pay her."

"No, please," Kay Dell said. "Just getting to be here and work with you guys and be around your animals is all I want. You just don't know how happy this has made me." And to show her appreciation, she stood up, went over to Alfred, who was still seated, bent down and hugged him.

Alfred beamed. Sparky got nervous when she then approached him. To his relief, she simply offered her hand, which he shook. Then she grinned and said with an exaggerated drawl, "I think I'll come on Friday, so I'll see you then, partner." Wow, she had a cool voice. He couldn't believe this was happening.

After the Finches were gone, Sparky and Alfred laughed together about what a hard time Alfred had had remembering what to call Sparky. "It will be even harder when Kay Dell comes to work with us on Friday. I hope you don't mind, but just remember, she is a Mormon—a member of The Church of Jesus Christ of Latter-day Saints. The leader of the Church, I've been told, doesn't like people to use the name *Mormon* anymore to refer to the Church. Anyway, the Church kind of likes their girls and boys to refrain from dating until they are sixteen, and even then they don't like couples pairing off."

"I don't have any plans of dating at all," Sparky said. At this point, that was the truth. All he planned to do was stay on Alfred's farm and work. And to be able to occasionally work with a cool girl like Kay Dell Finch was more than he could ever have asked for. None of the girls in Goodland had interested him very much, even though a few of them had tried to attract his attention.

Alfred wasn't through yet. "That will change. Someday soon, you will want to date. That is only natural. Just heed my warning, Sparky. Or I guess I should be practicing calling you *Walt*."

"I guess," Sparky said without enthusiasm.

"Anyway, another thing you need to know about this church is that they strongly encourage their young people to marry within the faith."

"Got it," Sparky said, marriage being the furthest thing from his mind. "Now, I've got some questions for you. Let's see, tell me what *ministering brethren* are, what a *prophet* is, why Bill calls you *Brother* Briggs, and what Bill meant when he said that Kay Dell has *mutual*."

"Let's sit down again, and I'll try to explain. Although I'm not what you'd call a good church member, I believe what the Church teaches. Me and Mama both did," Alfred began. "As I sort of mentioned a moment ago, *Mormon* is a nickname for The Church of Jesus Christ of Latter-day Saints. Our leader is a prophet like Moses was in his day. We believe that he speaks for God. Members of our church often call each other Brother and Sister so-and-so. Don't let that freak you out. Ministering brethren are men who visit the homes of other members and try to be helpful. Bill Finch and his partner are faithful about that. They usually show up at least once a month. Let's see, what else?"

"What is mutual?" Sparky asked.

"Oh, that's an organization within the Church for teenagers. I think they have classes and activities and the like," Alfred said.

"There is one other thing," Sparky said. "Does the church make them do activities as a family every Monday night? I think it's cool. My family hardly ever did anything together. But it seems strange that a church would require it."

"Oh yeah, that is another church thing. Families are encouraged to hold activities on Mondays or at other times during the week and to teach church lessons on Sundays and other times throughout the week as well. You'll have to ask Kay Dell about that sometime," Alfred suggested. "I really don't know that much about it."

"I guess I could do that, but Alfred, she worries me."

"Worries you?" Alfred asked, cocking an eyebrow. "She's a good girl, as good as they come, I'd say."

"Oh yeah, I get that. But I think she was beginning to suspect something. She makes me nervous. What if she thinks I'm a killer?" he asked.

"Then I guess you'll just have to show her by the way you treat me, her, and the animals what kind of guy you are. It'll be okay," Alfred assured him.

Sparky wasn't so certain.

CHAPTER SIX

"Dad, Walt seems like a really nice guy, but something about him really bothers me," Kay Dell said as they drove back to their home that evening.

"He clearly isn't a member of The Church of Jesus Christ of Latter-day Saints. Maybe you can have an influence on him. Teach him about the Church a little at a time," Bill suggested. "This could be a great missionary opportunity for you."

"I hope so," she said.

"Just remember who you are, and don't forget our standards," Bill began. "When young people in the Church get lax about whom they date, it often creates pitfalls for them."

"Dad, I know all that. I would never think of dating Walt. Frankly, I'm not boy crazy like a lot of other girls. I'm not really that interested in dating much, even when I turn sixteen. But maybe I can be Walt's friend."

"Yes, you can be his friend," Bill agreed. "You can be Alfred's friend, too. I'd sure like to see him come to church sometime. Maybe you can influence him better than I have."

Kay Dell puzzled over Walt all the way home. There was something about him that was a mystery. She thought it might have to do with his name. That night when she went to bed, she prayed that she would be able to be a good example to both Walt and Alfred. And she prayed for both of them.

***

The following evening, after once again viewing coverage on the national news about the search for the young killer, Sparky Graves, Alfred said, "Sparky, we've got to do something. There's now a reward offered for your arrest. Twenty-five thousand dollars and growing. And I constantly think about your younger siblings. I want to do something to help them but I don't want to put you in danger either."

"But I don't know what we can do," Sparky said, his voice shaky.

"I have an idea. I've been mulling it over for a couple of days. I'm convinced now that it's time to consider it."

"What's your idea?" Sparky asked.

"We need to hire a private investigator," Alfred told him. "And we need the best person we can find. Not just anyone will do."

"What can a private investigator do to help me or my brother and sister?" Sparky asked. "And what if the guy we hire decides to turn me in for that reward money? It won't help Johnny and Courtney if I go to jail."

"That's why we need the best, Sparky. We need someone who is totally honest and will keep your case in confidence."

"I still don't see what a private investigator could do for us."

"It appears to me that the cops are focused on you and only you. They are doing nothing to make sure they are after your mother's real killer. You need someone who will do that for you, someone who will dig and dig until he or she discovers a way to show that someone else killed your mother."

"It was Kal," Sparky said. "The more I think of it, the more sure I am."

"Then we need someone who can find the evidence that will prove that. But we also need someone who will spend time checking every place you stopped along the way while you were riding in the pipe on that semi. Every time you got out of the pipe, someone might have seen you. I could tell the cops that you were with me when your mother died, which is the truth, but that might not be enough to convince them," Alfred said.

"I can't see how that will help," Sparky said glumly. "I mean, I don't think anyone will remember me."

"I don't know about that. If we give our PI a picture of you, the one from your driver's license, he can show it to people, and sooner or later, someone will remember you."

"But wouldn't people already be letting the cops know if they remembered me?"

"Not necessarily. Remember, Kal claims you were there in Goodland when you were right here with me. I doubt many people this far from Kansas will give you much thought. It will be people close by who will be trying to remember if they saw you sometime. By showing your picture along the route you took, perhaps someone will remember you and that will help prove that you couldn't have killed your mother."

"Maybe," Sparky said doubtfully. All his life, his older brother had succeeded in pinning the blame on him for things he hadn't done—and would never do, for that matter. He couldn't see why that would change now. "Anyway, I'm sure PIs are expensive. I can't afford one."

"I can," Alfred said.

"You can't do that! It's not fair to you," Sparky protested.

"Sparky, you are a blessing to me. Without you, I don't know how I could keep this farm running another year. I want to do it—for both our sakes and for your family's."

"That girl, Kay Dell, wants to help you, and you don't even have to buy her food or clothes and stuff," Sparky argued.

"She hasn't proven to me that she can even do anything. It's one thing to love animals but quite another to do the hard farm work you've been doing. Sparky, I'm glad she wants to help, but I want you here helping me for as long as you are willing," Alfred said earnestly.

"I'll stay forever if you'll let me—if I don't get arrested," Sparky said somberly.

"Then let's see what it will take to get a PI located and hired."

"Only if you don't pay me. I'll work just for what you call my room and board."

"For now, that's fine if that's what you want."

"It is. So how do we find a good PI?" Sparky asked. "Should we look on the internet?"

"Might be a good idea . . ."

"I'll start by asking Siri." Sparky pulled out his cell phone. "Siri, I need a list of private investigators in or near Richfield, Utah."

In a matter of seconds, Sparky's phone said, "Okay, here's what I found on the internet," and Alfred looked on in amazement as the phone displayed a private investigation agency in Richfield and another in Spanish Fork.

"That blows my old mind," Alfred said. "I had no idea a phone could do that."

"Yup, pretty cool, huh? Anyway, here's a couple of agencies you can try," Sparky said.

"I want more than two agencies to pick from. Why don't you ask for some in or near Salt Lake City?" Sparky did and that inquiry produced a large list. "Okay, so let's make some calls."

"Won't we have to wait until morning?" Sparky asked. "It's nearly eight o'clock. We won't get anybody at night, will we?"

"You're probably right. It's just that once I make up my mind to do something, I like to get right after it. I'll just have to be patient. So I tell you what; after we get our chores done and finish with breakfast in the morning, we'll call until we find someone we feel good about."

***

Kay Dell Finch couldn't get Walt off her mind. Something wasn't right about him. Not that she believed he was a bad guy. No, it wasn't that at all. He seemed like a really nice guy. Again, it occurred to her that it was something about his name that didn't seem right. That night, she joined her parents when the national news came on. There was a brief story about the murder in Goodland, Kansas. The boy they wanted for killing his mother was named Sparky Graves. His picture was on the screen. And there was now a large cash reward for information leading to his arrest. He had neatly combed blond hair that hung over his ears and reached his collar. He had blue eyes. His height matched Walt's . . .

Surely Walt wasn't Sparky Graves. That would be horrible. Kay Dell shivered at the very thought.

Her dad said nothing, but then he was more interested in a book he was reading than in the news. And her mother hadn't seen or met Walt. But Kay Dell got a sinking feeling in the pit of her stomach. She quietly went to her bedroom and pulled out her phone. She Googled the name *Sparky Graves*. Once again, his picture came up with the story of the manhunt and the reward. She studied the face on the screen. The age was wrong. Walt was eighteen. *Or was he?*

She was thinking very seriously that Walt Piler and Sparky Graves were one and the same person. She thought about the reward. Twenty-five thousand dollars. That was a lot of money. That was more money than she knew what to do with. And it was expected to get bigger as more people donated to it. Mrs. Graves was someone who apparently many people admired.

Kay Dell suddenly felt guilty for thinking about the money. She decided she was wrong. It could not possibly be Walt. She read the article over again, then she looked closely at the date it occurred. *It couldn't be Walt.* Alfred had told them he hired Walt around two weeks ago. If that were true, she reasoned, then either Walt was who he said he was, or if he was Sparky Graves, who he looked so much like, then he was here in Utah when his mother was murdered. Either way, it could not have been him. The relief she felt was almost overwhelming.

She thought about talking to her father about it. But she decided to keep her suspicions to herself for now. If her parents had as much as even a tiny suspicion about Walt being a wanted murderer, there was no way they would ever let her go help on the farm. And that was something she wanted badly. It was her dream.

She studied the cute face on the phone again. She thought about when she'd met Brother Briggs and Walt. Something had bothered her then. Suddenly, it hit her. Bother Briggs had called Walt *Sparky*. He'd quickly covered up saying that he was too used to talking to Sparky the dog. And she remembered the look on Walt's face. He looked scared when Brother Briggs called him that and then relaxed when Brother Briggs tried to cover it up.

Once again, she looked at the date of the murder. She rubbed her eyes. There was something she had to ask her father. She found him still in front of the TV with her mother. "Dad, can I ask you something?" she said.

Bill looked up from his book.

"Dad, I am so excited about going out to Brother Briggs's farm. But I was just wondering how honest he is."

"Alfred Briggs may not go to church, but he's one of the most honest and honorable men I know," he said. "Are you worrying about being around him?"

"No, but I just wanted to know if he would ever lie to me," Kay Dell said.

Her father smiled and shook his head. "No, he will not lie to you."

"Thanks, Dad," she said and returned to her bedroom.

Kay Dell was troubled now. Brother Briggs had told them that Walt was eighteen. If Walt was Sparky, then he was the same age as her—fifteen. Had Brother Briggs lied? If he had, it didn't fit with what her father had just told her. On the other hand, maybe it was Walt who lied to Brother Briggs. Then she thought again about how he'd called Walt *Sparky*. She was pretty sure that Brother Briggs knew who Walt was and how old he was. If so, he'd lied.

Maybe he'd lied to protect Walt, *or Sparky*. If that were the case, then maybe it wasn't a *bad* lie. If Alfred Briggs knew what Kay Dell thought she had figured out, then it must be that he knew his helper was innocent. Brother Briggs was simply trying to keep something really bad from happening to Walt. She had to find out. She once again prayed, but this time, she prayed that she could figure out if she'd been lied to by both Brother Briggs and Walt. She also prayed that if Walt was Sparky Graves, then he would not get arrested for something he did not do. She was confused and unsure but still she felt no fear of either of them.

***

"I'll come down and meet you at your home," Detective Lys Grist told Alfred Briggs. "I just finished a case and haven't accepted another one yet, so I'm free today, and the drive would be nice."

Lys was a private investigator, the fifth one Alfred had called, and he had a good feeling about her after their short phone conversation. However, he was not going to retain her until he had a chance to meet her in person and make another assessment of her. He'd offered to drive to her office in Salt Lake, but he was relieved when she volunteered to drive down to Monroe. At his age, he simply was not comfortable driving in the city. His eyes were not as good as they used to be and his reflexes were slower. Plus, a long drive made his whole body hurt.

Sparky was out pulling and cutting more of the weeds. Alfred joined him and told him about Lys.

"Is that a woman or a man?" Sparky asked.

"A woman. So far, I feel good about hiring her."

"So what now?"

"She's driving down today to meet us here. We can decide after we get to know her if we want to hire her or not."

"Won't it be hard to tell her we don't want to hire her after she drives all the way down here?" Sparky asked.

"I won't be influenced by that," Alfred said firmly. "I will only hire her if she has the credentials I'm looking for and if we both feel like she is honest and will work for us with total confidentiality."

It was late afternoon when a black Chevy Tahoe pulled into the yard where Sparky was still cleaning up weeds. He was sweating and his back ached, but he was enjoying the work despite that. Alfred had helped for a while, but it was hard for him, and he'd left on a four-wheeler to start up one of the pivot irrigation systems.

The Tahoe stopped in front of the house and the driver got out and looked around. When she spotted Sparky, she waved at him and started walking in his direction. She was a pretty woman with short black hair and an athletic body. She walked with confidence, and when she reached where Sparky stood holding a shovel, she smiled and held out her hand. Sparky was hesitant, but he finally pulled off his glove and reached out as well and they shook. She had a firm grip. But the penetrating gaze she gave him with her brown eyes made him nervous. Even though at six foot one, he towered over her by seven or eight inches, she looked . . . well, *dangerous*, he decided, despite her smile. He felt the urge to cut and run. The only reason he didn't was the fact that he knew a female private investigator was coming to meet Alfred. He just hoped this was her and not some cop who had come to arrest him.

"I'm Lys Grist," she said. "I'm looking for Alfred Briggs. He's expecting me."

"He'll be back in a few minutes," Sparky said with a huge sigh of relief. "He went down to start one of the pivots running."

"Then I guess I'll wait. You must be his grandson," she said.

That caught him off guard. He didn't know what Alfred had told her when he'd talked to her on the phone. He supposed that Alfred might have told her that. Or he might not have mentioned why he even needed a PI. He was saved from having to make an answer when he heard the sound of Alfred's four-wheeler.

"Here he comes now," he said. "I'll get back to work here and let you talk to him."

She looked at him suspiciously, but Sparky simply turned away and began shoveling at a particularly large weed that was giving him trouble in the hard ground. He hoped she would take the hint and not try to speak with him anymore. She did speak, and what she said surprised him. "Here, let me help you with that," she said. She took hold of the dry stem and pulled while he shoveled.

They had barely gotten it out of the ground when Alfred pulled up and stopped. "Here he is now."

Lys smiled at him and then turned and offered her hand to Alfred after he'd climbed awkwardly from the four-wheeler. "You must be Alfred Briggs. I'm Lys Grist. Pretty place you have here."

"It's getting prettier," Alfred said, "thanks to the good help I have."

"Yes, I can see that he's a good worker," she said. "I'm sorry, but I didn't catch your name." She was looking right at Sparky with those piercing brown eyes.

Before he could decide what to tell her, Alfred spoke up. "That's what we need to talk about. Why don't we go in the house and sit down?"

Lys didn't bat an eye at the unexpected response. Sparky was relieved, but he was not sure if Alfred meant for him to keep working or to join him in the house. So he said, "I'll haul this load down to the goats and then get started on another one."

"No, that can wait," Alfred said. "This is about you and your future, so I want you involved in what we talk about." He looked at Lys for a moment and asked, "Just to confirm what you told me on the phone, will everything we discuss here today be kept confidential even if I don't decide to retain you?"

"Absolutely," she said. "I will even keep this young man's name to myself if and when you decide to tell me what it is." She smiled. "I'm guessing that the reason you're seeking my services has something to do with him."

"You are right about that," Alfred said with a firm nod. "When we get inside, we'll tell you all about it."

Sparky followed the other two into the house. He had decided that Lys Grist wasn't dangerous. At least she wasn't to him. Perhaps to some people she could be very dangerous. She had an air of both competence and confidence about her. He guessed she must have been about ten years older than his mother. If she was, that would put her in her mid-forties. He just hoped she could be trusted.

Once they were all seated in the living room, Alfred began by saying, "So tell us about yourself. What kinds of cases have you handled? That kind of thing."

"I conduct all sorts of investigations. It includes everything from divorce matters to murder," she said. "And what I mean by that is I've assisted in solving murder cases when the police have been having a hard time, or when a victim's family feels like the police aren't doing enough or are looking in the wrong places."

"I see," Alfred said as he and Sparky locked eyes for a moment. Sparky wanted to tell her that his case was exactly that, but he had made up his mind not to speak until he was specifically asked to do so.

"What kind of case are you thinking about having me work on?" Lys asked.

"May I tell you what our problem is before I tell you who my young friend is?" Alfred asked.

"First, am I to understand that he is not your grandson?"

There was an uncomfortable pause before Alfred finally said, "I'm afraid that's true, although he feels like a grandson to me."

"I can see that there is affection between the two of you. Okay, tell me about the problem, if you want me to hear it. After you do, you can decide if you want to retain me or not and I can decide if I want to take your case," Lys said. "I didn't drive all the way down here in an attempt to persuade you to hire me if you don't want to. I was intrigued when you told me that your case was a matter of life and death. That is what you told me, isn't it?"

Alfred nodded. "That's right. So here's our problem; my young friend here left his home because of danger to him posed by his older brother. He's been with me for a little over two weeks. He'd been here almost two weeks when we saw on the news that his mother had been murdered, and his older brother told the police that his younger brother did it. But that's not possible because that younger brother was with me, and anyway, he's not that kind of person."

"Intriguing," Lys said, glancing at Sparky for a moment. "I saw the reports on the news. Pictures of the young man the police are looking for do resemble you, but they show much longer hair."

"I cut his hair," Alfred said.

"So you're the missing and wanted boy?" Lys asked Sparky.

He exchanged glances with Alfred, who nodded, and then he said, "Yes, I'm Sparky Graves. But I did not kill my mother. I loved my mother." He felt himself choking up and fought to keep his emotions in check.

"Okay, you two, let's take this from the beginning. Tell me everything, including details of your family and why you chose to leave them," Lys instructed.

For the next half hour, Sparky opened up to Lys. She listened carefully, occasionally asked a question to clarify something, and then let him go on.

After he had finished and Alfred had told her what had happened since he'd picked Sparky up beside the road near Salina, Lys said, "Let's make sure I understand everything." Then she recited in abbreviated form what she had been told.

"Sounds like you've got it," Alfred said when she had finished.

"So what exactly, if you hire me, would you like me to do?" Lys asked, her eyes intently looking at Sparky's face. Her look was one of kindness and understanding.

CHAPTER SEVEN

ALFRED AND SPARKY EXCHANGED GLANCES, and then Alfred said, "Sparky, why don't you tell her?"

"Okay," Sparky agreed. "But first, do you believe me, ma'am?"

"Yes, Sparky, I do," she said firmly. "And you can call me Lys."

"Thanks, Lys," he said soberly. "I wish my father and the police in Goodland would believe the truth. They believe Kal. Everyone always believes Kal, and they never believe me. Anyway, I need to have proof that we can give the cops that will convince them I wasn't there and couldn't have done that to my mom."

"We have the word of Mr. Briggs," Lys said, smiling at Alfred. "Is that not enough?"

Alfred shook his head. "I don't think so. They could say that I lied to protect him."

"Okay, so I understand and agree that your word might not be enough, Alfred, even though I believe that you are an honest man. So you would like me to find others who can verify that you were not in Goodland at the time of your mother's murder? Is that right, Sparky?" she asked.

"Yes," he said.

"You know, there could be cameras at a lot of these places and they are always time stamped. If I could get your picture on some of them, that would be great proof of where you were and when," she said.

"I hadn't thought of that," Alfred said.

"It's my job to think of such things. But don't get your hopes up too much. Some businesses don't keep their videos for very long, and they often record over them. But it is worth checking, and I will."

"That sounds good," Alfred said.

"Is that all you need me to do?" Lys asked.

"No, I think we need to get proof of who actually did that to Mom," Sparky said. He was embarrassed when he had to wipe moisture from his eyes.

"You believe it was your older brother. You said his name is Kal. Is that right?"

"It had to be him," Sparky said with a sudden surge of anger. "And if it was, then my younger siblings are in danger. I . . . Alfred and I both want them to be safe. That's one of the reasons why we need your help."

"I think I understand, but let me ask you two this: did anyone else in this area know that you were here prior to the incident in Kansas?"

"He has been right here with me," Alfred said. "The only other people who know he is here with me just learned about it. A man from my church and his daughter came by. They think he is Walt Piler and is eighteen years old."

"Then let's make some decisions here. First, do you want to retain me?" Lys asked.

"Yes, I do," Alfred said. "As long as I know you will keep this confidential."

"I will, and I want to take your case. I was intrigued when you called me, but now I'm more intrigued than ever. So should we get some paperwork done?" Lys asked.

They both agreed. A contract was signed and Alfred gave the investigator a retainer. Then she said, "What I need now are some more details. Let's begin with your parents' names and their address in Kansas." After Sparky supplied that information, she asked him to detail the route he traveled after leaving his home. He told her, and then she said, "Okay, guys, this is what I'll do. I'll work backwards from here to Goodland. I'll see if I can find anyone in any of the places you stopped at along the way who might remember you when I show them your picture, one from before your hair was cut." She smiled.

"I don't know if anybody will remember me," Sparky said. "I tried not to be obvious."

"People did see you," Lys said. "You'd be surprised what people remember when I encourage them." She smiled again. "I'll find one of the old news reports and download it to my phone and then single out your picture."

"Okay," Sparky said doubtfully.

"One more thing. Tell me the name of the trucking company that you borrowed a ride from. If you noticed it on the door of the truck, that is."

"I didn't pay any attention to it," he admitted. "The pipe was being hauled to someplace near Las Vegas." Suddenly his eyes lit up. "Hey, I just remembered something. I actually talked to the driver one time. I was just trying to see if he suspected me of riding in the pipe on his truck. But he didn't."

"So the driver actually spoke with you?" she asked.

"Yes. He didn't know I was stowing away on his truck."

"Did you get his name?"

"No, I only talked to him for a few seconds. I asked him where he was hauling the pipe. That's how I knew it was going to Nevada."

"Then I've got to find him," she said. "He may recognize your picture and remember talking to you. Okay, I'll get to work. I'll talk to every driver of the trucks hauling pipe like that, and I'll be watching out for *your* driver in particular. Alfred, I'll keep you updated on any progress that I make."

***

Alfred wasn't the only one who was hiring a private investigator. That very afternoon, Donald Graves and his son Kal walked into an austere office in Topeka, Kansas. They had driven for the past four and a half hours in order to be on time to the appointment Donald had made to meet with Detective Brad Hagen. Donald had made a number of calls before deciding that Hagen would be a good choice for the work he needed to have done.

Brad was in his mid-fifties and was a retired FBI agent. He invited the two into his office and had them sit across from his desk. He was a stocky man with thick brown hair that was short and neatly combed. He studied the father and son with piercing green eyes for a moment. "What exactly do you two fellows need me to do?"

"Find my killer of a brother," Kal said angrily.

"Kal, let me handle this," Donald said. Then he turned to the investigator. "My wife was murdered several days ago. Kal here saw his younger brother push her from the deck on the second floor of our house, then take off."

"He pushed right past me, knocking me down," Kal said.

"Son," Donald said, "I'll handle this."

Kal frowned but sat back in his chair and folded his arms across his chest.

"Would this be the boy who ran away from home and then came back to kill his mother?" Detective Hagen asked. "I've followed that on the news."

"Yes, my adopted son, Sparky, has been a troublemaker in our family for a long time. He's a large boy, larger than Kal by quite a bit even though he is younger, and he has taken advantage of his size," Donald said. "The younger children are afraid of him. He always gave the appearance of being a nice boy, but he had us fooled. He constantly stirred up trouble for Kal."

Detective Hagen broke in. "Kal, you say you saw him push your mother to her death?"

"I sure did," Kal said. "We thought he was long gone. He disappeared like two weeks before he murdered my mother."

"I'll take it from here, Kal," Donald interrupted. "We did report it when Sparky vanished. But the police were unable to find him. It turns out he was hiding somewhere nearby. Frankly, we were better off with him gone, but of course, he's only fifteen and my wife and I didn't want him to get hurt out there on his own." He paused, his face growing dark, and he suddenly slammed his right fist into his left palm. "I just don't understand why he felt like he had to come back and kill his own mother. I knew he was trouble, but I never imagined he could do such a horrible thing to his mother." He choked back a sudden sob. "She was always so loving and kind to him."

Kal, seemingly incapable of keeping his mouth closed, butted in again. "He was arguing with Mom just before he pushed her over the railing."

"I see," Detective Hagen said. "I assume what you want me to do is help the police find him."

Kal snorted. "They aren't even trying to find him. We need you to do it and then let us know where he is so the cops can get off their duffs and go arrest him."

Donald gave up trying to get Kal to let him handle things with the detective. But he couldn't blame Kal. He couldn't imagine how hard it must be for his son to have seen his brother so brutally murder his mother and then disappear again with the unspoken threat that he could come back at any time and murder another member of the family. Unfortunately, he felt that Kal was right about the police. He didn't believe that they were doing nearly enough to find Sparky.

"That's right, Detective," Donald said. "I would like to hire you to find Sparky and bring him to justice."

***

Kal, though grim faced, was gloating inside. This guy had been an FBI agent. Kal was confident he could find Sparky. But when he did, Kal had no intention of letting the cops arrest him. Sparky would need to be silenced. And he would personally take care of that once he knew where Sparky was hiding out.

"All right then, gentlemen, let's get a contract signed. You did bring the five-thousand-dollar retainer I mentioned, did you not?"

"I have it," Donald said grimly.

The formalities out of the way, the investigator then spent several minutes with Donald and Kal, getting as much information as he felt he needed to begin the search. After they left his office, Kal said, "Dad, you'll be glad you hired him. He'll find Sparky."

"I hope so. Five thousand dollars is a lot of money. I just hope you're right, Kal. It would have never occurred to me that we might need to hire someone to help find him. I just wish you would have suggested this before Sparky came back and killed your mother," Donald said. "Maybe if we'd done that, your mother would still be alive."

Kal held his tongue. His dad was wrong. No matter what they did, his mother would still be dead. The only thing that might have been different was that Sparky might have been found sooner, and if so, he would also be dead.

***

Kay Dell was super excited. It was Friday afternoon. This would be her first time going to the Briggs farm to do some work and meet some of the animals. "I'll be glad when you get your driver's license," Elena, Kay Dell's mother, said as she got the last of the little boys in the car for the drive out to Alfred's farm.

"Me too," Kay Dell agreed. She felt bad that it was so much trouble for her mother. She'd offered to ride her bike, but Elena told her that she'd rather drive her out.

Alfred and Walt were shoveling and pulling weeds in the yard when Kay Dell arrived a few minutes later. It was not a terribly long drive, but it would have taken her at least twenty or thirty minutes on her bike. She would've been happy to do that if that's what it took to do what she had dreamed of doing for so long. She was pretty sure her mother would get tired of the two trips, one to take her out and the other to bring her back. When that happened, she would bike, unless the weather was bad.

Kay Dell got out of the car and promised to call when she was ready to come home. Alfred leaned his shovel against a tree and walked over to greet her. Walt looked up at her and responded with a smile when she waved at him, but he kept working.

"What would you like me to do?" she asked as Sparky the dog ran over to her and begged for her attention.

"As you can see, we've got the weeds about cleared here in the yard," Alfred said while Kay Dell petted the dog. "Actually, I should say that Walt has. He's a hard worker. As for me, I think I should go inside and take it easy for a little while. Thanks so much for offering to help. I just don't want you to feel obligated."

"Oh no, I don't at all," Kay Dell said with a huge smile. "I'm just so happy that you're willing to let me come out here. It's like a dream come true for me."

"Well, thanks, Kay Dell. Now if you don't mind, maybe you could help him finish up. This load will need to go to the goats pretty soon. Then there are some more fence repairs to be made way over on the far side of my farm. Walt knows what to do."

"Okay, I'll do whatever you want me to," Kay Dell said.

"Oh, do you know how to drive a four-wheeler?" he asked.

"I do," she replied.

"That's good. Then when Walt is ready to pull that trailer load of weeds to the goats, you can take the other four-wheeler. Do you have any gloves?" he asked.

It was pretty obvious that she didn't, but she said, "I'll be okay. I'll bring some next time."

"No need for that. I've got extra gloves in the house. I'll be right back out with them," he said.

Alfred walked off and Kay Dell glanced toward where Walt was working. She felt awkward. She had almost convinced herself that his name was not Walt, but Sparky. She wanted to talk to him about that and assure him that he could trust her. She just wasn't sure how to bring it up. She once again gave in to the dog's continued coaxing and knelt to pet him. She didn't hear Walt approach.

"He sure likes you," he said, startling her.

"He likes you too," she said as she stood up. "Hi. I hope it's okay with you that I'm coming out here to help a little."

"Why wouldn't it be?" Walt asked soberly. "It's not my place; it's Alfred's. But believe me, there is plenty of work to do." He glanced down at her hands. "You will need gloves. There's barbed wire where we are going to work. And it can be really tough on hands."

"I wasn't even thinking," she said, feeling her face begin to burn. "This is new to me. But Alfred went in the house to get me a pair. I'm sorry I wasn't prepared."

Walt's sober face finally lightened up and he grinned at her. "I was the same way, and he took pity on me. Another time you might want a hat. When I came to work for him, I didn't have a hat either. For you and me with our light complexions, we sort of need to wear hats."

Kay Dell felt some of the tension ease. "I promise I'll be more prepared next time. I need to get some better shoes too. These tennis shoes aren't the best. But those look like good work boots you're wearing."

Walt looked down at his feet. "Alfred bought these for me at a place he calls DI."

"Oh, yeah, Deseret Industries. That's what I need to do," she said. "Maybe I'll go there tomorrow and see if I can find a pair."

"You don't need to do that," Alfred said, surprising her. She had not heard him come up behind her. "I'll get you some before you come next week. I'll just need to know your size."

"No, I can get them," she said.

"Kay Dell, you are here helping me and you say you won't take any pay. The least I can do is buy you some work shoes and a hat," he said as he handed a pair of leather gloves to her.

"These are brand new," she protested. "I can wear a pair of old ones."

Alfred smiled at her. "You can wear new ones too. Now you kids go ahead. I'm going to go rest."

After Alfred walked away, she grinned at Walt. "At least I slathered myself with sunscreen."

"I've started doing that too," he said.

"Isn't Brother Briggs a nice guy?" she said.

Walt chuckled. "He likes us to call him *Alfred*. *Brother Briggs* makes him sound like a monk or something."

Kay Dell laughed. "Yeah, I guess you're right now that you mention it. I'll call him Alfred if you think he won't mind."

"I know he won't. Let's get going."

Kay Dell was on cloud nine as she followed Walt, driving one of Alfred's four-wheelers. They went down a long, narrow lane and eventually came to a gate and stopped. She laughed happily as the goats—a lot of goats—came running from across the goat pasture to greet them. "We'll throw these weeds in here and then go back for some tools and wire and a few steel posts," Walt said.

She pitched in, and they soon had the little trailer unloaded. "Look at them," Kay Dell said in delight. "They're eating like it's a treat or something."

Walt chuckled. "It is a treat to them. I couldn't believe it the first time I threw some in to them either. It's cool, isn't it?"

"It sure is. Are they tame?" she asked. "They won't hurt us, will they?"

"They are very tame. And no, they won't hurt you. Let's go in with them for a minute," he suggested. He opened the gate, stepped in, and she followed behind him. He led the way right into the middle of the goats. For the next ten minutes, Kay Dell petted one goat after another. Several llamas wandered close, but they mostly just watched as the young people fussed over the goats.

"I love them," she said as she picked up one baby goat and let it nuzzle her face.

"The little ones are called *kids*," Walt said.

While the mother goats, or *nannies*, as Walt called them, ate weeds, the dozens of kids frolicked around the two of them. Both of them laughed. Kay Dell was particularly delighted. In fact, she was more than delighted. She was ecstatic.

"I guess we better go work on that fence," Walt said as he led the way back through the gate with the goats following them. They had to be careful to get the gate shut before some of the goats got out.

"This is really kind of fun," Kay Dell said as they walked back to the four-wheelers.

"I love working here," Walt agreed. "I'm really lucky. And now, so are you."

Kay Dell felt more than lucky; she felt blessed, and regardless of who Walt was, she had a feeling that he was feeling equally blessed, if not even more so.

Back at the farmyard, the two of them loaded the fencing materials. "How do you know what to do?" Kay Dell asked.

"I've been here almost three weeks. Alfred has taught me a lot. I didn't know anything about this kind of work until he hired me. All I've done is mechanics. I used to help my dad work on cars at his garage."

"I don't know how to work on cars or how to farm. But I want to learn," Kay Dell said. "I mean, I want to learn the farming part. I don't think I want to be a mechanic. Anyway, I guess you'll have to teach me about farming."

"Alfred will teach you too," he said. "He just can't work nearly as long as he'd like to."

Kay Dell followed Walt, or *Sparky*, if that's who he really was, to another part of the farm, close to a mile from the farmyard. He finally stopped beside a piece of fence that was in pretty bad shape.

"That won't hold any animals," Kay Dell said.

"That's why we're here to fix it."

Kay Dell looked around. "I don't see any animals in this field here. I guess that's good though."

"This is a hay field and the animals are in the pastures. It was actually a couple of stray bulls that did all this damage. Alfred told me they belong to a neighbor. The guy felt bad but didn't offer to fix the fence. Anyway, here's what Alfred told me we needed to do."

He explained briefly. Kay Dell told him she thought she understood, and then the two of them went to work on the fence. They laboriously pounded several steel posts in the ground between bent ones that they straightened up using the winch on one of the four-wheelers. Once that was done, Walt showed

Kay Dell how to use a pair of pliers to twist wire as they used it to connect the barbed wire to the steel posts.

She caught on quickly and was grateful to Alfred for the gloves. As she worked, she kept thinking about a way to get Walt to talk about himself. She had an idea, and she finally worked up the courage to try it.

She said, "Sparky, can you help me here for a minute?"

CHAPTER EIGHT

"What do you need help with?" he asked from where he was doing the same thing she was with the wire.

She put her hands on her hips. "I need help understanding why you and Alfred want me to think your name is Walt when it's really Sparky." He started to say something, but she held her hand up to stop him. "Please, don't tell me that I'm not right. I just called you Sparky and you answered like you were used to being called that."

Walt's face flamed. He scowled. For a moment, she thought she may have made a terrible mistake, that he was angry with her. But after a moment, with no anger on his face or in his voice, just sadness, he said, "I'm sorry, Kay Dell, but it could be dangerous for you to call me Sparky."

She stood up and stretched before approaching him. "Dangerous for me or for you?" she asked.

"Kay Dell, you seem like a really nice girl. I'm truly sorry that we lied to you, but I've been accused of something that I didn't do, and if certain people—like cops, for example—knew who I was, I would be arrested and hauled off to jail."

"Sparky, I promise, I won't tell. I've seen the news and I know that your brother says you pushed your mother to her death. I know that's not possible," she said. "I may not know much about animals or about farming, but I am pretty good at math. From things you and Alfred said to Dad and me when we came here the other night, I know that there's no way you could have been in Kansas when your mother died. Unless, of course, you were lying to me about that too."

She felt tears fill her eyes. When Sparky said nothing, just stood watching her through eyes that appeared more gray than blue, she spoke again, fighting to keep the emotion that she was feeling from being displayed in her voice. "I'm so sorry about your mother. That must hurt something awful."

Finally, Sparky stepped closer to her, then sat down in the grass and pointed to a grassy spot directly in front of him. "It hurts a lot. And no, I didn't lie about that. Sit down, please. I guess I need to tell you the truth. I've never been any good at lying and neither has Alfred. And neither of us wanted to. I know that the cops in Goodland, Kansas, believe my older brother. So does my father. And my younger sister and brother are so afraid of Kal that they don't dare say anything that he doesn't want them to."

"That's terrible. How old is Kal?" Kay Dell asked.

"He's almost two years older than me."

"You're fifteen, right?"

"Yes, but I'll be sixteen in a few weeks."

"Really! I'll be sixteen pretty soon too. But Sparky, you really do look older," she said with a grin. "I would never have suspected that you and I were the same age. Unlike you, I look my age."

"You look nice," Sparky said, causing a blush in Kay Dell's face.

"Thank you," she said. "So are you going to tell me how you got here?"

"Yes, I guess so," he said after a moment. "I was adopted when I was almost two. I don't remember any family but the one I was raised in. Kal is older but a lot smaller than me, and he has always resented it. He learned a long time ago that he couldn't beat me up even though he wanted to. Kal is mean, but he has somehow always been able to hide that side of him from our parents."

Sparky went on for the next several minutes, and Kay Dell was a rapt audience of one. He finished his tale by telling her how Alfred picked him up when he was walking along the road near the Salina onramp. "I don't know why, but for some reason, he took a liking to me, and when we saw the newscast about the murder of my mother, he told me that he knew I hadn't killed her. I guess he's good at math too. And he promised to protect me."

"I don't know him very well, but my father says he's a really good man," Kay Dell said. "And I guess his wife was a good woman."

"He sure misses her," Sparky said. "She did a lot of the work on the farm. It was only when she got sick that he got behind on the work."

"Sparky, will you tell me about your birth parents?" Kay Dell asked in a sudden change of subject.

"I don't remember them. They were killed in a car wreck when I was really little. They were from Connecticut, but they crashed in Kansas. No one was ever able to find relatives, so I was a foster baby for a while and then the Graveses adopted me."

"Do you know what their names were?" Kay Dell asked.

Sparky grinned. "My mother's name was Karma Piler. My dad's name was Walt."

Kay Dell laughed. "So that's how you came up with the name you told Dad and me."

"Pretty original," he said with a grin. "Anyway, we'd better get back to work."

"Yeah, you're getting paid," Kay Dell teased. "I do have another question, Sparky. Who gave you your name? Was it the Graveses or the Pilers?"

"It was the name my birth parents gave me. My mom told me once that the cops had learned from a neighbor in Connecticut that my birth mother named me Sparky because she thought my eyes sparkled. I know, that's crazy. Mom says my dad wanted to change my name when they adopted me, but she wouldn't let him do it."

"Don't you like your name?" she asked.

"It's okay. How many guys do you know who have the same name as a dog?"

"I like your name," she said with a grin. "I like you, too. Thanks for sharing your secret with me."

"You're welcome, Kay Dell, but I do have one favor to ask of you," he said.

"Sure, what's that?"

With a straight face he said, "It's okay if you call me Sparky, just don't call me boy or dog."

They laughed together. "I promise," she said, and then they both got back to attaching the barbed wire to the steel posts. They worked closely together and talked back and forth. But Kay Dell worried about Sparky. She'd figured out who he was, and if she had figured it out, then surely others would too. She was convinced that the story Sparky had just told her was true, which meant his rotten brother, who had basically caused Sparky to leave home in fear of his life, was now attempting to get him put in prison.

"Kay Dell," Sparky said, bringing her out of her reverie. She straightened up as she opened and closed her sore hands. She'd never done this kind of work before. It was hard, but she was enjoying it. She looked over at Sparky without uttering a word, so he went on. "You won't give away my secret will you?"

"Not if you don't want me to," she replied.

"Thanks. I appreciate it."

"Hey, I know you are innocent. I just can't believe your brother would blame you," she said.

Sparky hadn't told her his suspicions about Kal, but as he gazed at her where she stood watching him from several feet down the fence, he said, "Kay Dell, I don't know this for sure, but I think it was Kal who pushed Mom off the deck."

"Oh, Sparky, that's terrible!" she exclaimed in horror.

"Like I said, I may be wrong, but why else would he say he saw me do it? If it was some burglar he saw, then why wouldn't he say so? Mom didn't have enemies. Everyone who knew her loved her. And if it was a stranger and Kal didn't see it, I still wonder why he would accuse me. I mean, I had already left; He'd gotten what he wanted. I was out of his life. He had no reason to ever think I'd come back."

"But why would Kal kill her if she was such a good person?"

"I don't know for sure, but I have an idea. Dad was always faster to take Kal's word against me than Mom. Mom always ended up going along with Dad, but I think she had doubts."

"Do you think she said something about it? I mean, might she have told Kal that she thought he may have lied about some of the things he'd done but had accused you of?" Kay Dell asked.

"Maybe. I know Kal better than anyone else does. If he got mad at her, I can see him pushing her like that." Sparky dropped his gaze and stared at the ground. "He will probably get away with it like he always has. And I will be the one to go to prison."

Kay Dell stepped over to him. "No, Sparky, you won't. Someone has to do something. Someone has to tell the police not to believe Kal."

"That would be a first. Everyone believes him. He's such a smooth liar."

"But, Sparky, you were here. Alfred can tell them it wasn't you," she said, suddenly feeling upbeat.

"Yeah, but if he told them and they didn't believe him, then they would know where I was at, and I would be in jail just that quick." He snapped his gloved fingers.

"This is crazy. Why wouldn't they believe Alfred?" she asked. "Or you, for that matter. It would be your word and Alfred's against Kal's."

"You've never met my brother, Kay Dell. He's lied his whole life and gotten away with it. He's really good at lying, which makes him a good actor. And there is one other thing that I've thought about . . ."

Feeling deflated, she asked, "What's that?"

"If Kal did kill Mom, someone he knew, what would stop him from killing Alfred?" Sparky asked bitterly. "I can't let that happen to Alfred."

Suddenly, Kay Dell had a thought that hit her so hard she felt her stomach rumble uncomfortably. She barely even knew Sparky, but she felt deep down that he was a special person, that he was a good kid who could become a great man one day. "Sparky, would Kal kill *you*?" she said, unable to keep the emotion she was feeling from her voice. "I mean, you are bigger and stronger. He must be afraid of you."

"Kal is a hater. He knows he can't beat me in a fair fight. One of the reasons I left home was I was afraid that he would figure out a way to hurt or even kill me. He pulled a knife on me a couple times and threatened to kill me. And my dad has guns." Sparky let that thought hang in the air.

Kay Dell stepped close to him and put a hand on his arm. "We've got to do something," she said passionately. "We can't let Kal win."

Sparky forced a chuckle. "You're a nice girl, Kay Dell, but this is not your problem. This isn't even Alfred's problem. It's *my* problem."

Kay Dell felt moisture fill her eyes. It was all so unfair. No, it was worse than unfair. It was *cruel.* She rubbed the moisture away, walked back to her post, and began tying the wire again. Sparky did the same. Thoughts flooded her mind. She felt so helpless. She wanted to think of something she could suggest that might help Sparky, but her mind was so troubled that she couldn't think of anything.

After they worked in silence for several minutes, Sparky finally spoke again. "I tried to keep Alfred from doing anything at first, but I was also worried about my little brother and sister. Kal could hurt them. So we both agreed that we needed to do something. Now, the more I think about it, the more worried I am for Alfred."

Kay Dell shoved the fencing pliers she'd been using in a back pocket of her jeans and once again walked over to where Sparky was working. "What is Alfred doing?" she asked.

Sparky faced her, his blue-gray eyes full of worry and his brow creased. "Promise you won't say anything?" he asked.

"Sparky, I like you, and I believe you. I won't do anything that will hurt you or Alfred. So, yes, I promise," she said firmly. "I'm on your side, Sparky."

"Thank you," Sparky said. "Alfred has hired a private investigator."

Kay Dell felt the knot in her stomach loosen. "That's great."

"I told him he couldn't afford it, but he said he could and he insisted and says he can. Anyway, the PI is going to try to find someone else who might remember me from one of the truck stops. But I don't think it will work. If it doesn't work, then I will only have one choice for Alfred's sake and for yours too."

"What do you mean for mine?" Kay Dell asked.

"I don't want you or Alfred to be in danger because of me. I will have to leave here," he said.

"Sparky, you like it here," she said urgently.

"No, Kay Dell, I *love* it here. But I can't let my troubles get somebody else hurt."

"Sparky, I think a PI is a great idea. I really believe that he will find someone who saw you and who remembers you."

"She," Sparky said.

"She?"

"The investigator Alfred hired is Lys Grist from Salt Lake."

"Your PI is a woman?" Kay Dell asked.

"Yes. And we both think she's really good. But I honestly have a hard time thinking she can really help me," Sparky said.

"She will. You've got to believe it," Kay Dell said fervently.

"I'm trying, but it's hard," Sparky said. Without another word, he turned away from Kay Dell and went back to work. She watched him for a moment and then pulled the fencing pliers from her pocket and walked back to the post where she'd been working.

Nothing more was said about Sparky's problem as they finished their task and loaded the tools. But before they got on the four-wheelers, Kay Dell walked up to him and looked him in the eyes. "Maybe your PI can figure out who killed your mother, and then you and your siblings can all be safe."

Sparky shook his head. "She's going to try, but I don't know how she can do that."

Kay Dell grinned. "That's because you're a farmer. She is a professional investigator. It's her job to know how."

Sparky shook his head. "Yeah, I guess I am a farmer now. Gee, I've never met anyone quite like you before. You're different from the girls back home."

"Is that a compliment?" she asked shyly.

"Yes, it is," he said, equally shyly.

"Thank you," she replied.

"I'm not much of a farmer."

"I think you are," she said. "I can tell you are enjoying fixing this fence. That makes you a farmer."

"Are you enjoying it?" he asked.

"You know what? I really am."

"Then I guess that makes you a farmer too."

Kay Dell laughed. "We both want to be, don't we?" she said. Their eyes met, and she felt a kinship with him like she'd never felt with anyone before. Then she remembered her father's warning about dating outside the church—

not that she was thinking about dating Sparky. Yet, against her best judgment, that idea appealed to her. Maybe she would get a chance to help him learn about the church. If he became a member then . . . She pushed the thought away.

Sparky approached his four-wheeler, but he turned back to her when she asked, "What are we going to tell Alfred? I mean, do I call you Walt and pretend you didn't tell me anything?"

He rubbed his chin and then looked at her with a serious expression. "I'd hate to keep lying."

"Then you should tell him. And it will be our secret—yours, mine, and Alfred's," Kay Dell said firmly.

Sparky took a deep breath. "Okay, let's go tell him. I hope it doesn't upset him, but he needs to understand that I trust you and that if you and I are going to be working together a little, we need to be honest with each other."

"Alfred is a wonderful man. He will agree," she said. As an afterthought, she added, "Or else he will fire me."

Sparky chuckled. "He can't fire you; you're a volunteer."

"Then I guess he could tell me I can't volunteer anymore."

"He won't do that," Sparky said. "He's a kind man. I've never known anyone as kind as he is."

The pair drove back to the farmyard. "Do you think Alfred's still inside?" Kay Dell asked.

"He must be," Sparky responded.

They found Alfred in the house reading a book. He looked up and smiled when they came in. "I'm lazy today," he said.

"No, you're not," Sparky said. "Neither is Kay Dell. We got that fence repaired. I'm sure it's not nearly as good as you could have done yourself, but hopefully it'll be okay."

"Actually, with these hands of mine, all arthritic and such, I'm sure you have done a much better job than I could have done," he said. "Thank you both for fixing that fence for me."

"We enjoyed it," Kay Dell said.

"Yes, we did," Sparky agreed.

Alfred studied the two of them for a moment. "You two look like you have something on your minds."

"We do," Sparky said.

"Then sit down and unload on me," the old man said with a grin.

After they were seated, Sparky said, "Kay Dell is not only a hard worker, but she's smart. She figured out who I am."

"Oh my." Alfred frowned. "That's not good."

"I'll keep his secret—and yours," Kay Dell promised immediately. "I know he didn't do any of the things he's been accused of." She grinned. "Well, I guess he did run away from home, but I don't blame him for doing that. In fact, I don't know what else he could have done."

For a moment, Alfred looked at his two young helpers with a sober face. Then, suddenly, he began to smile. "At least we don't have to pretend in front of you and try to make you think his name is Walt. I slipped up when I called him Sparky and tried to make you and your dad think I meant Sparky the dog."

"You sort of fooled me," she said. "Later I started thinking about it more. I'd seen the news and his picture with longer hair. And well, anyway, it just sort of all fit. Now I want to help if I can."

"I should have known we couldn't keep it a secret for very long, but we've got to keep trying so that Sparky won't get arrested," Alfred said. "Who's coming to pick you up tonight, Kay Dell?"

"I think Dad is. But I'll call Mom and let her know I'm finished here."

"That's good. Your dad is a very good man. How would you two feel if we let him in on our little secret?" Alfred asked.

Sparky looked at Kay Dell, who nodded her head. "All right. I trust him if you two do."

"Sparky, I promise that Dad would never do anything to put you in danger," Kay Dell said earnestly. "He's a good man, like Alfred is."

"Does he keep secrets from your mother?" Alfred asked.

Kay Dell slowly shook her head. "No, now that you mention it, I don't think he does. They talk about everything."

"Just like me and Mama used to do," Alfred said with a sudden sadness in his eyes. He paused for a moment, and both of the young people watched him intently. "Kay Dell, am I putting you in a bad spot by letting you come out here and help Sparky and me?"

"Not at all. I want to. I've had the most wonderful time the past few hours. Please don't make me not come anymore," she pleaded. "I love it here."

"That's not what I was asking for, Kay Dell," he said gently. "No, I was just thinking that if you want to do this, and I can tell that you do, then both of your parents need to know who Sparky is and the danger he is in if the wrong people find out who he is."

"I know that," Kay Dell responded. "They will want to help if they can. And they will keep our secret."

"Sparky, is it okay with you if we tell both of them?" Alfred asked.

He sighed deeply. "Yes. I want Kay Dell to keep coming. You and I could use her help. You should have seen her pounding those posts and twisting that wire." He grinned at her.

"You must be like my late wife, Kay Dell. She loved doing the same things I do. But for some reason, she would never let me help her can the fruit and vegetables or make the jam or juice."

"I know how to can," Kay Dell said brightly. "Maybe, if you don't mind, I could can some things for you."

"Oh my goodness, Kay Dell, that would be great. I was just telling Sparky the other day how I dreaded when all of Mama's canned goods were used up, and we had to start eating the store-bought stuff."

"I'll do it," Kay Dell said with a bright smile. "It's the least I can do."

"Thank you. Now, back to the matter at hand," the old man said with a tired smile. "When your dad gets here, we'll explain everything to him."

Kay Dell made her call and the three of them waited in the house for him to arrive. Twenty minutes later, Bill Finch was seated beside his daughter as Alfred explained who Sparky was, why he was in danger, and what steps he'd taken to attempt to clear his name. Bill reacted in the same way Kay Dell had.

"Surely if you're willing to testify about how Sparky came to be with you and that he was with you when his mother was killed, that would clear him."

Sparky was shaking his head as Bill spoke. "I'll tell you the same thing I told your daughter; you don't know my brother." He then told him all about Kal.

"I see. I'm sorry this is happening to you, Sparky. But my wife and I will keep this to ourselves until you direct us otherwise," Bill said. "You do understand that she needs to know, don't you?"

"Yes, of course," Sparky said. "Thank you for being so understanding. But if at any time I feel like I am putting any of you in danger, I will leave as quietly as I left my home."

"You don't have to do that, Sparky!" Alfred said in alarm. "The very thought of losing you after finding you in such a miraculous way makes me ill."

"I hope I don't have to. I just want you all to know that if I suddenly vanish, it will be to protect all of us," he said. "My being here and you knowing me could create a big danger for you. But I promise that I won't leave if I don't have to. I love it here."

"And I love having you here," Alfred said.

Kay Dell had to rub her eyes. She suddenly felt like she was in the presence of some very special people.

CHAPTER NINE

JOHNNY AND COURTNEY GRAVES WERE huddled in Johnny's room the next morning around nine. The death of their mother following the disappearance of Sparky had been a devastating blow to them. They knew Sparky had not come back and pushed their mother off the deck. They knew it because *they saw who did.* But they hadn't dared to tell anyone. Kal said he saw Sparky do it, and that was that. They were reconsidering now.

"Johnny, we have to tell Dad," Courtney said, her chin quivering.

"He won't believe us, Courtney," Johnny said. "He only believes Kal. Sparky always told the truth and Kal always lied and he always made us lie too. I think the reason Sparky left was because he always got blamed for what Kal did."

Courtney wiped tears from her eyes. "We have been praying that Sparky would come back. But we shouldn't do that anymore. If Sparky comes back, Kal will hurt him if he hasn't already," she sobbed. "We've got to do something. What can we do if we can't tell Dad?"

"We have to sneak out and go to the police station," Johnny said, trying to be brave despite only being eight years old.

"We can tell them that we can't go home if they don't believe us," Courtney suggested.

"They have to believe us," Johnny said. "They just have to."

"Dad was going to take us to dinner tonight," Courtney said. "But we can't let that stop us from doing what we have to do. We can't keep on lying for Kal."

The bedroom door burst open. Both children screamed in fright. Kal, his face purple with rage, grabbed Courtney by the hair and flung her across the room and into the wall. She bounced off the wall and landed on the floor. Kal grabbed Johnny by the front of his shirt and bashed a fist into his face. Blood spurted out of his nose.

"Kal, don't!" Courtney screamed, coming to her feet and attacking Kal with the fury of a mother cat defending her young. She tore into Kal, both hands pummeling him fiercely. But he once again grabbed her hair and swung her across the room. He grabbed her before she had managed to get to her feet again, then punched her in the face too.

Courtney and Johnny rushed to each other and clung tightly. Kal laughed. "That's just a sample of what will happen to the two of you if you say anything to Dad or the police or anyone else."

Bravely, Courtney said, "Dad will know you've hurt us this time."

Kal shook his head, his eyes glaring with hatred. "No, you two were riding double on a bike, like Dad always told you not to. You crashed. And that's how you got hurt."

Both children watched him fearfully. He stepped close to them. "How did you get hurt, Courtney?" he asked, venom in his voice.

"We . . . wrecked . . . the bike," she sobbed.

"That's right. Johnny, how did you get hurt?"

His chin quivered. "We wrecked on the bike."

Kal glared at them and stepped back. "If you say anything to anyone about how you stupidly think Sparky didn't shove Mom, you know what will happen to you, don't you?"

They both nodded and mumbled that they understood.

"If you tell anyone that I hurt you or threatened you, you know what will happen to you, don't you? Show me your fingers."

Slowly they each lifted their hands, fear tearing at them.

"I'll break every one of them. And that might not be all. Do you two understand?"

Again, they both nodded and mumbled that they understood.

Kal pointed a finger at them. "Say it. Promise me you won't say anything other than what I've told you to say."

Courtney and Johnny glanced at one another and then they said in unison, "I promise."

"If Dad asks you why you were riding double on Courtney's bike, just tell him that Johnny's has a flat tire," Kal said.

"It doesn't," Johnny said.

"Wanna bet?" Kal asked.

"Ooh," Johnny moaned.

"You little brats," Kal said. "Don't you ever even think about crossing me again. So help me, I will do what I have to do if you don't obey me." With that, he spun on his heels and stormed out, slamming the door behind him.

The two children clung to each other for a long time. It was Courtney who finally spoke. "We need to run away."

"Yes, we have to," Johnny agreed. "Kal is so mean. He must have let the air out of my tire."

"Forget about it. It doesn't matter now. Let's pack some food and clothes in our school backpacks and take off," Courtney said.

"I'm scared, Courtney," Johnny confessed.

"So am I, but we need to try to be brave. We can't stay here anymore."

"Where will we go?"

"Somewhere far away from here," Courtney said. "Sparky did it and so can we."

Just then, Kal appeared at the door again and the two of them huddled together. "You two little brats shouldn't have come in with your noses bleeding after wrecking on the bike. Clean up that blood. Clean it all up."

He made no further verbal threats. He didn't need to. The menace on his face and in his voice was all that it took. Once again, he left, slamming the door so hard the room shook. The children didn't make a move until they heard the living room door slam and their mother's car start up and squeal away.

"Let's get ready and leave," Courtney said.

"We have to clean up the blood," Johnny countered, his entire body shaking with fear. "Kal said we have to."

"No, Johnny. We don't have to do what Kal says. Not anymore. Not ever again. Get your backpack."

Ten minutes later, the Graves children were out the back door, running across the very spot where their mother had died. Then they passed through the gate at the back of the yard. "We can do this," Courtney called back to her little brother. "We can do it for Sparky and for Mom."

They had a plan now. It was a desperate one, but they were determined to carry it out. In their young minds, nothing out in the unknown world where they were headed could be more dangerous than Kal.

***

"Where are Johnny and Courtney?" Donald Graves asked Kal when he came into the house a little before six that evening.

Kal was slouching in a chair, his eyes on the TV, a can of Pepsi in his hand. "How would I know?"

"How long has it been since you saw them, Kal?"

"I don't know. They're probably in their rooms." He didn't look at his father. He just took a long swig of his Pepsi. "The last thing I remember about them was when I heard them crying this afternoon."

"Crying about what?"

"I dunno. Maybe it was because they wrecked on the bike. Earlier I heard Johnny say to Courtney that you would be mad when you found out that they'd been riding double and wrecked."

"Were they hurt?" Donald asked with concern.

"They both had bloody noses when I saw them come in the house and head for their rooms. That's when I heard Johnny say to Courtney that you would be mad that they were riding double. I offered to help them clean their faces, but they said they were fine and not to tell you."

"The little buggers," Donald mumbled as he stormed past Kal and out of the room. "Those kids are getting more like Sparky all the time. I don't know what your mother and I did wrong with those kids."

Donald left Kal slouched in the chair and went to Courtney's room. She wasn't there. He went to Johnny's next. There was dried blood on the floor and on his bed—quite a bit of blood. They'd been told not to ride double a hundred times, but they did just as they pleased, just like Sparky always did. He sat down on the edge of his son's bed, his head in his hands.

He was discouraged. It was hard without his wife. He loved those kids, but they couldn't be allowed to turn out like Sparky.

He didn't know what he was going to do. He'd planned to take the kids out for dinner tonight, but he knew he had to punish Courtney and Johnny. He couldn't let them get away with their disobedience. They'd have to make themselves peanut butter and jelly sandwiches after they cleaned the blood off the floor of Johnny's room and washed the bedding. He didn't feel much like going out anymore, but he couldn't punish Kal. He hadn't done anything wrong. Finally, he stood up and started looking through the house for the children.

Kal joined him helpfully. "They've got to be here somewhere, Dad," he said. "They're hiding from you. They knew they weren't supposed to be riding double on Courtney's bike."

Failing to find them after searching for ten minutes in the house and the yard, Donald said, "You and I are going out to dinner like I promised. Those kids will just have to fare for themselves when they come sneaking back." He hated doing this, but his parents had always punished him when he did anything wrong. At times he'd resented it, but he felt like it had made him a stronger man.

He was determined that the younger kids would turn out more like Kal and less like Sparky, and letting them off easy was not the way to accomplish that.

***

Kal hid his evil smile from his dad. He had those two right where he needed them to be. They had to be hiding nearby, and when they came back, they would know that they'd better keep their mouths shut. It had been hours since he'd warned them last. They always did what he told them to. They knew they had to.

***

"I gotta pee," Johnny whispered to Courtney.

"Me too," she said. "But we gotta hold it."

"I can't much longer," Johnny whispered.

"She'll need to stop soon, and when she does, we'll get out of the car," Courtney promised.

They had been on the floor in the backseat of a blue four-door sedan that they had found by the gas pumps in a service station near the freeway. They had watched the driver, a woman with gray hair, walk into the convenience store after filling her car with gas. She looked to them like a nice lady, so they had looked around, and when they were quite sure no one was looking in their direction and that the woman was out of sight in the store, they climbed in and hid themselves and their backpacks on the floor in front of the backseat. They had both been fearful that she would see them, but when she'd returned to the car, she had not looked back there. She'd just started the engine and drove away.

The car had been driving east ever since then. They both felt a huge relief when they felt the car slowing. After a little while it stopped, and they heard the lady get out and close her door. Courtney peeked out. "We're in a rest area. She went inside. Let's get out and use the bathroom. But we need to hurry."

They both rushed into the appropriate restrooms. When they came out a little later, the car was still parked there. By mutual consent, they climbed back in. "Did you take a drink of water?" Courtney asked.

"No, you told me not to, that we wouldn't have to go to the bathroom so soon again if we didn't," he said. "But I'm hungry and thirsty."

"So am I," Courtney said. "But this is better than letting Kal hurt us again. The lady we saw, the one who is driving this car, talked to me in the restroom. She was really nice. She asked if I was going somewhere with my parents, and I told her I was. She smiled at me and told me she hoped I had a nice trip."

Five minutes later, the car started up again, and once more, they were eastbound on the freeway.

***

"Where in the world could those kids be?" Donald asked worriedly when he and Kal got home from the restaurant. He'd already checked their rooms and found that they were not in them. Nor was the blood cleaned up. "Let's see if we can tell if they found something to eat."

It only took a minute to determine that the kids had not made a mess eating, but Donald became suspicious when he saw that a whole loaf of bread was missing and so was the peanut butter and a bottle of jam.

"I'll bet they did just like what Sparky did and ran away," Kal said smugly. "I wonder if they took anything else."

It didn't take long for them to discover that several bottles of water were gone, some candy bars, and both their school backpacks. Donald had not noticed that when he'd found the blood on the floor and bed in Johnny's room. Donald was suddenly very worried. This was not normal behavior for his two younger children.

"They've run away, just like Sparky did," Kal repeated, feigning concern. "Even with him gone, he is still a bad influence on them."

"I hope you're wrong. The trouble is, Sparky is smart enough to hide out. I mean, even the police can't find him," Donald said. "But Johnny and Courtney won't be able to take care of themselves. They'll get hurt for sure. I've got to call the police."

Kal had another one of his bright ideas. He honestly hadn't thought they would actually run away, but he knew why the kids had left, and he was glad to see them gone. "Dad, I just had a horrible thought," he said deviously. "I wonder if Sparky has been back again and if he talked them into running away with him."

Donald's worried face grew more creased than before. "At least if they're with Sparky, they will be safe. He apparently knows how to take care of himself, and he will do the same for them."

"Dad, think about what you just said," Kal said, repressing the smirk that he was feeling. "Sparky shoved Mom to her death. What makes you think the kids would be safe with him, with a killer?"

Donald's hopes were dashed. "I hadn't thought of that. I have to call the police. Maybe they will try harder to find Sparky if they think that the children have been taken by him."

"Dad, the cops are hopeless. They don't care about our family," Kal said. "They don't have time for us. They've proven that already."

"They need to know anyway. I can't just do nothing. They are my children, Kal. And they are in danger." Donald pulled out his cell phone and made the call.

An officer showed up at the house within minutes. He had a lot of questions for Kal and Donald. Then he finally left, after assuring Donald that he and the other police officers would do all that they could to find the three children.

"I'm telling you, Dad," Kal said when they were gone. "The police don't care."

"I think they do, but they don't know where to look," Donald said helplessly. "I need to call Brad Hagen. This is terrible."

"Yes, that's a good idea," Kal said. He was of the opinion that the younger kids had run away. If he could make sure his dad believed Sparky had taken them, then that would make his search for Sparky more intense. And Kal wanted Sparky found—so he could silence him. He knew full well that Sparky had not taken the other kids, but he intended to pretend otherwise.

***

Brad Hagen had concentrated his efforts to the east. Knowing that Sparky had been born in Connecticut made him think that possibly the young man, after killing his mother, was heading to the only other place where he had a history, even if he had no memory of it. But when Donald Graves called him, pulling him out of his motel bed, he decided that he needed to rethink his plan. If Sparky had returned to Goodland long enough to snatch his younger siblings, then he must have been hiding somewhere in that vicinity all this time.

Even though it was very late, and he had only gone to sleep a few minutes before, Brad got dressed and checked out of the motel. He had to return to Goodland and make more inquiries there. The thought occurred to him that Sparky might have a friend whose family was willing to shelter him and his younger siblings. He was coming to believe that Sparky Graves was a very devious young man and perhaps quite persuasive.

When he'd had his initial discussion with Sgt. Abel Bone, no mention had been made of the idea that Sparky might have sympathetic friends whose parents might be foolish enough to protect him. Bone had mentioned that Sparky was shy and a bit of a loner, but he had to have some friends. That would be Brad's first consideration now.

He called Donald back as soon as he was on the road. "Donald, I'm returning to Goodland tonight. I'll contact you in the morning. Here's what I need from you: Make me a list of all of Sparky's friends that you and Kal can think of. Get me addresses and phone numbers if you can find them."

"What good will that do?" Donald asked.

Brad explained what he was thinking. "I'm just feeling like that is an avenue we need to explore before I do anything else."

"Okay, if that's what you think, then I'm good with it. I should have thought of it myself. I don't think the list will be very long because Sparky was a loner," Donald said. "I know of only one or two guys who might have been his friends. Maybe Kal will know some more."

"I suspect that he will. Now, Donald, I also want to talk to all of your employees."

"What good would that possibly do?" Donald asked, sudden anger in his voice.

Brad was surprised by Donald's change in attitude.

"They could tell me of people who might have come to see Sparky at the shop when he was working there. Or maybe one of your employees is sympathetic toward Sparky."

"Not a chance!" Donald thundered. "They all know what a lazy kid he is, how he always shoves his work onto Kal and then claims he did it."

"Nonetheless, I would like to speak with them," Detective Hagen said firmly.

"I think that is a total waste of your time and my money," Donald responded.

"I can't in good conscience fail to talk to them when your little ones are missing," Brad shot back. "Think about it. Sparky can't have gone far. I mean, he came back to kill your wife, and now you believe he came back to take your younger children. That being the case, we simply have to concentrate locally before expanding the search again."

"I don't think Sparky would have stayed close after taking the kids," Donald argued.

"We have to make sure," Brad said firmly.

For a moment, Donald said nothing. "Okay," he said finally, his voice breaking. "I guess that's why I hired you. You're the expert. I just hope that Sparky doesn't hurt my little ones. Do whatever you need to do as quickly as you can, but I wish you wouldn't waste time with my employees."

"I fully understand your concern. I'll see you in the morning. Have the list ready when I get there," Brad instructed. "And please include your employees."

Kal had already gone to bed, but feeling the urgency of Brad's request and knowing that, to a degree, it made sense, Donald woke him up so they could work on the list together. Kal's reaction was the same as his father's. "Dad, that's stupid. There's no way Sparky is going to stick around here after taking the little kids."

"I told Brad that, but he thinks he should check anyway."

"You've got to argue with Brad. You can't let him spend precious time talking to the guys at the shop. That would be a total waste of his time."

Kal, as usual, had a valid argument. Donald decided that he would talk to Detective Hagen about it in the morning. For now, he would ignore the names of his workers and, with Kal's help, see if he could make a list of as many of Sparky's friends as they could come up with.

CHAPTER TEN

DETECTIVE LYS GRIST HAD STARTED checking with the businesses near the Salina exit off I-70. That was where Sparky had slipped out of the semi he'd been stowing away on. She did not tell any of the people she talked to who the boy was that she was showing them a picture of. All she cared to tell anyone was that she needed to know if the boy in the picture had been seen. She looked at some video, but as she'd feared, anything over two weeks had been copied over. A couple of places that did have video did not show anything conclusive regarding Sparky.

She was careful to skate around the issue of Sparky's being wanted by the police in Kansas. A couple of people asked for the name of the boy in the picture, and she had just told them he was Walt Piler from Connecticut. Lys was thorough. She was not satisfied with just talking to one or two people at the various establishments and locations she stopped at. She spoke with every employee who was on the premises in each place she stopped.

The information she was accumulating was proof that Sparky had been heading west, as the times and dates given to her by the people that recognized the photograph were earlier and earlier the further east she traveled from Salina. She took names, phone numbers, and addresses from anyone who had seen him or even thought they had. It was all helpful but probably not enough to prove his innocence.

She'd also shown Sparky's picture to a number of truck drivers in rest areas and truck stops along I-70 as she worked her way east. It was time-consuming work. Since a young man's life was in jeopardy, she was determined to find others who could back up her client's story. She needed reliable witnesses, not half-baked or unsure ones. And the timeline she was writing down needed to be as reliable and accurate as possible.

Lys was taking particular care to speak with the drivers of the semis that were hauling large pipes on their way to that project in Nevada. It wasn't just one company that was hauling the pipe but several independent truckers. Whenever one of those particular trucks, loaded with large pipes, was parked in a rest area or truck stop, she would wait beside that truck until the driver appeared. Then she'd engage him in conversation. She described the trucker with the long moustache—the one who drove the truck Sparky had stowed away in—but none of the other truckers seemed to know him, even though they were hauling to the same place he was. A couple of times, the drivers were women. She showed them the picture of Sparky anyway, but she did not disclose to them that the young man might have been riding in the pipe on the back of a truck. What she did ask them was if they'd seen the young fellow in any of the areas where they'd stopped and if they knew the driver with the long moustache.

She took more time questioning the male drivers. It was mid-morning after a couple of days of diligently searching that one of the drivers, a man about five ten with longish brown hair, a black ball cap, a large stomach, and a very large moustache was approaching his truck. She felt that familiar rush she always felt when an investigation took a positive turn—this could be the driver Sparky had described.

She approached him, explained what she was doing, and then held up the picture of Sparky. He took it from her hands and looked closely at it. "Yeah, this kid looks familiar," he said. "Why are you looking for him?"

"He had trouble at home and ran away almost three weeks ago. He rode in the back of a truck hauling pipe just like yours," she said. "I'm a private detective, and I've been retained to locate anyone who might have seen him."

"You're telling me he rode back there in one of those large corrugated pipes?" he asked. "I can't imagine. That would be terribly uncomfortable. I suspect it gets hot in there on a very sunny day although when I'm on the freeway, there would be a stiff breeze blowing through, so maybe it wasn't so bad. He would need to drink plenty of water, but if he did, I guess it would have been doable."

"I guess he was desperate, but yes, he rode in one of those pipes," she affirmed.

He walked around his truck and peered into one of the bottom-level pipes as if expecting to see a stowaway there now. He still had the picture of Sparky in his hand. He looked at it again, very closely this time, and scratched his chin with his free hand. "You know, I do believe I saw this kid. And not just once. Can't anyone find him?" He'd no sooner asked that than he said, "Wait, he couldn't be missing if you know he was riding in one of these pipes. You know where he is, don't you?"

Detective Grist smiled at him and said, "I can't disclose the details, Mr. . . ."

"Granberry," he said when she paused and looked at him expectantly. "Rick Granberry."

"It's nice to meet you, Rick," she said. "I'm Detective Lys Grist." She showed him her ID. "This young man's life is in jeopardy. If the wrong person found him, it would be tragic. If you are sure you've seen him, I'd like some details."

"Well, I don't know how much help I can be," Granberry said hesitantly.

"Please, are you sure that you saw him? It's very important."

"Okay, if you say so. Yes, I'm quite certain I saw him at least a couple of times. I thought nothing of it. I figured he was traveling with someone and that they were driving at the same rate I was." He paused, studied the picture again, handed it back to Lys, and then fingered his long, waxed moustache. He closed his eyes, deep in thought. "Okay, I know I saw the kid, and I'm pretty sure that's the kid who spoke to me one day. He asked me where I was hauling the load of pipe to."

"And you told him you were taking it to Nevada," Lys supplied.

"Yes, I did. I wondered why he wanted to know that, but he didn't say. He just thanked me and walked off."

"You didn't see where he went?" Lys asked.

"No, but I wasn't really paying any attention."

"So he could have jumped up in the pipe and you wouldn't have known it?"

"That's right," Rick replied. He reached again for the picture, and after she'd handed it to him, he studied it closely. "Is he about six feet, slender but strong looking?"

"That's right," Lys confirmed.

"This is the kid. I'm sure of it now. Seemed like a nice kid. I'd say he was probably about eighteen or so."

"He's actually fifteen, just short of sixteen. But he does pass easily as eighteen," Lys told him.

"That young? That's worrisome. Okay, Detective, how can I help?" Mr. Granberry asked.

"First, I need to know what day you talked to him. Can you figure that out for me?"

"I think so. Let me see if I can remember exactly where I was when he approached me," the truck driver said. He climbed into his truck, got out his logbook, climbed back out, and then consulted it. "It would have been about here," he said, pointing to a date on the logbook. Then he told her what he thought the location was.

"That's great. Very helpful," Lys said. "Can I get you to give me your contact information so that if I need to talk to you again, I can?"

Rick quickly complied. "You say he is in some kind of danger? Would you mind telling me what it is?"

"I'm sorry, but I can't do that. But you have been very helpful," Lys said. She thanked Rick and handed him one of her cards. "I may be in touch with you again."

"Anytime you need me just call my cell phone. I'd be glad to help if I can."

With that, Rick climbed in his truck and headed to the onramp. Lys was thoughtful as she watched him go. The truck driver had recognized Sparky and could testify to that if he had to. But she wasn't sure how much help that would be. Even though Rick believed the boy would have continued west, that wasn't proof that Sparky did, in fact, go west.

Theoretically, he could have left Rick's truck and headed back to Goodland the same way he had come west. Lys knew that he hadn't done that, but it was still only Alfred Briggs's word that Sparky was in Utah when his mother was killed. She feared she might be wasting her time and Alfred's money with these efforts.

She climbed into her car, thinking it through for a minute. All the sightings were adding up. They *had* to help. She decided to continue to make her way back to Kansas. That was where her real work would begin; Sparky and Alfred had asked her to identify the real killer, and that was exactly what she intended to do. If that killer was his brother, as Sparky suspected, then Lys needed to find proof.

***

It was mid-morning on Sunday when Detective Brad Hagen rang the doorbell at Donald Graves's house. He was extremely tired, but worry over the welfare of Donald's children had helped keep him awake and alert as he drove.

Donald looked about as tired as Brad was when he answered the door. His hair was disheveled, and his breath reeked of stale alcohol. "Come in," Donald said as he held the door wide. "I have the list ready for you, but there are only four names on it."

"Have the police found anything about the children?" Brad asked.

"No, and they won't, I'm afraid. Sparky seems to be pretty good at avoiding being seen," Donald said.

"Are you sure he has them?" Brad asked.

"Pretty sure," he said, but Brad detected a bit of doubt in his voice.

"You don't sound totally convinced," the detective prompted. "Could they have just run away?"

Just then Kal entered the room. He was a bit bleary eyed and his hair was a mess. "We don't think so," Kal said, giving his dad a look that Brad wasn't sure how to interpret.

"They did have a little accident on one of their bikes," Donald said. "They were riding double, and they knew I didn't allow that, but they would never run away over something that trivial."

"You've got to find Sparky, Detective," Kal said. "I'm almost certain they're with him."

"And what makes you so certain?" Brad asked, watching the Graves boy's expression very carefully.

"If you knew Sparky like I do, you'd understand," Kal said.

To Brad that was a very lame reason. "I'll check with the people on your list." He looked at it briefly. "Does this include your employees?"

"No, I'll talk with all of them when they come into work in the morning," Donald said. "None of them would know anything that will help anyway."

"Yeah, leave them out of this," Kal said. "We hired you to find Sparky, not harass our friends and the guys who work for Dad."

"Is that how you feel, Donald?" Brad asked.

He was slow in answering. "Yes, it is," Donald said, but his eyes didn't meet Brad's, and that bothered him.

Brad wondered who was making the decisions here—Donald or his son. Experienced investigator that he was, he sensed in Kal Graves an expertise in manipulation that he had seen so often in the criminals he'd dealt with over the years. He said nothing about it, but it would most certainly be something to be kept foremost in his mind as he interviewed the people on the list.

He left the Graves's house, but his mind was made up about one thing: he would find a way to contact Donald's employees. Someone in town must know at least one of them. After all, this was not a large town. And when he found one of them, he'd soon learn who the rest of them were. Sunday was a good day to locate and talk to them since he didn't want to speak with them at Donald's shop. He suspected that most of them were probably at home. If they were at church or out somewhere, he reasoned they would be back by evening.

As was his practice, Brad drove to the police station before he began contacting people. He did not like working behind the backs of local law enforcement unless it was necessary. His many years with the FBI had taught him how sensitive local officers could be when they thought someone might be treading on their toes.

Detective Hagen walked into the Goodland Police Department's building. He wasn't surprised that there weren't a lot of officers there, since it was Sunday. So when he saw one young officer, he immediately approached him and introduced himself. He explained to the officer, Lawrence Snepper, that he was looking into the disappearance of both Sparky Graves and his little brother and sister.

"You need to get your nose out of police business," Snepper snapped at him. "We are doing just fine without your help."

Brad had not intended to antagonize anyone, and he apologized for doing so. "I know what a tough job you have. And I know I might not learn anything you don't already know, but I've been asked to try."

"I can't stop you from doing that, but don't even think about interfering with my work or that of my fellow officers," Snepper said firmly.

"If I learn anything, would you like me to let you know?" Brad asked the young officer briskly.

"I don't know what makes you think you can accomplish anything we can't. And I certainly won't hold my breath until you do. But if, by some stroke of luck, you do come across some information, you'd better give it to us right away."

"Has anyone in the department received any leads on the whereabouts of Courtney and Johnny? I'm really worried about those kids."

"If we had, it would not be proper to give that information out until we had acted on it," Officer Snepper said.

Just then, an office door opened and Sgt. Abel Bone joined them. He nodded at Brad and introduced himself before asking, "Lawrence, have you followed up on that information I gave you about the missing children?"

Lawrence looked at Brad and said, "Thanks for coming in. You'll have to excuse my sergeant and me now. We have things to discuss."

"You can finish your conversation with Mr. Hagen in a moment, Lawrence. I just need to know if you've learned anything."

Brad's years of experience had made him very observant; he noticed a slip of paper on the counter where Officer Snepper had been standing when he first saw him. It was upside down, but Brad didn't have any trouble reading it. It mentioned a possible sighting of the children and had a name, Leeann Boyer, and a phone number. It also mentioned Topeka. He quickly memorized the name and phone number so he could follow up on it later.

"I don't have anything to discuss with this guy," Officer Snepper continued. "He's a PI, and he's snooping into our cases."

"Sorry, Sergeant, but I don't mean to snoop. I am a private investigator and former FBI special agent. I have been retained to look into the disappearance of the Graves kids. I was just explaining to Officer Snepper that I would be happy to share any information I come up with if you folks would like me to."

"We don't need your help," Lawrence snapped.

"Actually, Officer Snepper," the sergeant began, "we would welcome any help we can get. The disappearance of these kids is a serious matter."

"PIs aren't any help," Lawrence said, his face going red.

"They can be, especially if they are former, experienced law enforcement folks," Sergeant Bone told the young officer. "Sorry, Detective. I hope you can come up with something. These missing kids are a big concern to me. We're afraid that the missing brother has come back and snatched them. We believe he is a dangerous young man, and we have redoubled our efforts to find him in addition to the young kids."

"Well, if I can help with anything, I'll be glad to," Brad said.

"Thanks, Detective," Sergeant Bone said.

Brad walked away but kept his ears tuned to the resumed conversation between Officer Snepper and his sergeant. He wanted to know what exactly the sergeant was asking him regarding a lead. He did hear the young officer say, "It was nothing."

Back in his car a couple of minutes later, Brad jotted down the phone number and name he had memorized from the note he'd seen. He planned to call that number but not before he had left the parking lot. His noisy stomach reminded him that he needed to stop somewhere to get a bite to eat and a cup of coffee to keep him awake. When he parked at the café, he pulled out his cell phone and tried the number. The response he got was that it was not a working number.

Frustrated, he put his phone back in his pocket and went inside. As he was eating, he studied the rather short list Donald Graves had given him. He planned to begin contacting each person on that list as soon as he finished his lunch. But at the same time, the name *Leeann Boyer* would not leave his mind. In fact, not only did it not leave his mind, but he began to feel a sense of urgency. Perhaps, he thought, the officer who had written the note had jotted down the number wrong. When he left the café, his mind was made up. He would spend a few minutes trying to see if there was a better number for Leeann and if there was, he would call her.

CHAPTER ELEVEN

THE FIRST THING BRAD DID upon reaching his vehicle after he had finished his lunch was to ask Siri on his iPhone what the area code for Topeka, Kansas, was. The number he found was 785. The number he had memorized from the note at the police station was 784. He dialed again, this time using the 785 area code. He got a working number, but he also got a recording informing him that he had reached the home of Mrs. Leeann Boyer and that if he would leave his name and phone number, she would return his call. He did so and then added, "I am a private detective looking into the matter of two missing children from Goodland."

There was nothing more to be done with that until he received a return call. The woman may not be of any help, but if she was, he wondered what Sergeant Bone would think of the sorry effort that Officer Snepper had made. The young officer needed to learn a few things.

Brad then called at an address listed on the sheet of paper he had received from Donald. There was no one home, and Donald had not listed a phone number, so he went to the next listed address. He found a woman at home, but she informed him in no uncertain terms that she had not heard from nor seen young Sparky Graves since he had disappeared.

The woman's name was Patty Grow. She was middle aged, looked tired, and admitted that she was a bit under the weather.

"I won't take much of your time," Brad told her. "I'm a private investigator, and I'm looking into the disappearance of Sparky Graves."

The lady's eyes narrowed. "And his little brother and sister too?"

"Yes," he said.

"Well, I can tell you one thing for sure," she said. "If those kids are truly gone, it didn't have anything to do with Sparky. He's been in my home a few times, and I'll tell you he is one of the nicest young men I've ever met."

Brad leaned forward, frowning. "Apparently there must be another side to Sparky that you never saw. You see, his older brother saw him kill Mrs. Graves, their mother."

"Now that is simply *not possible*. Sparky would never hurt his mother," she said firmly. "I don't understand why anyone would believe that. I can't understand how our police officers would believe it."

"But the older brother saw Sparky push her off the deck," Brad said.

"If someone were to push his mother off a deck, Kal Graves would be the one," she said hotly, and then she began to cough.

Brad waited until she got her breathing under control and then said, "According to Donald, their father, Sparky was always causing trouble and blaming things on Kal."

"Kal is trouble, I'm telling you," Patty said with fire in her eyes. "Kal has always managed to pull the wool over people's eyes and put blame for the bad things he did onto this younger brother. But he didn't pull any wool over my eyes."

"This is very different from what I've been told," Brad said, even as serious doubts about both Donald and Kal Graves began to take root in his brain.

"My husband is friends with one of Donald Graves's mechanics," Mrs. Grow said. "Would you like to hear what he says about Kal and Sparky?"

"I certainly would," Brad said as he thought about Donald's and Kal's refusal to give him the names of the men who worked in his shop. "But before you tell me what he says, I'd like to have his name, address, and phone number if you have that information."

"I don't know if I should do that," she said hesitantly, her face troubled.

"Why not?" Brad asked.

"Because he told my husband that he believes Kal is capable of violence. He's afraid that if Kal found out he'd told the truth about him to the authorities or anyone else that his life would be in danger," Mrs. Grow said. "My husband would probably be angry with me if he finds out I spoke to you about this."

"Mrs. Grow," Brad began.

"Please call me Patty. *Mrs. Grow* makes me feel old."

"Patty it is," Brad said with a smile. "Now, you have my word that our conversation will not go to anyone else. I will not tell the police. I will only use the information that you give me to enable me to reach the truth through other means. I have been led to believe that Sparky is an extremely dangerous young man, and my job is to find him so he can be arrested."

Patty's eyes grew wide with alarm. "If you find him and bring him back here, it will be the end of a very fine boy!"

"What do you mean by that?" Brad asked, though he had a feeling he knew.

"I mean that he will be brought back here and be convicted of a murder he did not commit. He would then probably spend the rest of his life locked up somewhere."

"You really believe he's innocent, don't you?" Brad asked.

"I'm sure of it. So is my husband and his friend from Donald's shop," she said with great feeling and emotion. "I don't know who hired you, but if it was Donald or Kal, and you tell them where he is, I would fear that Sparky might never even get to have a trial."

"Meaning what?" Brad asked.

"Meaning that if Kal were to learn where Sparky is hiding, he would go there and kill him, just like I think he killed his mother."

"That is a pretty extreme statement," Brad said, starting to wonder whom he should trust.

"If you knew Sparky and Kal the way I do, you would believe me," Patty said. "Now, let me tell you what my husband's friend says about those two young men."

"Sure, go ahead," Brad said.

"This will not go beyond the two of us?" Patty asked, an anxious look on her face.

"You have my word," Brad assured her.

"Well, it's like this: Kal was always taking credit for work that Sparky does, but Kal convinced his father that Sparky was always taking credit for what Kal did. Much of the work the boys did was in the evenings and on the weekends— but not always. There have been a couple of occasions when my husband's friend knew it was Sparky who did the work because he saw him do it, but Kal got the credit for it, and Sparky got punished for loafing and for lying."

Brad was very concerned. Patty Grow seemed to him to be a trustworthy person. "Do any other mechanics think the same thing?"

"I'm sure they do, but they don't dare say anything. Donald always takes Kal's word, and the couple of times my husband's friend attempted to defend Sparky, Donald got upset and wouldn't hear it. He even told this friend that if he valued his job, he would not go around creating trouble for Kal. Donald honestly seems to believe that Sparky is a troubled young man and that Kal walks on water."

"Thanks for telling me this," Brad said. He believed Mrs. Grow despite the information Donald and Kal had fed him. And the fear that he might bring disastrous consequences to an innocent boy by doing the job he'd been hired to do gave him serious pause. "What would any of Donald's coworkers say if I approached them?"

"Please, don't do that!" Patty cried out in alarm.

"No, I don't mean I'd use what you told me, but just in the course of my investigation, if I spoke with any of them, do you think they might tell me much the same thing that you have just told me, or are they too afraid of losing their jobs?"

Patty slowly shook her head. "I don't think they would dare tell the truth. They're afraid of Donald ending their jobs, as you suggested. But I believe they are also afraid of Kal ending their lives or, at the very least, harming them in some way. Did you plan to talk to some of them?"

"I wanted to, but I don't have their names or addresses," he said.

Patty perceptively said, "Donald probably told you not to talk to them."

Brad neither confirmed nor denied that, but it certainly seemed likely that Donald and Kal—mostly Kal, he presumed—feared what they might say. "Thanks again, Patty. I assure you that I will keep what you have told me in the strictest confidence."

That meant, to Brad at least, that he would not be reporting what he had just learned to Donald.

"Detective, there is one more thing my husband's friend told him; He—the friend—always keeps a loaded pistol in his car. He has a permit for it, but anyway, that pistol is missing. He thinks Kal might have stolen it, but he can't prove it and doesn't dare mention it to his boss," Patty said. "If Kal does have that gun, he could be more dangerous than ever."

"I'll keep that in mind," Brad promised, his worry building.

After leaving Patty's home, he drove out of her neighborhood and then parked on the side of the road while he considered what to do about the disturbing information he had just received. He couldn't shake the feeling that he was an unwitting pawn in the hands of an extremely dangerous young man, Kal Graves, who might now be armed. He considered contacting Donald, returning the retainer he had received, and walking away from the job.

Then he thought about the two children who, like their brother Sparky, were missing. He wondered if maybe Sparky had come back and taken the kids, but not for the reason Kal had stated. If Sparky had his younger siblings, it could be to protect them from Kal. Another thought, a disturbing one, entered his anxious mind. What if the two had fled out of fear of Kal? He thought about the comment Donald had made about them having been hurt riding double on one of their bikes. They only had Kal's word to go off of. But what if the injuries to the children that led to all that blood in the bedroom were inflicted by Kal? Would they leave home and go out into a dangerous world to flee what they perceived as an even more dangerous situation at home? An even worse thought hit him. Could Kal have killed the children and hidden their bodies?

Brad's phone rang, interrupting his worrisome thoughts. When he saw that it was Leeann Boyer returning his call, he quickly answered. Brad explained who he was, and she dove right in with, "You called about what I told the police dispatcher in Goodland?"

"I did," he replied.

"They never called me back. I don't think they want to talk to me," she said.

"That may not be true," he said, "although the officer that was given your number was not very enthused about your call. It's possible he may even have attempted to call you."

"If he did, he did not leave me a message, and I haven't seen any missed calls on my phone," she said rather hotly.

"That's because someone there wrote your phone number down wrong," Brad explained.

"Then how did you reach me?" she asked.

"I did more than they did," he admitted. "I wondered if someone had written it down wrong, so I checked and found out they were calling using the wrong area code. At any rate, would you tell me why you called them? I am looking for the children independently of the police here in Goodland, although I did promise to share any pertinent information I find with them."

"Thank you. This may be nothing," Mrs. Boyer said, "but I saw a little girl in the restroom at a rest stop along the freeway. She was very pretty. She had long blonde hair and blue eyes. I spoke to her. I asked her if she was on a trip with her parents. She said she was, but as I've thought about it, she seemed really nervous, afraid even. I think she may have had a bloody nose, because she had blood on her shirt and pants. She kept looking around like she was afraid of someone. I wondered if a brother or sister had punched her in the face."

Brad nodded to himself. *A big brother.* "What else did she tell you?"

"Nothing. She very quickly left the restroom after that. I didn't think much about it until after I got home and saw the news on the TV about two children missing from Goodland. I had stopped for gas in Goodland," she said. "I'm sorry. I'm probably wasting your time. I mean, the news said that they may have been kidnapped by their brother who is wanted for killing their mother. I wouldn't have called the police in Goodland, but I have always tried to be a good citizen. So I felt that I should do so even though they might actually be with their brother like the news is reporting."

Brad's heart raced. He knew right then what he would do. "Mrs. Boyer, do you think it might have been possible that they were stowaways in your car?"

"It might sound crazy, but I did wonder, either my car or someone else's who had stopped at that same rest area."

"That seems like too much of a coincidence. What kind of car do you drive?" Brad asked.

"It's a Toyota," she responded.

"A sedan, not a van?" Brad asked.

"That's right. It is a four-door sedan. I had my luggage in the trunk so I never looked behind the front seat. And I had my radio on, so if they made any noise, I probably wouldn't have heard it. Even after I got home, I got my suitcase from the trunk and took it in the house," she said.

"Have you looked since then to see if there was any evidence someone may have been on the floor back there?" he asked.

"No, should I do that?"

"Yes, and would you do so now while I am on the phone with you?" he asked.

"Okay, I am walking out to my car now," she said. It was silent for a moment. He heard a door open and then close. He could hear what sounded like footsteps on concrete. After a moment, the walking stopped and Mrs. Boyer spoke again. "I'm at my car now. I'm unlocking it." A pause, then, "I'm opening the back door on the passenger side."

Brad smiled at the running dialogue, but his smile faded rapidly when he heard her gasp.

"There's a candy wrapper on the floor. I didn't put it there. And there are crumbs. Oh, Detective, I think those poor frightened children rode with me, and I didn't even know it. Should I call the police again?"

"Let me take care of that," Brad said quickly. "I would like to visit with you in person, if that's okay. I'm in Goodland right now, but I'll head your way immediately and call the police on the phone as I drive. Will you please give me your address? You will be there, won't you?"

The lady's voice was shaky now as she said, "I'll make sure I am. Thank you so much. I'm just so upset now that I'm shaking like a leaf."

"Try to be calm, Mrs. Boyer. Go inside your house and lie down. I'll be there as soon as I can," he promised.

After he hung up with her, Brad then dialed the police department and asked to speak with Sgt. Abel Bone. When he was told that the sergeant was not available, he asked, against his better judgement, about Officer Lawrence

Snepper. Snepper took the call, but as soon as Brad identified himself, he said, "Not you again. I don't have time for your interference in my work."

"I'm sorry, but I have a lead on the children that I wanted to pass along to you," Brad said.

"Oh really? Did Donald Graves call you too?" the officer asked.

"No, but I do have some credible information," he said.

"Then go look into it, for all the good it will do you," Officer Snepper told him. "We now know for a fact that Sparky Graves kidnapped his own siblings."

"Did Mr. Graves just tell you that?" Brad asked.

"Not that it's any of your business, but yes, he did. One of the kids got away from Sparky and found a phone and called Kal. It was the little girl. She told Kal that she was scared and that Sparky had taken them. She had managed to get away from him and was using a phone she borrowed from someone in a rest area to call. But before she could say anymore, she screamed and said Sparky was coming after her."

"That was it? Nothing from the person whose phone she was using?"

"Use your brain," Officer Snepper snapped. "Sparky probably took the phone, beat the guy senseless, and then took off with the kids."

"And you seriously believe that?" Brad asked.

"Of course I do. Sparky is a dangerous young man, but we will find him. You go ahead and chase your wild geese." He hung up on Brad, who, by then, was seething. Kal Graves was unbelievable. It was obvious now that he was a liar, and Brad was afraid he might be much worse than that. Once again, he thought about giving Donald back his retainer. First, however, he would see what he could do to find his younger children.

Several hours later, Brad pulled up to a pale-blue house in a nice, clean neighborhood in Topeka. He was met at the door by a small woman with clear blue eyes and gray hair that she wore tied in a bun on the top of her head.

"I found more things in the car after you called, Detective," she said before he had even introduced himself. "Come, let me show you."

She was an energetic, friendly woman. They walked to where the car was parked in her driveway in front of a single-car garage, and she chattered the whole way.

"My late husband was a school teacher just like I was. We both always loved children. We only had one of our own, but after he grew up, he joined the army. He's made a career of the military. He's a good man, but I don't see him very often. He does call regularly though, so I can talk to him and to my two grandchildren."

They reached the car. She grabbed the door handle to the back seat on the driver's side, but did not open it. She looked into Brad's eyes. "I love my grandchildren—a boy and a girl. They're almost grown now, but I remember what they were like when they were about the ages of the ones who are missing. Do you have grandchildren, Detective?"

"I have two as well, and they light up my life," he said as he thought about them, safe and sound in a happy home with loving parents.

"Then you worry about these two missing children just like I do."

"I sure do," he said as he thought about how he'd considered dropping the case. He hadn't gone through with it because he cared about the missing Graves children.

Leeann opened the door and stepped back. "I didn't touch anything. I just looked. But as you can see, there's a candy wrapper and crumbs on the floor. Look over on the other side."

Brad leaned in. There on the floor, against the far door, was a bright-yellow hair clip in the shape of a butterfly. And next to it was a stick of gum, still in the foil. He leaned back and stood upright.

"Those two poor little kids were in there, weren't they?" Leeann asked.

"Someone was," he said. "And one of them was a little girl. Have you checked your yard?"

"No, I didn't think to do that. I just supposed that they would have hurried from here as soon as they got out of my car," she said sheepishly. "I guess it was good I was a school teacher, not a cop."

"Lock the car and then let's go around back," he said.

"I guess they could be in my garden shed or my late husband's woodworking shop. I have no reason to go in his shop anymore. And I haven't been in my little shed since I got home from my trip."

The door to the garden tool shed was unlocked. After a quick inspection, Brad determined that there were no children hiding inside. He did spend a couple of minutes carefully inspecting the interior but couldn't see any sign of someone having been in there. "Do you see anything out of place?" he asked Leeann as he turned to face her.

She'd been waiting at the door, but she joined him inside and looked around. She put her hand to her mouth. "I'm sure the lawnmower was tight against that back wall. It's out a couple of feet now. Detective! They must have hidden behind it for a while and then left."

"You're probably right. So why don't we go take a look in the woodworking shop now?" he said.

She shook her head. "I suppose we can do that, but I don't believe they could have gotten in there. I keep it locked. I haven't been in it for a long while, but my husband was very fussy about keeping the shop locked."

"Let's look anyway, if you don't mind," Brad said.

"All right then. I'll go in the house and get the key." She scurried away.

Brad tried the door anyway, but it was indeed locked. He walked around the building. At the back there was a window. The glass had been shattered. He was very quiet as he peered inside, but he couldn't see any children. However, he saw dried blood, a fair amount of it, on the window sill. It could not have come from any injuries Kal might have inflicted on his siblings. It could mean only one thing: someone had climbed through the window and had been cut in the process.

He quietly walked back to the front and met Mrs. Boyer, who handed him the key. In a quiet voice he asked, "How long has the window at the back been broken?"

Her eyes grew wide, but taking a cue from how quietly he was speaking, she whispered, "I didn't know it was."

He inserted the key in the lock and turned it. Then he opened the door as quietly as he could and, signaling for Leeann to follow him, stepped inside. It didn't look like anyone had done any work in there for a long time, probably not in the time since Mr. Boyer had passed away. There were lots of tools—hand tools, an assortment of large saws, a drill press, and other big items. There was a partially finished cupboard of some sort in the middle of the floor. But he couldn't see where any children could be hiding unless they were behind the door at the back east corner of the large room.

"What's through that door?" he whispered, pointing at that door.

"A bathroom," Leeann whispered back.

Brad turned the doorknob and pulled it open. "Ah, what have we here?" he said as he peered into the bathroom.

CHAPTER TWELVE

IN THE BACK OF THE bathroom was a shower. The opaque door was closed, but through the door, Brad could see what could only be the distorted images of two children. He opened the shower door, and saw a young boy and a slightly older girl. They were huddled together, holding each other tightly. He could see dried blood on both of them. They began to cry when they realized they had been found.

"It's okay now, kids," Brad said gently. "No one is going to harm you. I am Detective Hagen, and I have been looking for you."

"Do we have to go to jail?" the girl asked, her chin quivering.

"No. Why do you think you would have to go to jail, Courtney?" he asked gently.

"You know who we are," she said. "You know we ran away from home."

"Yes, and like I said, I have been looking for you. I'm relieved to see that you're both okay."

He squatted down and held out a hand. "You're a policeman," the little girl said. "We broke the window. We're sorry. But we needed a place to hide. We couldn't find anyplace else. Now we're in trouble, aren't we?" Her little chin quivered, and her hold on her sobbing brother tightened.

"Why did you need a place to hide?" Brad asked, keeping an encouraging smile on his face and his voice low and tender.

"So we wouldn't have to go home," she said. Suddenly, her eyes grew wide as Mrs. Boyer knelt beside the detective. "You talked to me in the restroom. I'm sorry I lied to you."

"That's okay. I understand. Come on, you two, let's bring you in my house and get you cleaned up and fed. I'll bet you two are really hungry. Those cuts on your hands need to be cleaned and bandaged, and we need to wash the blood off your faces. Your clothing also needs to be washed to get the blood out. I'll help you with all of that. You poor, sweet little children."

"We tried to clean off the blood but we had to use our hands," Courtney said. "We couldn't find a washcloth or towel. I'm sorry, but we got blood on stuff."

"It will clean up just fine," Leeann said. "And by the way, my name is Leeann Boyer. I love children. My late husband and I were school teachers."

Neither child had moved, and they still clung tightly to each other. But for the first time, little Johnny spoke up. "We are really hungry, but please, don't tell Kal where we are. He might kill us like he did our mom."

Courtney shushed him with a worried look on her face.

Brad should have been shocked, but he was not. He, like others, had been taken in by Kal Graves, but not anymore. He knew that what Mrs. Patty Grow back in Goodland had told him was the truth. Kal might be relatively young, but he was a ruthless killer and a smooth talker. "You have my word that I will not let Kal near you, kids. You're safe now."

He stepped back as Leeann reached for the children, took their hands, and led them from the shower. "You're at my home now," Leeann added. "I'll keep you safe. Are these your backpacks?" They mumbled that they were, and she said, "We'll take them in the house with us."

Courtney was still worrying about the window. "We'll work to pay you back for the window."

"Don't you kids worry about that old window," Leeann said lovingly. "Let's go in the house now."

"Just a moment, Leeann," Brad said. "I want to talk to these two for just a minute."

"Don't tell our dad," Courtney cried out.

"Hey, kids. I'm here to keep you safe. You don't need to worry," he said gently. For the next couple of minutes, he quizzed them about Kal, Sparky, and their father. Then he let Mrs. Boyer lead them from the shop.

As soon as the kids were in the house, Brad dialed the Goodland Police Department again. He asked for Sgt. Abel Bone. This time, he got him. "Sergeant, this is Detective Hagen. Have you got a moment?"

"If you have something to report, I have. If not, then I am very busy," Bone said tersely.

Brad chuckled. "I do have something to report. I know where the Graves children are."

"Are you sure?" Sergeant Bone said quickly. "And do you believe they are with Sparky?"

"They are not with their brother. They know nothing about his whereabouts. And yes, I am sure. I have seen and spoken with them."

"Excellent work, Detective. I can't imagine how you found them. We've tried everything we can think of," the sergeant said.

"Everything except returning a very simple call to Mrs. Leeann Boyer," Brad said, not hiding his disgust very well.

"What are you talking about? I turned that matter over to Officer Snepper. He tried to call, but it was not a working number. Just another hoax," Sergeant Bone said.

"It was not a hoax, and whoever took the call wrote down the wrong area code. After a couple of minutes, I solved that problem and was able to reach her."

"How did you know she had called here?" the sergeant asked suspiciously.

"I'm a detective," Brad said. "I observe things, and I follow up."

"Snepper is not very efficient, I'll admit," Bone said. "But I thought he'd tried to call. I'll have to speak to him about that. Now, tell me about the Graves children. Where are they and are they okay?"

"They are doing well considering what they've gone through. As to where they are, I can't say just yet as they are petrified that their brother will kill them," Brad said. Knowing that the cops in Goodland had Mrs. Boyer's name, he added, "I have them in a secure place which I will not, at this point, disclose."

"So they aren't with Sparky, but they fear he will do them harm?" the sergeant asked.

"No, that's not how it is at all. It's *Kal* they're afraid of. *They saw Kal kill their mother.* He threatened to kill *them* if they told. They believed him. And they did not wreck a bike. Kal beat them both up and threatened them with their lives if they didn't say they had been riding double and wrecked. They felt they had no choice but to leave," Brad said. "They're afraid that no matter what, their father will always take Kal's side. They say he always has. They're petrified of Kal, and they miss Sparky terribly."

"I see. Are you sure of that?" the sergeant asked suspiciously.

"Totally! Yes, Sergeant, Kal is the killer, not Sparky."

"Frankly, I'm shocked to hear you say that. That goes against what anyone else has told me."

"Then you haven't talked to the right people in Goodland," Brad said. "I did. But at any rate, they are safe now."

"Okay, give me their location, and I will send someone to pick them up and bring them back here."

"Not on your life, Sergeant. I just told you I have them taken care of. They're safe where they are."

"You can't keep them from me," Sergeant Bone said angrily. "I'll keep them safe."

"You might try, but I worked hard to find them, and I will not risk them being in danger until you have that brother of theirs, Kal, locked up tight," Brad told him. "I will make arrangements for you to meet them and question them, but it will be at a place of my choosing, and I will be with them."

"I want them here in Goodland," Bone said stubbornly.

"It's not going to happen. You and your department had the chance to find them and failed. I did the leg work, I found them, and I will keep them safe. Now, do you want to come yourself, or will you send someone else? And if you send another officer, it'd better not be Snepper, because I won't let him within a hundred miles of those kids."

Bone finally backed down. "I'll come. And Snepper will be nowhere near this investigation from here on out."

"Very well," Brad said. "You will understand why I feel so strongly after you have a chance to interview the children. I'll call you back with a place to meet. Then you can tell me what time you can be there tomorrow. I want to give them time to rest until they talk to you."

Although he didn't say so, Brad did not plan to have the meeting occur anywhere near where he had located the children. It wasn't that he had anything against Detective Bone, but he did fear that someone in the department who was so pro-Kal that they were blinded by their prejudice would inadvertently learn where Bone was going and then interfere.

The biggest dilemma he had was what to do about his clients, Kal and Donald Graves. He'd found the missing children, but he was nowhere closer to finding Sparky. His motivation to locate the young man was strong, but there was no way he could tell his clients if and when he did find him. He was conflicted because he owed his clients to complete his mission, but he would never do anything to further endanger Sparky. At this point, he was considering simply contacting Donald Graves and telling him he could not continue, that he would have to hire someone else.

If he did that, he felt morally bound to continue, on his own, to search for Sparky in order to protect him as he was protecting his younger siblings. He had no doubt that Donald would hire someone else, and if he did, that person might not be concerned about what could happen to Sparky if he was located. He pulled out his phone. He planned to call Donald before speaking further with the younger children. His goal at this point was to reunite the younger children with Sparky and to somehow eventually get them back together with Donald if and when their father came to his senses about his dangerous oldest son. And then only when Kal was behind bars for killing his mother.

***

Donald Graves answered his cell phone that evening as soon as he saw that the caller was Brad Hagen, his private investigator. "You found my killer son yet?" he asked as his way of answering the call.

"I have not found Sparky, and I have made no progress in that regard," the investigator told him.

"Well, you better do so and fast or I will find someone else who will," he threatened as he felt anger begin to boil.

"You do that," Brad said to him. "This has been a dead-end job from the beginning as far as I am concerned."

That infuriated Donald, who sat looking at his son, Kal, who mouthed, "Is that Hagen?" Donald nodded and put the cell phone on speaker mode.

"Don't you dare threaten to quit me," Donald shouted.

"Is he thinking about quitting?" Kal asked. "He can't do that. We paid him to find Sparky. And you better do that, Hagen. You hear me? This is Kal."

"I know who it is," the investigator said in a voice that was calm enough to further infuriate both of them. "But I don't feel that it would be fair to either of you to continue since I have made no progress, and it is clear that I do not have the confidence of either of you that I can actually find Sparky."

"You are fired!" Kal shouted.

"Not so fast, Kal. We paid him," Donald said.

"I know. I just said that," Kal argued.

"I think we should give him a few more days, and then we can fire him if he doesn't produce," Donald said, his voice calmer now.

"I don't," his son argued loudly. "We got the wrong guy. We need to find someone who will do a better job."

"Hey, you two, I'm still here," Brad's voice on the phone said. "I'll send you back your money minus what expenses I have already accrued."

"You can't just quit," Donald shouted.

"I can't continue working for the two of you if you aren't unified on my employment," Brad said.

"I don't like your attitude," Donald burst out. "Kal is right. You are fired."

"Fine," Brad said, and the call was terminated.

"Did he just hang up on you, Dad?" Kal asked, his face red.

"I think he did," Donald agreed. "So I guess we need to start looking for another investigator."

"And you'd better get a good one this time," Kal said. "We can't let Sparky get away with what he's done. We have to find him. I'm sure he took those two innocent little siblings of mine. You can't let him get away with that or with killing my poor mother."

Donald looked at Kal for a moment, and then he said, "We won't Kal. He's destroyed my life. Believe me, we won't."

***

Brad heaved a sigh of relief. He'd been fired. That was better than quitting. He felt like new life had just been breathed into him. He shut the door to the woodworking shed behind him and strode toward the house. He tapped on the back door, and Mrs. Boyer opened it with a smile on her face.

"They are such sweet children," she said.

"What are they doing?" Brad asked as she ushered him into her clean and orderly house.

"They're eating," she said with a radiant smile. "I wanted them to both have a bath, but they asked if they could please eat first. The little tykes are starved. And yes, they did say *please*."

"I suppose they are very hungry," he agreed.

Mrs. Boyer steered him into the living room and then said quietly, "The children can't hear us from in here if we talk quietly. And we do need to talk." Her face had become very serious. "Please, sit down, Mr. Hagen."

"Thank you, Mrs. Boyer," he said as she showed him to the end of the living room that was the farthest from the kitchen.

"I think you should call me Leeann," she said.

"And you should call me Brad," he countered.

"Yes, that would be nice, Brad," she agreed. "Now, please tell me who you told about where the children are." Brad detected a note of deep concern in her eyes. "I would like to take care of them for as long as I am allowed to. You can't let them go back to their father as long as their brother Kal is there."

"I agree with you on that," Brad said. He then told her about his conversation with Sergeant Bone and what he had planned to do in regards to letting the officer speak with them but not letting his client know. He also explained that he had not been hired to find the children, only Sparky.

Most of the concern faded from Leeann's eyes and she smiled. "You are a good man, Brad. Now, tell me, if you didn't tell the person who hired you to find Sparky that you found the children, do you still plan to?"

"No, I do not. I called with the intention of telling him that I could not continue to search for Sparky, but my client made it easy for me. I was fired."

For a moment, Mrs. Boyer was silent. "So . . . you don't have a client anymore? What about the children's poor brother, Sparky? Someone must find him for Johnny and Courtney's sake as well as for his own."

"I agree," Brad said. "But at this point, the last thing I think needs to happen is for my former client to find out where Sparky is."

"Who is your former client?" Leeann asked. Before Brad could tell her that he probably *shouldn't* tell her, she went on. "It was their father, wasn't it? Probably the older brother as well."

Brad simply smiled, but neither confirmed nor denied it. "My concern now is for the safety of the three innocent children."

"Mr. Hagen," Leeann began.

"Brad, remember?" he reminded her.

"Yes, Brad," she agreed. "Will you work for me? Will you let me pay you to safely reunite the three children?"

That surprised him. "I can't take your money."

"I am well enough off," Leeann informed him. "And it seems to me that you need a client."

"I can do this on my own," Brad said.

"Please, Brad. Let me pay you something. I feel responsible for these kids. After all, I brought them here to Topeka."

"Not that you knew you were doing that," Brad reminded her.

"Maybe not, but I did. How much do you charge?"

Brad thought for a moment. It would be good to have a client. It would make his search for Sparky Graves more legitimate. "Okay, I will work for you, Leeann. My fee will be ten dollars."

She shook her head. "Don't insult me, Brad. I can pay you. Will you take a thousand dollars?"

Leeann clearly had no idea what the cost of an investigator was, so it was probably best he took her up on the offer before she could find out how low her estimate was. "Okay, I'll agree to that. But not one penny more, no matter how long it takes me or how high my expenses get."

Leeann nodded. "Now, let's talk more about these children. Since you will be working for me, I need to keep them here."

Brad really quite liked this retired teacher. "Okay, for now. And since I work for you now—"

Leeann cut him off again. "Let me get my checkbook. I will write you a check, and then we can talk about what happens next." Ten minutes later, he had a check and she had a contract. "By the way, I don't even know where you live," Leeann said.

"Same city as you do. I'm also from here in Topeka," he said.

"I thought you must be from Goodland or around there," she said. "So how did Donald Graves . . . I mean your former client, locate you to hire you?"

"I'm not sure how my former client found me," he said.

"Well, I'm glad to know you're from here," she said, as if that meant something. And maybe to her it did.

Even though he had never told her who his former client was, it was clear that she knew, and that was good enough for both of them. United in their desire to reunite Sparky with Johnny and Courtney and hopefully at some point with their father, they began to lay out a plan. It was mostly Brad's plan, but he wanted Leeann to feel part of it, so he listened to her ideas and expressed his own. Their goal was the same.

Late the next morning, a Monday, Brad and Leeann sat in the front seat of his car, driving to Salina, Kansas, while the two young Graves children sat in the backseat. It was well over a hundred miles from Topeka, but it also made the drive for Sergeant Bone a reasonable one. Sergeant Bone had assured Brad that he would meet them at a hotel where Brad had made a reservation. There, he would be allowed to interview the children in the presence of both Brad and Leeann. Brad had not revealed Leeann's name to the officer, nor did he intend to. If she were to care for the children in her home for the near future, he didn't want anyone figuring out who she was or where she lived.

The children, well fed, bathed, fresh from a good night's sleep, and dressed in new clothing that Leeann had purchased for them, were quiet as they rode. Both of them seemed nervous about telling their story to the police, but they also seemed confident in the promise of both Brad and Leeann that they would be protected from Kal.

Brad felt like he could trust Sergeant Bone, but he did *not* trust Officer Snepper. Bone had promised to tell Snepper to stay away from the case, but as far as Brad knew, the sergeant hadn't had much luck contacting Snepper, since the officer was off duty until that evening.

Thirty minutes into the trip, Brad's cell phone rang.

"Detective, this is Sergeant Bone. I just wanted to assure you that I finally reached Officer Snepper by phone and ordered him to stay away from this investigation. He assured me that he would."

"Thank you, Sergeant," Brad said.

"How are the children?" Bone asked.

"They're doing fine. They're nervous about meeting with you, but I have assured them that you want to listen to what they have to say and will take steps to see to it that Kal will be arrested and will be of no further danger to them."

Brad bristled when Bone said, "I still think you should let me take them and provide protection for them on my terms."

"Not until the threat has been removed," Brad said, trying to keep his anger in check.

"All right. I'll have to go along with that for now," the sergeant said reluctantly.

The two spoke for a couple more minutes, and then the call ended. Brad was left with an uneasy feeling in the pit of his stomach. His trust of Sergeant Bone was a bit shaky now. He wasn't sure why, but he felt like he had to be careful of what he said, what he did, and where he went.

CHAPTER THIRTEEN

DETECTIVE LYS GRIST WAS HAVING some success doing what she'd been hired to do. She needed to prove that Sparky had been nowhere near Goodland, Kansas, when his mother had been shoved to her death. Lys was making some progress on that front.

The second responsibility she had accepted would likely be a lot more difficult to accomplish; she had to find the evidence necessary to prove that someone, likely Kal Graves, was the real killer. With the information she had gained, mostly from Rick Granberry, the trucker who had inadvertently hauled Sparky for many miles, she headed to Goodland. The most important thing now was to prove Sparky was innocent.

She also had another concern. Alfred had called to tell her that Sparky's siblings had gone missing and the media had named Sparky as the prime suspect. She knew that Sparky being involved was simply not possible. Regardless, she was very concerned about the two of them. Even though Alfred had not hired her to find the younger children, she felt compelled to attempt to find them as well.

When she drove into Goodland, she went straight to the police station. She was not at all sure how she would be received, but she always tried to work closely with local authorities—when they would let her. She identified herself to the receptionist and asked to speak with someone involved in the investigation involving the disappearance of Sparky Graves. She was stalled for nearly an hour but did not leave or back down. Finally, an officer by the name of Lawrence Snepper approached and introduced himself.

"I'm handling the investigation of the wanted killer Sparky Graves," he said coldly. "And I don't welcome the interference of people like you and Brad Hagen."

Lys was taken aback. She knew Brad well. In fact, she was very fond of him. They'd worked together on a case and had corresponded regularly since then. He'd even flown to Salt Lake twice and taken her out. She felt a shiver of delight when she heard his name.

She looked at the officer's angry face. "I am not trying to interfere. I want to help if you will let me. I have solid evidence that Sparky Graves did not kill anyone."

"I have the investigation under control, lady. I do not need your help," he said, his face slightly flushed. "Believe me, I have solid evidence that Sparky is a killer, and I intend to find him and bring him to justice."

Lys shook her head. This was not the reception she had hoped for. In an attempt to keep this visit from being a total bust, she said, "I would like to speak to your supervisor."

"Won't happen. He's out of town."

"Then let me talk to the chief of police," she suggested.

"Nope. He's not here either. Sorry, lady, but you'll have to leave now. And I am warning you to refrain from interfering in my investigation." Before she could reply, he turned and briskly walked away.

Back in her black Tahoe, she sat and pondered the altercation she had just experienced. It was clear to her that the investigating officer had no intention of considering anything other than Sparky being a vicious killer. His mind was closed to there being any other possibility. With that kind of attitude at the police department, her task of proving that Sparky was innocent and that Kal was the likely killer became much more difficult.

She sat in the vehicle with the motor running while considering her next move. There was a tap on the window. She looked over and saw that it was Officer Snepper, and she could tell from the frown on his face that he was angry. She rolled the window down. "Is there something you need, Officer?" she asked calmly.

"Yeah, lady, there is. I need for you to beat it." He jerked his head toward the road.

"Hey, this is a public parking area. I just needed a few moments to consider what I should do since you clearly don't want to allow me to help you," she said.

"It's public unless I tell you to leave. Then for you, it is no longer public. If you stay here even one minute longer, I'll have to take you into custody for trespassing," he said. "So leave right now, and I don't want to see you or this Tahoe of yours around here again. Am I making myself clear?"

Lys checked her anger. "Yes, sir, I understand." She put the Tahoe in gear and pulled away, leaving the young officer standing there, still shaking his head. She had a hard time understanding how a case so important could be turned over to such a young, and clearly inexperienced, officer. It made no sense.

She stopped at a restaurant a few blocks away and went inside. She ordered a cheeseburger and glass of milk and then thought about what Officer Snepper had said to her about her very good friend Brad. Snepper had told her that he didn't want people like her and Brad Hagen to interfere. Did that mean he was involved in this case somehow? She needed to find out where Brad was and what he was up to.

She called the number for his office, and a moment later, she was told by an electronic voice that the call was going to be forwarded to his cell phone. She waited as the cell phone rang.

"Detective Brad Hagen," a slightly muted male voice said. "I'm currently busy, but if this isn't an emergency, please leave a message and I'll call you back."

Lys hesitated, then left a message. "Brad, this is Lys. I need to speak with you about the Sparky Graves case. I think we're both working on it from opposite ends. I'll anxiously await your call." If Brad didn't call back in the next hour, she would call him again. In the meantime, she would snoop around town after she finished her burger and see if she could find anyone who would talk to her about Sparky Graves and his family.

***

Brad Hagen looked at his phone for a moment. He was seated beside Leeann Boyer in a hotel room he had retained in Salina and was listening to the interview Sergeant Bone was conducting with the Graves children. So far, the children had told their story to Bone exactly as they had to him and Leeann. Bone was gentle with the children and appeared to have gained their confidence. As for Leeann, when Bone asked who she was, Brad gave a fake name just in case Bone did somehow recall who had called his officer about the children. He refused to tell him where she lived, only that she was watching the children for him. He'd straighten it all out later with Sergeant Bone.

A shiver of excitement passed through him when he saw who had called him. He and Lys had become very good friends over the past few months, perhaps even more than friends. He was anxious to speak with her. He leaned over to Leeann and said in a soft voice, "I need to return this call. Please listen carefully to this interview. I'll be back as soon as I can. I'll only be outside the door, so if something happens that you don't feel good about, come out and get me immediately."

"I will," she whispered. "But so far, I think the kids are doing great."

"So do I," he said and then slipped out. He called the number Lys had called from, a number he knew by heart, and waited while it rang.

"Hello, Brad. That was fast. I appreciate it. It's good to hear your voice. It's been a few days." Lys took a breath. "We need to talk."

"It's good to hear your voice too, Lys," he said sincerely. "Your message mentioned Sparky Graves."

"Yes. Brad, I've been retained to work on his case."

"I won't ask who retained you, but I'm guessing it was Donald Graves," Brad said.

"You know I can't tell you who hired me, but I can tell you who didn't. It was not Donald Graves."

"Interesting," he said. "Where are you calling from?"

"I'm in Goodland, Kansas. I just went to the police station and was very rudely rejected by an Officer Snepper a little while ago."

"Snepper? Why were you speaking with him?" Brad asked.

"I offered to help him locate Sparky Graves," she said. "I was told to keep my nose out of his investigation."

"Did Snepper honestly tell you that it was *his* investigation?" Brad asked as he thought about what Sergeant Bone had told him. Now he wondered who was telling the truth—Officer Snepper or Sergeant Bone. He hoped it was Bone.

"He told me that he was investigating the matter and to stay out of his way, or words to that effect. He even told me that if I didn't leave the parking lot, he would arrest me for trespassing."

"That's a new one," Brad said. "The officer is a jerk. But I find this quite interesting. I'm working with an officer by the name of Abel Bone. He's a sergeant, and he told me that he had instructed Snepper to have nothing to do with the case."

"Then somebody is lying," Lys said.

"That's for sure. How did you know to contact me?" Brad asked.

"Snepper told me that he didn't appreciate people like me and *Brad Hagen* interfering with his investigation. He had no idea that you and I were good friends. So I left, assuming you'd been hired by someone to look into the matter. That's why I called you."

"I was hired by Donald Graves to find Sparky, but then he fired me. I am still on the case, however, just with a new client."

"An amazing coincidence," Lys said. "I was hired to work on a case involving Sparky Graves. But I don't think I should tell you more than that."

"It seems that you and I are on the same page," Brad said. "We need to get together. I've missed you, Lys."

"And I've missed you," she said wistfully. She really did care for this man. It was just too bad they lived so far apart.

"By working together, we may be able to prove who the real killer is, Lys. I personally believe it is Kal Graves. And maybe together we can locate Sparky. Although . . ." Brad chuckled. "I get the feeling you already know where he is."

"I didn't say that," she replied, but he could also detect a smile in her voice.

"I didn't say you did," Brad said, laughing outright. "I'm in Salina, Kansas, at the moment. I'll be coming back to Goodland tomorrow, and then we can get together."

"I can head for Salina right now," she offered.

"I won't be here much longer, and I shouldn't tell you where I am going when I finish what I'm doing here. I'll call you tomorrow before noon, and we can meet."

"Okay. In that case, I'll get a room here and simply wait for you," she said. "Thanks for getting back to me. I can't wait to see you."

"Same here," he said and broke the connection.

He stood outside the hotel room door for a moment while he pondered what he had just learned. Someone had hired Lys. And he couldn't help but think that whoever it was knew exactly where Sparky was or, at the least, where he had been at some point in the recent past. Perhaps when they got together, he could learn more about what her mission was, if she could tell him. In the meantime, he needed to speak with Sergeant Bone. Either he had not pulled Snepper from the case, or Snepper was a maverick who was out to make a name for himself despite orders he'd been given to the contrary.

Brad slipped back into the hotel room where Sgt. Bone was still speaking with the children. The sergeant looked at him when he took his seat again. "I think I'm about finished here," he said. "Could you and I talk while your friend stays in here with the children?"

"Sure, we can do that," Brad said. Then to Johnny and Courtney he said, "Are you two okay waiting here with her for a little while?" They both nodded in agreement. Brad had very pointedly told them that he didn't want anyone to know Leeann's real name or where she was from. He had repeated the instruction for them to not reveal that information several times. They were smart children, and they promised they would not say her name. So far, they had complied. He then spoke to Leeann. "We won't be long, ma'am." She, too, nodded in agreement, so he and Bone left the room together.

"Let's go down to the restaurant and talk while we have a cup of coffee," the sergeant suggested.

"Sounds good to me," Brad said.

Once they had made their order, Sergeant Bone said, "You're right, Detective. These kids are scared to death of Kal, and they love Sparky. It looks like I have some work to do, and I expect that when I change the focus of my investigation, I will meet a great deal of resistance from Donald Graves."

"No doubt about that," Brad said. "And from the lead investigator on the case, Officer Snepper."

"What are you talking about?" Bone asked with a touch of anger in his voice. "I told you that I instructed him he was to have nothing further to do with this case. He is not now nor has he ever been the lead investigator. I am. Are you saying you don't believe me?"

"Sergeant, I don't know what to believe. You see, I just had a conversation with someone who spoke to Snepper a short while ago. He told her he was the lead investigator in the disappearance of Sparky and that she was not to interfere. He mentioned my name to her in what was apparently a rather derogatory fashion."

"Was that who you were talking to in the hall a few minutes ago?"

"It was. Her name is Detective Lys Grist. Like me, she is a private detective. It just happens that she and I are very good friends. Lys informed me that she spoke to Snepper, and he told her to bug off, that it was his case. He even ordered her to leave the parking lot under threat of arrest for trespassing."

Sergeant Bone was silent for a moment as his anger faded. "I'm sorry, Brad. Snepper is way out of order here. Is it okay if I call you Brad?"

"Sure, if it's okay if I call you Abel."

"It seems like we're going to need to work together, so I think we need to be on a first-name basis," Abel explained. "But first, I suppose I need to earn your trust. Believe me, I ordered Snepper off the case in no uncertain terms. At this point, I have no idea what he's up to, but clearly he is going off on his own on this case, and I need to speak with the chief of police to have him put an end to whatever Snepper's up to."

"I think that's a good idea," Brad agreed.

"Can you be back in Goodland tomorrow, Brad? The chief has been out of town for several days, but he will be back tomorrow, and I can take care of this matter of Officer Snepper. I realize that you need time to make sure the Graves kids are secure. I was miffed with you at first, but I'm okay with that situation for now, even though I would normally be calling child services. Would you be willing to meet with the chief tomorrow?"

"If you want me to," Brad said.

"I do. That way you will know I'm being straight with you," Abel said with a grin. "This is a serious matter, and if you and I are going to work together, we need to be able to trust one another."

Brad could not have agreed more.

***

Kay Dell was having lunch with some of her friends in the school lunchroom on Monday when the subject of Alfred's farm came up. "Where did you go Friday after school?" one of the girls, Jordan Spiker, asked.

"I've started working on a farm," she said. "I was out there Friday after school."

"Whose farm?" Jordan asked.

"Oh, you probably don't know him. He's an old man whose wife died last year. He needs help and I'm trying to help him," Kay Dell said evasively.

One of the other girls said that she might know him and asked his name.

"It's Alfred Briggs," Kay Dell reluctantly told the other girls.

"Why would you want to do that?" another girl, Nova Heylep, asked.

Kay Dell and Nova were not exactly friends, just classmates. Kay Dell didn't approve of some of the things Nova said she did. Nova was a very attractive girl and she often bragged about her association with some of the boys in their school. And Kay Dell did not like the language Nova often used. She avoided her when she could, but sometimes it couldn't be helped since Nova was friends with some of the girls Kay Dell hung out with.

But she was afraid she couldn't avoid Nova's question without being rude, so she said, "Because my dad is his church friend and because I really love animals. Alfred lets me spend a little time with his animals for helping him."

"You guys know that my family and I don't need churchy things," Nova said with a nasty tone in her voice. "It's a waste of time and just plain stupid."

Before Kay Dell could answer, Jordan spoke up. "I'm sorry you don't like church, Nova, but we do," she said, sweeping her hand to include the other girls in the group.

"You don't really understand our church, but you would be welcome to go with me some time," Kay Dell said, trying to be a missionary. She was quickly rebuffed.

"No thanks. Church doesn't do anything for anybody. So who needs it?"

Kay Dell tried not to look hurt. "I respect your feelings, Nova, but the invitation is there. If you ever change your mind, I'll be glad to let you go with me."

"Don't hold your breath, girl," Nova said nastily.

For the next few minutes, the tension at the table wouldn't be dispelled. Finally, Kay Dell got up. "I think I'll go to class."

As she and one other girl were walking away, she heard Nova say, "She's lying, you guys. There's no way she would go out there and work on a dirty old farm with some old geezer who probably slobbers when he eats and can't walk without staggering."

Kay Dell hid a blush and tried to hurry on her way, but she heard Jordan's response.

"Nova, Kay Dell is honest. If she says she's working for Mr. Briggs, then she is."

"I don't know about that. Kay Dell is a little weasel. She's such a—"

To Kay Dell's surprise, Jordan and the rest of the girls parted company with Nova before she had completed her disparaging statement. Nova was mean-spirited, and it seemed they didn't care to hear any more slams against Kay Dell.

***

Alfred Briggs was having a hard time getting used to his iPhone. He and Sparky were fixing dinner together when it began ringing and buzzing in his pocket. "That's your ringtone," Sparky said as Alfred dug in his pocket. "Someone is trying to call you."

"Oh, sorry," he said. "Who has my number besides you and Lys?"

"Probably only Kay Dell and her parents," Sparky said with a grin. "I'm not calling you, so it must be one of them."

Alfred fumbled with the phone for a moment, then Sparky took it from him. "You push this right here to answer it."

"Oh, yeah, that's right."

Sparky accepted the call and handed the phone back to Alfred as he said, "Oh, it's Lys."

Still puzzled, Alfred asked, "How do you know that?"

"I'll explain later. Talk to her," Sparky instructed with a grin.

Alfred lifted the phone to his ear and said, "Hello."

"Alfred, this is Lys Grist," she said. "Is Sparky there with you?"

"Yes. He's trying to help me figure this blasted phone out."

"Put it on speaker, so I can talk to both of you."

"I don't know how to do that."

"Give the phone to Sparky, please," she instructed.

"Okay," Alfred said and handed the phone to Sparky. "She wants it on speaker." To his amazement, Sparky pushed something on the screen, and Lys's voice was immediately amplified.

"Can you both hear me now?" she asked.

"Yes," they answered in unison.

"Good. Let me bring you up to date on what is happening and what I've learned," Lys said.

After Lys had explained what she knew, Alfred said, "So is Kal going to be arrested soon?"

"That I don't know. Your little brother and sister claim they saw Kal shove your mother from the balcony, but they are terribly scared," she said. "And frankly, I'm not sure if the police believe them."

"Where are they right now?" Sparky asked.

"I don't know. The other private investigator, a close friend of mine by the name of Brad Hagen, feels that it's best if he keeps their location secret for now to protect them from Kal."

"I'd like to see them and talk to them," Sparky replied. "I love them and I want to make sure they know it."

"They're safe for now," Lys confirmed again. "We need to trust Detective Hagen for the time being. They are safe, and so are you. We need to keep it that way until the cops finally decide to arrest your brother. I will continue to work to prove his guilt. I will make sure, when I can, that your siblings know you love them."

Sparky rubbed his short hair. He was perspiring profusely, and he felt half sick to his stomach. He had known for a long time that Kal was a bad person, but knowing just how bad he was made him ill. Lys Grist was right; he needed to be patient and trust her and this other investigator, the one she called Brad Hagen, despite how hard it was.

CHAPTER FOURTEEN

"THIS GUY WAS EXACTLY WHO we needed, Dad. You should have hired him," Kal said after Donald had refused to sign a contract with a rough-looking PI by the name of Fredrick Belina on Tuesday morning.

Belina was a stocky man with a large stomach, shaggy brown hair, and a short but uneven beard. His hazel eyes carried a hard, unforgiving look in them. They'd found him listed as a PI in Dodge City. After a short conversation on the phone, he had agreed to meet them about halfway between Goodland and Dodge City along I-70 near the small town of Russell.

"I don't think so," Donald said doubtfully after parting company with the PI. "He seems kind of rough to me. We can find someone better."

"He's what we need, Dad. The police won't run all over him," Kal insisted. To him, Fredrick Belina was a kindred spirit. He could sense in the guy a mean streak, and he liked it.

Donald shrugged. "I didn't care for him. We'll keep looking."

Kal bit his tongue. He had his father right where he wanted him. Right now was not a good time to lose his temper and show his true colors. The two spoke very little on the way back to Goodland.

Once back home, Donald told Kal that he would get on the phone later and attempt to locate another PI.

"Okay, Dad," Kal said, "but we need to hurry. Sparky needs to be in jail where he can't hurt anyone again."

"I just hope he hasn't already done something terrible to Courtney and Johnny," Donald said, shaking his fists in anger while trembling with fear for his younger children.

"I have some work I should do at the shop," Kal told him. "I'll get back with you later."

"Thanks, Kal," Donald said. "I'm sure glad I can count on you. I'll be in myself in about a half an hour."

Kal had no intention of working. But he knew that there was quite a bit of money in the safe at the shop since his dad hadn't made a deposit in several days. A half hour should give him enough time to do what he planned to do. Making sure none of the employees at the shop saw what he was up to, he took most of the cash and three of the checks from the safe and stuffed it all in his pockets. He then made sure he was seen in the work bays. He pretended to work for a few minutes, and then he told the others that he was feeling ill and was going to go home and go to bed. In fact, he was so ill, he almost hadn't come in at all. Then he asked them to tell his father that he'd gone home sick when he came in.

Kal did not go home except to park nearby and watch until his father left the house. Then he hurried to the bank his father used and cashed the checks. The teller knew him and never questioned it when he told her his father needed the cash right away.

She was sympathetic about his mother and siblings, and Kal used that sympathy to his advantage to keep her from questioning his actions. When he left the bank and went back to his mother's car, which he had pretty much claimed for himself, he counted the money. He had nearly ten thousand dollars. He drove to another town not too far away and bought a new phone, a cheap one. After smashing the phone his father had given him, he threw it in a garbage bin. He wouldn't need it anymore.

Ten minutes later, he was on his way east again. As he drove, he called Fredrick Belina and convinced him that he needed to meet with him.

"Why isn't your father coming instead of you?" Fredrick asked suspiciously.

"He's behind at our shop and had to work. He told me to hire you if I wanted to," Kal lied. "He said to tell you he was sorry that he didn't hire you earlier."

***

Donald had been unable to reach any other PIs and decided it could wait. He had to check on things at his shop. He knew Kal wouldn't like it, but he was sure he could convince him that waiting another day was for the best. When he got there, he was surprised to see that his dependable son was not there and then felt bad when he was told Kal had gone home sick. He had clearly just missed him. "This whole thing is really getting to him," Donald told his workers. "I'll let him rest. The poor kid needs it."

He was told that he looked pretty rough himself and that he should go home and rest too. "I'd rather work for a while," he responded. "Sitting at home only makes things worse. I worry less when I'm busy."

His employees sympathetically accepted that, and he busied himself in his office.

***

The meeting with Fredrick Belina went pretty much the way Kal had planned. He'd been thinking about it since his father had told him he didn't want to hire Belina. When the two met, Kal succeeded in convincing the rugged PI that it was not his father that was hiring him, but that Kal was doing it on his own with his father's blessing. "My little brother must be brought to justice, and that can't happen until you find him."

Fredrick accepted the job but only after Kal offered him two thousand dollars on top of the original three-thousand-dollar retainer he had asked for. Once that was done, Kal proceeded to tell him what a dangerous person his little brother was, and then they talked strategy. Kal was satisfied that Belina would work hard at finding Sparky. When he handed Fredrick the five thousand dollars in cash, the PI seemed quite anxious to get to work.

Kal, recognizing a kindred spirit in Fredrick, wasn't sure how much he trusted him. He decided on the spur of the moment to trail after him as the fellow began his investigation. So before Fredrick left, he insisted that the PI agree to fill him in daily on his activities and let him know his location each time he called him. Kal, although ruthless and conniving, was very smart. He gave Fredrick the number of his new phone, and said nothing to him about the phone his father had given him, the one he'd trashed.

He watched as Fredrick drove off in his blue 2007 Chevy Monte Carlo, and then Kal drove quickly back toward Goodland. Kal knew it would not be smart to continue to drive his mother's car. He intended to make his dad believe that Sparky had once again come back and that his dangerous little brother had forced Kal to go with him. To do that, his mother's car needed to be left behind. He thought hard about what to do, then decided to leave the car at his home and hitchhike west on I-70. Then he'd steal a car in some town along the freeway.

***

Kal had not done much in his father's mechanic shop in the few years he had pretended to work there, but he had learned how to hotwire a car. He put those skills to use in a motel parking lot about a hundred miles from Goodland after a couple of girls in a sporty car gave him a lift. He stole a green Ford pickup—an older model—then slept in it a couple miles off of the freeway in a grove of trees. He had roughly five thousand dollars in his pocket, but he wanted to save it as long as he could. If he eventually needed more money than that, he would not hesitate to steal it any way he could. Anything he needed to do was okay if it would lead to getting rid of Sparky for good.

Fredrick's instructions from Kal was to stop at every truck stop and rest area along I-70 in an attempt to pick up on the cold trail the two of them hoped Sparky had left nearly three weeks earlier. Kal had convinced the PI that Sparky had originally left and then came back to kill his mother. But he also told the fellow that his father was wrong about his siblings, that he didn't really believe Sparky had taken them, that the kids had been so distraught over their mother's death and the lack of attention they got from their father that they must have run off.

He told Fredrick that he was afraid something terrible had happened to them. Kal had also informed Fredrick that he was afraid Sparky was hundreds of miles away. As far as why he chose to look to the west, it was just a gut feeling Kal had. He reasoned that if *he* were running away, he would go west toward California.

Fredrick offered to look for the two children, but Kal had quickly hatched another lie and told him that his father was hiring someone else to look for them. Kal's lies were so numerous that he had to constantly remind himself of what he'd told different people in order to keep his story straight for his PI.

Fredrick called Kal, told him the places he'd checked, explained that so far he had not learned anything, and then, when reminded by Kal, he told him his current location. Unbeknownst to Fredrick, Kal headed that way in the stolen pickup.

***

Lys Grist and Brad Hagen met with a hug and a kiss on Wednesday morning before entering a small diner for breakfast where they spent a few minutes catching up with what they each had been doing in their personal lives. Then they began exchanging information.

Brad's phone rang. It was Sergeant Bone.

"I just finished visiting with Donald Graves," Bone said. "He is highly agitated this morning. He's convinced that Sparky has been back in town. He can't find Kal and says he's not answering his cell phone."

"That's suspicious," Brad said, thinking that Kal must be up to something nefarious. Even though Lys had assured him that Sparky was alive and well a very long ways from Goodland, she had not told him where. She couldn't tell him until she had permission from her client. Since he knew that Lys worked out of Salt Lake City, he assumed the young man was somewhere in or near Utah, but he said nothing about his deductions.

"That's not all," Sergeant Bone went on. "Donald says that Sparky got into his shop, opened his safe, and stole several thousand dollars. He doesn't know when, but he says it had to have been during the night as he wouldn't dare show up in the daytime."

"How does he know it was Sparky?" Brad asked.

"He didn't say. But he seems awfully sure. And he fears that Sparky has done something to Kal as well as his younger children."

"Don't you think it's time to educate Donald on the true state of affairs?" Brad asked.

"I tried to reason with him without telling him that you had found the younger kids, but he doesn't believe that Kal would ever do anything wrong, and he told me to just shut up and find Sparky," the sergeant said. "He is drinking a lot and was quite drunk when I spoke with him. He seems to be drowning his sorrows and worries in liquor. Where are you at now?"

"I'm in Goodland. I'm having breakfast with Detective Grist," Brad replied. "Perhaps the three of us should meet."

Ten minutes later, Sergeant Bone strode into the restaurant and sat down with the two PIs. They chatted for a moment before getting down to the serious business at hand. "I'm pretty sure it was Kal, not Sparky, who stole the money from his father," the sergeant told the others.

"Was it only cash that was stolen?" Lys asked.

"Some checks too. As soon as the banks open, I'll check to see if anyone came in to cash or deposit the checks," Abel told the others. "Having seen the younger Graves children with my own eyes, I know that Sparky didn't take them, and I believe them when they say that they saw Kal shove their mother to her death."

"I know that as well," Brad said and glanced at Lys. She nodded.

"Tell me who you are and where you're from," Abel Bone said as he looked with suspicion at Lys.

"I am a private investigator and a good friend of Brad's. My name is Lys Grist," she said. Without stating where she was from, she asked, "What kind of man is Donald Graves? I'm not getting the feeling that he is an upstanding citizen or he would want to hear the truth."

"He is convinced that Sparky is rotten to the core and that the sun rises and sets on Kal," Abel answered. "He's a decent man as far as I know. He runs a good business and is well thought of in the community. Unfortunately, it looks like he drinks too much. At least, he does now."

"And yet he's been blinded by a son who, as you say, is rotten to the core," Lys said with a touch of bitterness in her voice.

Sergeant Bone studied her for a moment. "You said you were a friend of Brad's, but what exactly is your interest in this case and who are you working for?"

"I am interested in the killer of Mrs. Graves being apprehended and brought to justice. As for who hired me, you know that is confidential. I cannot and will not divulge who my client is. I haven't even told Brad."

Abel continued to stare at her as Brad quietly watched the two of them. "What proof do you have that Kal Graves shoved his mother from the balcony?" he finally asked.

"None, except a source vouched for Sparky's character. And I know Johnny and Courtney Graves were not abducted by Sparky. I know they ran away on their own out of fear of their other brother, Kal," she said. "I also know that you're convinced of the same, since you've interviewed the children. So let's see what we can do about finding where Kal has gone and what he's up to."

"Detective Grist, do you know where Sparky Graves is hiding?" Abel asked pointedly.

For a long moment, she did not answer. Brad wondered what she would do and say. He was quite certain that she knew exactly where Sparky was even though she had not shared that information with him. He also felt strongly that she would not divulge that information if she thought there was any chance at all that Donald Graves would find out.

"He's safe at the moment," she said finally. "That's all I can tell you." She rose from her chair but looked down at Sergeant Bone. "Sparky Graves is not my client, if that's what you're thinking. I was hired by someone else to try to find out who killed Sydney Graves. I know now who did it and so do the two of you. Those younger children are not lying. Sergeant, you'd better find Kal and arrest him before he does more damage."

"We are working on that," Abel said defensively.

"You'd better be." She leaned down until her face was close to the sergeant's. "And I would suggest you find out exactly what Donald Graves's agenda is. Now, I have work to do. I need to go, but I'll catch up with you sometime, Brad."

With that, Lys dropped a twenty-dollar bill on the table, spun around, and left the restaurant. Brad watched her until she had disappeared through the door. He sure was fond of that woman. She had spunk. And she was very smart. Beautiful, too, which had been what had first attracted him to her when they'd met. But he had soon learned that there was a lot more than looks to be admired about Lys. He wished he could have talked with her longer, but she had clearly not liked being pressured by the sergeant. Still, he'd catch up with her later.

Abel Bone had also watched until Lys had vanished. He turned to Detective Hagen. "I know you two are friends, but are you sure that woman is to be trusted?"

"Absolutely. I'd trust her with my life," Brad said.

"Then why won't she tell me where she's from?" Abel asked.

"She's looking out for the interests of her client, I suppose," Brad said.

"If you know her so well, you can tell me where she's from," Abel said.

"I'm sorry, I would but I have to respect her wishes."

Abel shrugged and didn't pursue the matter. Brad wasn't sure, but he had a feeling that since Lys knew Kal had dropped out of sight, she was probably heading for Utah to make sure Kal did not find Sparky. It was what he would have done if he were in her shoes.

"I'm looking for a killer," Abel Bone said as he, too, stood. "I'll get back with you if I learn anything else of interest."

Brad also stood up. "Would it do any good for the two of us to sit down with Donald and force him to listen to us?"

Slowly, the sergeant turned to face the PI. "Would you be willing to let me tell him that the younger children are safe and where they are staying?"

Brad smiled. "You don't know where they are."

"No, but you do, and I think we need to let Donald know that they are safe and that Sparky had nothing to do with the murder of his wife or the abduction of his children."

"You just said he wouldn't listen to you when he called this morning, that he was drunk," Brad reminded him. "Maybe if he sobers up. . ."

"I'm sure he was drunk, and no, he wouldn't, but I wasn't trying to tell him anything specific. Maybe if the two of us sat down with him, drunk or not, we could get his attention," Sergeant Bone said.

"It is possible." Brad thought for a moment. "That's why I suggested it. Is there any chance that Kal did what he did with his father knowing all along and perhaps even at his request?"

"Are you suggesting that Donald Graves wanted his wife dead?" Abel asked with doubt evident in his voice.

"I'm not suggesting anything, but I am wondering," Brad said.

"I see. Brad, I know where Donald does his banking," the sergeant said as he looked at his watch. "Would you mind going with me to have a talk with that bank?"

"What would that accomplish?" Brad asked.

"Some of the money taken from the safe at Donald's business was, as I mentioned, in the form of checks from customers. If Kal stole the money, I would think he would want to cash the checks, and I think there's a good chance that he went to that bank. It's worth checking out."

"Could he do it without Donald's signature?" Brad asked.

"More likely with his forged signature. If Kal Graves is as bad as I'm beginning to believe he is, I can see him doing something like that."

"Then let's see what we can find out," Brad said.

Fifteen minutes later, they left the bank, armed with the knowledge that Kal Graves had, in fact, cashed the checks, and he had either forged his father's name or his father had signed them himself and sent Kal to cash them. Donald swore to Abel earlier that Sparky had gotten into the safe. But they were convinced, now more than ever, that he hadn't. Both men were now prepared to take a closer look at Donald Graves and his own motives regarding the death of his wife.

"Let's find Donald and bring him in," Sergeant Bone suggested. "I would like you with me when I question him, if you don't mind."

"I would be glad to help," Detective Hagen said, "but I'm not sure that Donald will be very cooperative. He and I have a history, and it's not a good one."

"He hired you to find his son Sparky, but then he fired you," Sergeant Bone said.

Brad didn't answer, but he knew that Bone knew that was exactly what had happened. So the two of them went looking for Donald, hoping he had sobered up some.

CHAPTER FIFTEEN

FREDRICK BELINA WAS NOT A very good investigator, but he was persistent when he got on a case. He was talking to truckers at every stop he came to. He always got their names and then spoke to them about Sparky and showed them pictures. One of the drivers he spoke with was a man by the name of Rick Granberry. "Yeah, you're the second PI that's asked about him," Rick told Fredrick. "I'll tell you the same thing I told that lady PI; I saw the kid a few times at places like this—truck stops and rest areas. I didn't know it at the time, but it turns out he was riding in one of the pipes I was hauling." Rick chuckled. "He was a modern-day stowaway."

"Where and when did he leave your truck?" Fredrick asked with a quickening pulse.

"That I don't know. I'm pretty sure it was somewhere before the place we're hauling this pipe to."

"Where is that?"

"Near Las Vegas."

Fredrick rubbed his already mussed hair for a moment. "This other PI, the lady you talked to, what was her name?"

"Just a moment," Rick said. "She gave me her card." He dug out his wallet and extracted Lys's card.

Fredrick took it and looked it over. "I'll need to keep this. I want to get in touch with her."

Rick shook his head. "No, I plan to keep it. You can write down the information if you want to, but I can't let you have it."

Fredrick felt a rush of irritation as Granberry held his hand out for the card. Finally, Fredrick pulled out his cell phone. "Here, I'll just take a picture of it then, although I can't imagine what you would need of it now." He held the card in his hand, snapped a photo, and handed it back to the truck driver. "Now tell me, what was Lys Grist's interest in Sparky Graves?"

Rick Granberry looked around himself nervously. "You have her number; you can ask her yourself. She can tell you if she wants to."

"She didn't say why she was looking for him?" Fredrick asked angrily.

"No, she didn't. I gotta get back on the road." Rick shoved Lys's card back in his wallet and the wallet in his pocket.

Fredrick watched Rick as he headed for his truck, working to keep his anger in check. He knew the stocky truck driver could have told him more, and probably would have if there weren't people around. He knew how to get people to tell him things they didn't want to, but this wasn't the time or the place.

He glanced at the photo of the lady PI on the screen of his phone. She was from Salt Lake City. That meant there was a good chance the fugitive was in Utah. He was pretty sure Lys Grist had at least an idea of where Sparky Graves was hiding. If she started in Utah, and it made sense that she would have done that, then she was going the wrong direction. That meant, he concluded, that she was simply looking for information about Sparky. He decided he'd move on to Utah and continue his search there.

Fredrick called Kal and updated him. "He's somewhere in Utah, Kal. I'm pretty sure of that. I'm getting close."

"Where are you right now?" Kal asked.

"I'll be in Grand Junction, Colorado, tonight. I'll spend the night there and then continue to Utah in the morning. I'm going to find your brother, Kal. You can be sure of it."

After talking to Kal, he went inside the truck stop and got something to eat. Something about his young client wasn't feeling right. He didn't mind breaking rules to get his job done, but at the same time, Kal Graves was a juvenile, not yet eighteen. He had worried about this for some time. He'd never taken on a job where he'd been hired by a juvenile. In this case, he didn't want to run afoul of Kal's dad, who the kid said gave him permission to retain Fredrick. That wouldn't be smart. If Donald Graves got upset, he could file a complaint with the state of Kansas, and Fredrick didn't need that. A complaint could jeopardize his license and, thus, his livelihood. So after he had finished eating, he walked back to his car, wondering if he should call Donald Graves.

***

Donald Graves had found a sympathetic ear in the form of Officer Lawrence Snepper. The two of them were in Snepper's private vehicle, since Snepper was off duty. He didn't tell Donald that he was not just off duty for the day, but that he had been given a two-week suspension by the police chief for disobeying the orders of his sergeant.

"What did Sergeant Bone say when you reported that Sparky had stolen your money?" Snepper asked.

"He asked how I knew it was Sparky," Donald said.

"How did you answer that?" Snepper asked.

"I told him he was the only one it could have been."

"I take it that didn't satisfy him."

"He had the gall to ask me if there was any chance Kal might have taken it," Donald said angrily. "Kal is the good son. I'm offended that you police officers would dare to suggest otherwise."

"Now wait a minute. *I* have suggested no such thing," Snepper told him. "Do you fear for Kal's life?"

"Of course I do. Sparky killed his mother. What would stop him from killing his brother?" Donald asked, rubbing his eyes, which were filling with moisture. "I wish I would have realized a long time ago how sneaky and conniving Sparky was. All of this tragedy in my family could have been prevented if I'd known. The kid is smart, that's for sure."

"What about Courtney and Johnny?" Officer Snepper asked.

Donald sobbed. "I'm afraid they might be dead by now. Why else would Sparky come back here for them?"

Snepper felt his anger rising. Sergeant Bone and the chief of police had not told him anything about how the search for the children was going. All they had done was told him that he was being suspended for continuing to investigate the case after being told not to. He could not understand how they could be so uncaring about those two children. They needed him on the case. They were just too proud to admit it.

"Will you help me find Sparky?" Donald asked. "I hired a private investigator, but he turned on me, just like your sergeant has on you. I had to fire the guy. I interviewed another PI, but I didn't like him, so I didn't give him the job."

"You don't need a PI. They aren't to be trusted. You have me, Mr. Graves," Officer Snepper said. "I will do what I can to find him and bring him in. He must be hanging around Goodland somewhere."

"Thank you," Donald said as water filled his eyes again and he wiped it away. "I'm glad someone believes me and is willing to do something."

The two of them were interrupted by the ringing of Donald's cell phone. He answered it and was surprised to hear the harsh voice of Detective Fredrick

Belina. "Mr. Graves, this is Detective Fredrick Belina. I thought I should call you even though I'm sure you already know what I'm doing."

"How would I know that?" Donald asked. "You don't work for me. You have no reason to call me."

"Well, I know it was your son who hired me on your say-so, but he's under eighteen, so I thought I should report to you as well as to him," the detective said.

"What are you talking about? Nobody hired you," Donald said.

"Actually, your son Kal did. He told me that you told him to hire me," Detective Belina said. "Apparently . . . that's not true?"

"I don't know what kind of game you are playing," Donald said, "but I find no humor in it. My younger son killed his mother and kidnapped his little brother and sister, and now, it seems he's also done something to Kal. He is missing, and I can't get ahold of him."

"You're confused about one thing," Belina said. "Kal is fine. I just reported to him five minutes ago on the phone. I have a lead on the area where Sparky is hiding out. I'm on my way to determine his exact location, and then I'll have him arrested."

Donald's head was spinning. "Where is Sparky?"

"I just told you, I don't know exactly, but I believe he is somewhere in the state of Utah. You and Kal need to just sit still and wait until I have him arrested," Belina said harshly.

"Listen, I haven't spoken to Kal since shortly after we got home from meeting with you yesterday. He's not answering his phone. In fact," Donald said angrily, "it seems to not be working. So I know you are lying. What's your game? Are you after more money or what?"

"Kal paid me enough for now. As for his phone, it is working perfectly well. Are you telling me he isn't there with you?" Detective Belina asked.

Officer Snepper reached over and jerked Donald's phone from his hand. "This is Officer Lawrence Snepper speaking. I am here with Donald at the moment. I am investigating the murder of Mrs. Graves and the disappearance of Sparky and his little brother and sister. Who are you and what exactly are you doing?"

"I am a PI. Detective Fredrick Belina is my name. I've narrowed the search for Sparky Graves. I was hired by Kal Graves, and I thought that Donald knew that and that the kid was with his father."

"Clearly Donald didn't know that. Detective, I need to meet with you as soon as possible. We can work together. Once we find Sparky, I'll make the arrest and bring him back here to face murder charges. About Kal, are you implying that he is okay?"

"I'm not implying anything. I know he is. I just spoke with him on the phone a few minutes ago. He's very concerned about his father and his little brother and sister. If Sparky had the young ones, there's a good chance they're with him still. At least, I hope that's the case."

"Where can I meet you? We'll proceed together from this point. Donald is nodding his head at me. He is in agreement."

"We need to get right on it, but I'm not waiting for you. If you catch up with me, fine. For tonight, I'll be staying in Grand Junction. I need to go to Utah tomorrow. I'm close," the PI said with confidence in his voice. "But I'm not waiting for anyone."

"I'm on my way, and I will catch up with you," Snepper said. "I'll call you at this number when I get to Grand Junction. In fact, I think I'll text you my number as soon as we finish this conversation, so you can call me if you learn something more before I meet up with you."

Snepper hung up and Donald leaned forward.

"Are you sure this Fredrick Belina guy is being straight with us?" Donald asked.

"I can't say for sure because he's a private investigator, and they generally aren't to be trusted. If he is, however, then he's onto something. I want to catch up with him and stick close to make sure he doesn't pull a fast one on you. If this guy is for real, then that means Kal is okay. We need to try to call him again. Maybe now that Belina has an idea of where to look for Sparky and the children, Kal will answer your call."

"I'll try him in a minute. But right now, you and I need to get going," Donald said.

"No, you have to let me handle this. I will keep you posted."

Donald argued, but Snepper was firm, and soon he was on the freeway speeding west in his full-sized Toyota pickup.

***

The last thing in the world that Detective Belina wanted was for a snotty young cop to interfere in his search for Sparky Graves. He didn't know the officer, one Donald referred to as Officer Lawrence Snepper. Furthermore, he didn't want to get to know him. Instead of staying in Grand Junction that night, he decided to stay somewhere nearby but where Snepper couldn't possibly locate him. And he was determined not to answer any calls from the cop. He'd worked with a few police officers in the past, but he avoided it if at all possible. And in this case, it was possible.

Fredrick Belina did answer when he got a call from Kal Graves, but not because the call didn't irritate him. Kal was calling way too frequently. He didn't appreciate clients constantly checking on him. He preferred to do his work and report when he had something substantial. He was particularly miffed as it had only been a few minutes since his last report.

"Hey, Kal," he said as soon as he'd answered the phone. "You need to let me work. Why don't we do this: let me call you when I have something to report, and you wait patiently for my call. I work better that way, and you'll get the results you're after a lot quicker."

"Hey, it's my five grand that's paying your way, and don't you forget it. I'll call whenever I want. You got that? I'm your boss," Kal shouted. "Have you learned anything new?"

Inspiration didn't strike Fredrick Belina very often, but since his client's attitude ticked him off, inspiration did come, and it came quite vividly. "Yes," he said. "As a matter of fact, there's a cop that's trying to catch up with me and help me look for your brother. Do you know an Officer Lawrence Snepper?"

That got the reaction Belina had anticipated.

"Yes, and I don't want no cops involved. I mean, you know, until you find Sparky and all. You don't tell anybody where he is when you find him but me, and then I'll call the cops myself." Kal spoke so loudly that Belina had to hold the phone away from his ear.

"Sorry, but according to your dad, he's involved whether you or I like it or not. Now, if you really want to help me, you could do something to get him off my tail," Belina said.

"How do you know what my dad thinks?" Kal asked, his voice getting louder and higher.

"I spoke with him on the phone, and, Kal, he didn't seem to know that you were going to hire me. Is there a reason you're going behind your father's back? Did you lie when you told me that he had changed his mind and asked you to hire me?" the detective asked.

For a moment, he seemed to have silenced his less-than-trustworthy young client, but not for long. "It doesn't matter why I hired you or who knew. You took my money, and so now you work for me, and that's that!" he shouted. Then, before the PI could make a response, he went on. "Do you have a phone number for Officer Snepper?"

"As a matter of fact, I do," Belina responded and recited the number to Kal. "Why don't you call him and discourage him while I find your little brother?"

"Okay, I'll do that. And if you talk to my dad again, tell him to bug out, that you and I are getting the job done, that we'll find Sparky and make him pay for what he did," Kal said, his voice finally toned down enough that Belina could put his phone to his ear again without endangering his eardrum.

After the contentious call had ended, Fredrick sighed and thought about Kal. The kid was a loose cannon. However, the five grand, no matter whether Kal's father had known about it or not, was money in his pocket, and he would do what he was hired to do despite Kal's lies. He'd told Donald that Kal had hired him, and Donald hadn't told him that he was fired or to give the money back. In his mind, that validated his working for Kal. He wondered if Kal would actually contact Officer Snepper and if he could convince him to back off and let the PI do his job. He shrugged and put his phone away. He'd find Sparky. Of that he was quite confident. No way would he allow the young police officer to interfere.

***

"I'm sorry, Alfred. It's my fault. I should have made sure we both had our phones where they couldn't fall out of our pockets. Now they're wet. I just hope they aren't ruined," Sparky said with disgust at himself.

The two of them had been working to dislodge a beaver dam in the stream that was causing the stream to flood onto a hay field. They'd been working from on top of the dam, pulling sticks out and throwing them onto the bank. Alfred's phone had fallen into the stream behind the dam, and in Sparky's haste to retrieve the old man's phone, his own had slipped from his pocket and it too landed in the water. Sparky had pulled off the rubber irrigating boots he was wearing, threw them onto the shore, and jumped into the water. It was not a large stream, but behind the dam, it was well over waist deep. And to make matters worse, the bottom of the stream was very muddy.

"We've got to find them and I hope they will still work when we do," Sparky said as he desperately searched in the water.

"I'd better come in there with you," Alfred said as he carefully made his way off the little dam and stepped onto the bank.

"No, let me do this," Sparky said. "I'm stirring up the mud as it is, and two of us would only make it worse."

"I guess you're right," Alfred reluctantly agreed.

"When I find them, we'll take them back to the house and see if there's a way to dry them out," Sparky said. "Maybe you could call Mr. Finch and see if he knows if there is a way to get them working again."

Alfred watched helplessly as Sparky searched. Sparky would wait for a moment each time he brought his head out of the water for the water to clear, and then he would try again. He couldn't see clearly and was using his hands to sift through the mud. Suddenly, his hand felt what he believed was one of the phones. He grasped it tightly and pulled it from the mud. "I got one of them, Alfred," he said triumphantly. Then he rinsed the mud off of it, stepped toward the bank, and handed it to the old farmer. "This is mine, but yours has got to be close."

Alfred shook the phone and rubbed it on his shirt, trying to dry it. Sparky moved back to where he'd found it as he said, "Yours has got to be close to where mine was."

"Actually, it's probably two or three feet farther that way," Alfred said, pointing in the direction of the far bank.

"You're right," Sparky agreed and moved past the point where he had found his.

"I hate to leave you, but I need to drive back to the yard and check on the cow, Bossy. She should be having her calf real soon. I'll come back as soon as I check on her." With that, he drove off on his four-wheeler.

Another half hour of searching for the cell phone brought no results, and soon enough, Alfred returned. "No calf yet," he said, "but you just as well give up here, Sparky. At least we got this one. Let's go back and see if we can find out a way to dry it out."

Sparky crawled out of the stream and Alfred handed him the phone. He tried to turn it on, but to no avail. "It doesn't work yet. I sure hope it will work again when it dries out."

"Let's go back to the house right now and see if we can get it to dry out faster," Alfred said. "Maybe I could put it in the oven with the temperature low and the door open. If we can't get it to work, at least we still have the house phone. And I can always buy a new one—or two if I need to."

"We can't go yet," Sparky argued. "The water is going to make a huge mess in the field. You said you need to cut the hay in a couple of weeks. We can't let it mess that up for you. It won't take me long to finish getting enough of this dam torn apart to lower the level of the water."

"I guess you're right, Sparky," Alfred said. "I can help. I'll put this phone on my four-wheeler where the sun will hit it and maybe dry it out, although the sun is sinking fast."

It only took the two another half hour to get enough of the dam torn out to lower the level of the stream. It would be enough to stop the flow of water onto the field. By then, the sun was setting. "Maybe I should look for your phone a little longer now that the water is not so deep and before it gets dark," Sparky suggested. Alfred did not argue, so Sparky once again waded in.

But after another few minutes, Alfred told him to give it up. "It'll be dark soon. I'll get a new phone sometime," he said. "They can keep my same number on a new one, can't they?"

"I think so," Sparky said as he once again waded to the bank and got out.

Back at the house, Alfred asked Sparky to get the evening chores done while he went in and fixed them some supper. "I'll call Bill Finch in a few minutes and see if he can suggest what to do. While I'm doing that, Sparky, please check the milk cow and see if the calf is coming yet."

Sparky got to work, checking the cow first. She seemed restless, wandering around the stall Alfred had put her in a couple of days before, but other than that, he couldn't tell anything. According to Alfred, if she was having her calf, she would be lying down. So, he started on the other chores.

Sparky was feeling terrible about the phones. He wasn't sure there was a way to get his phone to work again. He was just glad Alfred had a house phone. At least he could call Bill Finch and find out if there was any way to fix the phone. He hated to see Alfred have to spend so much money. He already felt guilty over all the money his elderly friend had spent trying to help him.

He left feeding the pigs toward the end. After filling Sherman's trough with some soaked grain, he watched the animal for a moment. Sherman seemed nice enough, though he was large, and Sparky could see those razor-sharp tusks sticking out from either side of his mouth. He believed Alfred about Sherman being dangerous to get in the pen with, but he couldn't help but admire the pig.

He finally turned away, gathered the eggs, took another look at Bossy the cow, and headed for the house. Hopefully Alfred had learned of a way to get the cell phone working again. He really wanted to get on the internet and see if there were any updates on the hunt for him. It was constantly worrying him. He didn't want to put Alfred in any kind of danger. Even though he did not want to go on the run again, he would if he had to. The very thought of leaving this farm and the wonderful old man made him sick to his stomach.

When he got back to the house, he could smell fried onions and potatoes, and his stomach growled. He was starved after such a hard afternoon. He left his rubber boots on the porch along with his wet socks. His other clothes had dried out a lot while he'd been doing the chores.

"What did you see when you checked on the milk cow?" Alfred asked. "She should be calving soon. I'm getting tired of drinking this nasty pasteurized milk and not having any fresh cream."

"I checked on her, and there still isn't a calf. She's just walking around the pen seeming like she's nervous or something. I hope she has it soon. I want to try milking her," Sparky said.

"We'll go out and check her again after dinner. That calf is several days past due now. It worries me because the last time she calved, I had to help her."

"Help her how?" Sparky asked.

"I had to get hold of the calf and pull to get it out. That's why I am keeping such a close watch on her," Alfred responded.

"I'll stay out there with her tonight if you want me to," Sparky suggested.

Alfred shrugged his shoulders. "Let's see what she looks like when we check her a little later. We may need to do that."

"I will do whatever you need," Sparky said. "So what did Bill Finch tell you about the cell phone?"

"He wasn't at home, but Kay Dell told me that we should put it in rice," Alfred responded. "So I did that. She offered to come out tomorrow and help look for the other one again."

CHAPTER SIXTEEN

AFTER DINNER, JUST AS THEY were getting ready to go out to check the milk cow, the landline rang. Alfred answered, and after a moment, he said, "Yes, I put it in a bowl filled with rice."

Alfred listened to Kay Dell for a moment before speaking again. "Sparky and I are just going out to check on my milk cow, Kay Dell. She is way overdue. She should have had her calf days ago. We may have to spend the night with her just to make sure she's okay. I sure would hate to lose her or her calf."

"Can I come out tonight and watch her too?" Kay Dell asked. "I'll ask Mom if she'll let me. Dad isn't at home."

"If you would like to for a little while, that would be fine, but only if your mother agrees."

"I'll call you right back," she said. True to her word, she did call back a moment later and said, "Mom says I can come for two or three hours. She'll bring me out. I hope I get to see it being born."

"Me too," Alfred responded. "But it may not come that soon."

***

Nova Heylep was sitting in her car in a parking area just off of the main street in Monroe. She was parked opposite another car that had a couple of girls in it. They had the driver's side windows down and were talking and laughing when suddenly Nova said, "Hey, isn't that Kay Dell Finch and her mother that just went by? I wonder where they're going. Kay Dell is never out after dark like this."

One of the other girls made a remark about her being chaperoned by her mother and laughed. But Nova wasn't listening to what she was saying. "Hey, I think I'd better go now," she said and started her car. The other girls looked at her with puzzled faces, but she said nothing more. She just pulled her red Corvette onto the street and headed the same way Kay Dell had gone.

Nova giggled to herself when the Finch car left the town heading south. She followed for a while. Surely Kay Dell wouldn't be going to the farm she claimed to work at so late, but Nova was going to follow until she knew. She disliked Kay Dell but had a feeling she was up to something, and she wanted to know what. The other girls seemed to like Kay Dell better than her, and she thought that if she could figure out what she was up to, she could lie and make it look like something bad. That would make Kay Dell less popular. At least, that was Nova's hope.

They traveled some distance, and pretty soon, Mrs. Finch turned onto a narrow graveled lane. There was no other traffic, and Nova did not want to be spotted, so she turned off her lights and followed at a distance. When she noticed the lights of a farmyard up ahead, she pulled off the road, shut off her lights, and watched as Mrs. Finch drove to the house. Someone, Kay Dell probably, got out and ran toward the house.

A minute later, Mrs. Finch drove toward Nova's car on the lane, her lights on bright. Nova ducked out of sight on the seat until Mrs. Finch's car had passed. When she looked up, the tail lights were far down the lane.

She had found the farm where Kay Dell worked. She grinned to herself and was about to start her car and head back toward town, but then she had a better idea. She wanted to know more, so she could make up a reasonable lie. She exited her car, locked it, and hiked up the semi-dark lane. There was just enough moonlight that she could see where she was going without stumbling.

As she approached the house, a dog barked and bounded in her direction. She froze. Nova did not like animals, especially dogs. Fear drove her to start backpedaling. But the dog stopped short when the voice of an old man shouted, "Sparky, cut it out. Come back here."

The dog watched her for a heart-stopping moment before it turned and ran back toward the house. She waited where she was for several minutes, then curiosity finally overcame fear. Nova picked up a sturdy stick from the side of the lane and proceeded slowly toward the yard. She didn't see or hear the dog again. But she did see three people come out of a door at the side of the house and walk with flashlights to the south. She moved slowly forward again, keeping a sharp eye out for the dog while wielding her stick.

She tried to keep in the shadows but kept moving. Three people—the old farmer, Kay Dell Finch, and a young man—entered a large barn and shut the door behind them. Nova waited for several minutes, and when they didn't come out, she gave up and headed back to her car. She had no idea what was happening in that barn, but one thing was for sure; Kay Dell did know an old farmer, but more intriguing yet, she also knew a young man. Kay Dell hadn't mentioned him.

Oh what gossip Nova could start now. She'd say that Kay Dell had a secret boyfriend. She giggled as she walked back to her car.

***

Lys was frustrated and worried. She had tried calling Alfred's cell phone a dozen times over the past few hours as she worked her way west. She was checking at the same places she had earlier. Only this time, it was Kal's picture she was showing. She didn't think Kal would be heading that way, but she wanted to find out if he was just to ease her mind.

Alfred's phone went to voice mail each time she called. It had been doing that ever since she had first tried to call Alfred in the late afternoon. She tried Sparky's cell phone with the same result. She had even tried Alfred's landline, but no one answered.

She looked at her watch. Almost ten o'clock. Surely they would be in the house by now. She dialed and listened as it rang over and over again. She finally ended the call and hoped they were all right. She hated the idea of Kal being out there somewhere, even though she couldn't imagine that he had any idea where Sparky was or, if he did, that he could have reached Alfred's farm already.

She was exhausted and knew she needed rest, so she found a room in a motel at a truck stop in the middle of Colorado.

***

Detective Hagen and Sergeant Bone finally located Donald Graves a little after ten that evening at his house after searching for him all day. No one at his work had any idea where he was. So what had he been doing? Finally, they'd simply parked near his home and waited until Donald showed up. Then, after a couple of minutes, they went to his door.

The first thing Graves said when he saw Detective Hagen was, "Get off my property. I fired you. My affairs are no longer of any concern to you." He was staggering, and his breath reeked of alcohol.

"Actually, they are. I now have a new client," Brad said.

"Who's that?" Donald asked angrily.

"You know I can't tell you that, but Sergeant Bone and I need to talk to you."

"I have nothing to say to you," Donald said, his face turning red. "All you two want to do is blame my son Kal for all the misery that Sparky has brought into my life. Kal's a good boy. Leave him alone. Go find Sparky and bring him back. I want to see him in jail for what he's done."

"You're wrong about Sparky," Sergeant Bone said as he spoke up for the first time. "He did not take your children. They are—"

"Get out! You're lying!" he interrupted in a drunken rage. "Do your jobs and leave me alone."

"Where is Kal?" Abel asked.

Donald balled his fists. "I wish I knew. Only Sparky knows that."

"Sparky did not steal your money. Kal did," Abel said as calmly as he could.

"You are both liars! Get out of my house right now! Officer Snepper will bring my sons back. At least he cares. Now go. Leave me to my grief."

"What is Officer Snepper doing?" Abel asked, his face also going red.

"He's doing what you won't. If you were half the cop Snepper is, you'd have found Sparky before he could do so much damage," Donald said, and with that, he turned and rapidly walked deeper into his house with a staggering gait.

Brad and Abel walked outside, slamming the door behind them. "That went well," Brad said blandly. "There is something off about that guy, something besides the fact that he's been drinking pretty heavily, or I miss my guess."

"That's probably why we couldn't find him. He's been at a bar," Abel said. "Perhaps all the sorrow and stress has gotten to him. I feel for him, but alcohol isn't going to solve his problems." They walked toward the car, each pondering the situation. "I wonder what Snepper is up to. He's on a two-week suspension. He has no business doing anything regarding this case or any other police business. You heard the chief when we talked to him. I don't think it will take much more of Snepper's nonsense to get the chief to fire him."

"Clearly he's up to something," Brad agreed.

The two men got into Sergeant Bone's car, and as they pulled into the street, the sergeant said, "Let's go to Snepper's apartment. I need to have a serious talk with that young man."

When they reached the apartment, the officer and his private vehicle, a full-size Toyota pickup, were gone.

"This is all we need," Abel said, frustrated. "First Kal is out there somewhere doing who knows what and now that idiot, Snepper, is up to something."

"Speaking of Kal, I hope he hasn't somehow figured out where the children are. It seems impossible to me, but as a precaution, I think I'd better call our friend." As soon as Brad parted ways with Abel and was back in his own vehicle, he dialed Leeann's number. "Sorry to call so late," he said as soon as she answered her phone. "I just felt the need to check on the children and make sure they're okay."

"They are both asleep in bed," Leeann said. "You sound worried. Are they in danger again?"

"I hope not, but things are not going well in the search for Sparky Graves. The officer who was originally supposed to contact you after you called the Goodland Police Department—and didn't do it—has gone rogue on us." Brad went on to explain what had happened since he'd spoken with her last. "So, you see, we don't know where either Kal Graves or Officer Snepper are at or what they're up to."

"Could they be coming here?" Leeann asked, suddenly sounding very worried.

"I don't think so," Brad said slowly.

"But you never know, do you? You must fear that or you wouldn't have called me at this time of night," she said. "What should I do?"

"You're right. I am worried about exactly that. I think you should wake the children up and take them somewhere else," he said.

"But I don't know where I would take them," Leeann responded.

"To a hotel, perhaps," Brad ventured.

"Okay. That sounds like a good idea. I can do that."

"Don't let anyone but me know where you take them, Leeann. Please keep me advised," Brad instructed her.

"We'll leave as soon as I can wake them and get the three of us packed," she said, sounding like the strong woman Brad believed her to be.

"Thank you. You are a gem. Keep in touch, and that includes calling me as soon as you get checked in somewhere."

"I will. Thanks for calling me, Brad. I promise that I'll do everything within my power to keep these children safe," she said.

Brad thanked her and then he made another call. It was to Lys Grist.

***

Lys was rousted from a deep sleep by the ringing of her cell phone. It took her a moment to clear the sleep from her head and answer the phone. "Hello," she said groggily without even looking at the screen.

"Hi, Lys, it's Brad. I'm sorry if I woke you, but I need to speak with you for a moment."

She sat up and swung her legs over the side of the bed. "I'm sorry I took off on you like I did, but that sergeant was getting to me. What's going on?"

"Donald Graves has been drinking, and he won't talk to Sergeant Bone and me about his kids. We both feel that something is amiss. I just asked the lady who is watching his younger children to move them since we have no idea where Kal's at or what he's up to," he said. "Donald seems to think that Sparky kidnapped Kal, which we know didn't happen, but we get the feeling there is something important that he isn't telling us."

"Are you wondering if he is somehow guilty of something?" she asked.

"We don't know what to think about Donald. Maybe all the tragedy has tipped him over the edge mentally. We do know that he's tipping the bottle very heavily. We also know that Officer Lawrence Snepper, who has been suspended for two weeks, has been in contact with Donald, and Donald seems to think Snepper is searching for Sparky," Brad told her. "Where are you and what are you doing?"

"I was sleeping until you woke me," she said with a tired chuckle. "In all seriousness, Brad, I'm headed back to check with my client. I'm very worried. I've been trying to make contact for hours, and he isn't answering his cell phone or his landline. I tried just before I went to bed a little while ago. Something is definitely wrong, and I worry that somehow Kal Graves might be involved."

"Surely you don't think Kal's figured out where Sparky is?" Brad asked.

"I don't know what to think," Lys answered. "Since I'm awake, I'm going to try calling again."

"Would you call me back and let me know if your client is okay?"

"Of course I will. But first, you had more on your mind, didn't you?"

"Actually, I wanted to coordinate with you now, since the younger ones are east and I suspect that Sparky may be somewhere west of Goodland."

"That sounds reasonable to me," Lys said. "I'll call you back shortly." When she did, it was not good news. "My client is still not answering his cell phone or his landline. I'm going to get a little more rest so my mind and my body are functioning fully, and then I'm heading out."

"Keep me advised," Brad said, "and I'll do the same for you. Oh, and you might also ask people you happen to come across in any stops you make if they've seen someone who meets the description of Officer Snepper. I know you know what he looks like since you had a run-in with him like I did." He told her what vehicle he was driving, and after Lys agreed, the call ended.

For a moment, Brad sat and thought about Lys. From the moment he'd first seen her all those months ago, he'd been attracted to her. She was a decent woman and was fun to be around. He'd enjoyed the few dates they'd had and the many phone calls. He hoped that he could soon move their relationship ahead. He was tired of this lonely life he was living and would like nothing better than to share it with her.

***

Alfred, Sparky, and Kay Dell were all sitting on the stall floor behind Bossy, Alfred's Jersey milk cow. Kay Dell's allotted time had long since passed, but she had called on her cell phone and begged her mother to let her stay with Alfred and Sparky and watch the cow. Her mother had finally agreed when Alfred promised to drive her home after the calf was born. None of them were willing to leave Bossy when she seemed so distressed.

Alfred had gone in the house and brought out some blankets and pillows so that two of them could rest while the third one kept an eye on Bossy. Sparky and Kay Dell shared Alfred's ever-increasing worry, and yet they were both fascinated, each wanting to witness the birth of the calf.

As four o'clock rolled around, Alfred was sleeping soundly, but the teenagers were quite wide-awake. They'd each had a little sleep, but neither one of them wanted to sleep now. Bossy kept getting to her feet, turning around in the stall, and then laying back down. She was the most restless she had been all night.

Another half hour passed, and Bossy suddenly began to moan and straighten her feet out. The light from the alley outside the stall was bright enough that they both saw a small hoof appear. Kay Dell gasped with excitement. "It's coming! Should we wake Alfred?"

"No, not yet, let's just watch for a bit."

The hoof withdrew and then appeared again a couple of minutes later. The little Jersey cow strained and grunted, but nothing more happened. Finally, Sparky said, "I think she's having trouble. I'll wake Alfred."

He crawled through the clean straw and touched Alfred's arm. The old man drew it back. Sparky crawled a little closer and shook his shoulder. This time the old farmer woke with a start. "What is it?" he asked, sounding confused. Then as his eyes opened and focused on Sparky, he said. "Oh, it's you. How's Bossy?"

"She's trying to have the calf, but I think she's having trouble," Sparky said.

Alfred slowly got to his feet and stepped over to the cow and then stood watching for a moment. "It's good we stayed out here, kids, because it looks like she needs some help," he said as he wearily knelt down behind her.

"What can we do to help her?" Kay Dell asked. "I feel sorry for Bossy and the calf."

"We get a hold on the calf and pull," Alfred said. He grabbed the one foot that was sticking out and then pushed his hand into the cow, and for a couple of minutes, he worked hard, moving his arm farther into the cow. "There, I found the other foot." He pulled and the cow strained, but nothing happened.

"It's stuck," Kay Dell said.

"It is that," Alfred agreed. "I'm afraid I'm not strong enough to pull it out. We may need to get a veterinarian out here." He let go of the calf and pulled his hand out.

"Let me try," Sparky said.

"Sure, you do that," Alfred agreed as he moved aside and then stepped out of the stall.

Sparky sat behind the cow and repeated what he had just seen Alfred do. Kay Dell leaned over his shoulder and encouraged him as he worked his arm in and then began to pull. He worked for a couple of minutes and then relaxed. Alfred had returned with a couple of rags. He was wiping his hands on one of them as he moved up to the front of the cow and began making soothing noises to her. Sparky began to pull again. After another minute, he was able to pull the second foot out.

"Good job, Sparky," Kay Dell said excitedly from over his shoulder. "Keep pulling."

Encouraged, Sparky pulled ever harder on both feet. Slowly, the calf came out. First its nose appeared, and then more of its head. Kay Dell cheered. Alfred continued to soothe his cow. Sparky continued to pull. Soon the calf's head was clear out. The cow strained hard, bawling loudly as she did. Alfred petted her head. Slowly the calf came farther out, and finally, the front shoulders cleared.

Sparky relaxed for a minute. "Do you need me to take a turn?" Kay Dell asked.

"Sure, I'm exhausted," Sparky said as he moved aside and Kay Dell took his place. She pulled with all the strength she had. The cow strained, and suddenly, with a swoosh, the rest of the calf slid out. "We did it!" she cheered. "This is so amazing! I'm so glad Mom let me stay."

Alfred got to his feet and stepped behind the cow. "Thanks, kids," he said as he reached down and cleared the calf's mouth so it could breathe easily.

"Is it okay?" Kay Dell asked as she and Sparky shared a rag, wiping their hands.

"I think it's fine. Let's step back and give Bossy a chance to get up and clean the baby off."

They all stepped to the back of the stall. Kay Dell was fascinated. She had never felt so exhilarated in her life. She glanced at Sparky. His face was glowing, and he had a huge smile plastered on it. Alfred simply smiled and then sat down against the wall of the stall. Bossy got to her feet, turned, and immediately began to clean her baby off with her long tongue.

Within just a few minutes, the calf began struggling to get on its feet. "Do we need to help it stand up?" Kay Dell asked.

Alfred smiled. "No, it'll be okay now. It'll be sucking before you know it."

"Is it a boy or a girl?" Kay Dell asked.

Sparky had figured that out already. "It's a girl."

Alfred chuckled. "A female calf is called a heifer."

"Okay, so it's a heifer," Sparky said and he laughed.

Before long, it was on its feet, and it worked its way instinctively to the back end of its mother and was soon sucking. Kay Dell and Sparky were both amazed and delighted. Kay Dell's phone rang. It was her mother. "The calf is born now. It was so exciting, Mom. I helped pull it out!" Kay Dell gushed.

Her mother asked her to tell Alfred that she would come get Kay Dell in a few minutes. Before long, she arrived, and after Kay Dell had gone, Alfred and Sparky went to the house and ate a quick breakfast before returning to the barn to check on the new heifer calf and the milk cow. After finding that all was well, Sparky talked Alfred into returning to the house to get some sleep, and he began to work on the morning chores. He was tired, but his excitement gave him energy. And for a short while, his troubles had been driven from his mind.

CHAPTER SEVENTEEN

"Have you been able to make contact with your client yet?" Brad asked Lys on the phone in the middle of the morning.

"I have not, and I'm worried sick," Lys responded, feeling a lift at the sound of Brad's voice. There was just something about him that touched her like no one else had ever done before. It was so hard for both of them to develop a relationship while living so far apart. "Something is going on, Brad, and it can't be good."

"Would you like me to come that way instead of going east?" he asked.

"If you don't mind," she responded, excited at the prospect of seeing him again very soon. "I'm on the freeway now and am heading west. I talked to a waitress at the truck stop where I spent the night who is pretty sure she waited on Kal Graves yesterday. She identified his picture with absolutely no hesitation."

"That clinches it. I'm coming to join you, Lys."

"I would like that, Brad." *A lot*, she thought, but she didn't say it. "I'll continue to do what I'm doing while you hurry this way. Once you get here, we'll decide what we need to do next," Lys concluded.

At the very next stop Lys made, she learned something that added even more concern. There was someone else, a man who identified himself as a private investigator, who was showing pictures of Sparky and asking for information about him. As she digested what she had just learned, she thought about who might have hired him. Only one name came to mind: Donald Graves. That might explain why he was refusing to cooperate with Sergeant Bone and Brad. Donald had fired Brad Hagen, who, in her biased opinion, was one of the best PIs in the country. This other guy was probably not the outstanding type of man that Brad was.

She spoke with several other people in a variety of businesses before she found someone who was able to tell her who the other PI was. The woman had a business card identifying Fredrick Belina, a Kansas man. Lys was not surprised when that woman did not paint a very flattering picture of him. In fact, she said that he had rubbed her the wrong way from the very first word he spoke. The woman had been surprised when he'd given her a card and asked her to call if she remembered anything.

Lys called Brad a few minutes later to report on this development.

"I wonder if he and Officer Snepper are working together," Brad said.

"Goodness. I never thought about that. I suppose they could be. I think you and I need to hurry and make sure Sparky is safe," she said.

"You're willing to let me know where he is?" Brad asked.

"At this point, yes, I am. Brad, there is no one I like or trust more than you. I will also introduce you to my client, with his permission, of course."

"Great. So have you talked to him at last?" Brad asked her.

"No, I'm afraid not, and I am getting more worried by the hour. My client is a responsible man, and this just isn't making sense. I'm going to try calling him again as soon as I finish talking to you."

"I'm pushing it as fast as I dare. You've got me worried too."

"Where are you now?" she asked.

He told her.

"I'm making great time. I'll reach Green River, Utah, before too long, and I'll wait for you there." After the call ended, Lys thought about Brad. He really was a wonderful man. She could hardly wait to see him again. And working with him again would be delightful. She smiled to herself. She thought back to the meal, a long, slow, superb one that they had enjoyed together after he had finally made it back to Goodland.

With an effort, Lys quit thinking about Brad and once again tried Alfred's phone numbers, without success. She hadn't mentioned to Brad that she also had the number of a phone Sparky Graves was using. She had tried it several times as well and tried it once more. She still had no answer. It made her stomach churn. As she continued driving west, Lys decided to attempt to contact the third private investigator working on the Sparky Graves matter. First, since she had hardly eaten anything so far that day, she entered a café and ordered. Then, while she was waiting for her food to arrive, she attempted to call Detective Fredrick Belina.

***

Staying up with an animal in distress was not as easy as it used to be for Alfred Briggs. He was grateful beyond words that his two young helpers had been there with him. Had it not been for them, he might have lost both his cow and her calf. He sat up from his bed and looked at his watch. He'd been sleeping for several hours, and if it weren't for his ringing phone, he might have gone on sleeping a lot longer.

He fumbled for his bedside phone, forgetting that he had moved it to the other side of the bed after his wife had died. She had always been the one to answer the phone. After her death it seldom rang.

By the time he oriented himself, the phone had quit ringing.

He shrugged and thought about getting a little more rest, but then he thought about how he was leaving Sparky with everything and climbed out of his bed and got dressed. He found Sparky in the barn with the new calf and its mother. He was near the little heifer, sound asleep in the straw they were both laying on. His heart swelled with love for this boy who had so miraculously come into his life.

He left Sparky sleeping there and went outside and checked his farm, riding from one end to the other on his four-wheeler. He loved this place. But even with Sparky as company, he was lonesome. He missed his wife as much as he had the first while after her passing. Tears wet his eyes, but he wiped them away with a bandana. He didn't want Sparky to see him cry.

When he got back to the barnyard, Sparky was outside pulling a few new weeds that had sprung up. "Hey, looks like the calf is okay," he said.

"Yep," Sparky said. "It's eating really well."

"That's what you and I need to do, Sparky. We need to eat. We both missed our breakfast, unless you came in and grabbed something while I was having my nap."

"No, I didn't. I got the chores done, then stayed with the cow and calf quite a bit. But now that you mention it, I am hungry."

"Let's go fix something, and then we better come out and relieve old Bossy of some of that milk. She gives a lot, and she will be feeling some pain if we don't milk her pretty soon," Alfred said. "Her calf can't use but a fraction of what she produces."

As they entered the house, the phone was ringing, but by the time they got to it, it had quit. "Darn phone," Alfred said. "That's what woke me from my nap."

***

Fredrick Belina ended his call to Kal. He was becoming increasingly leery of the young man's motives. Kal's hatred for his younger brother came out in practically every other sentence. He was wishing now that he hadn't called him, and he regretted telling him that he was in Salina, Utah, where he had found someone who remembered seeing Sparky walking along the side of the road a short distance from the freeway a few weeks ago. Surely Kal wouldn't follow him, would he? At this point, he was not too sure.

A waitress by the name of Kimberlee Owings, from a Denny's that was situated close to the freeway, recalled wondering what the handsome kid whose picture she looked at was doing with only a small bag and no hat. She had looked at the picture, studied it closely for a moment, and then said she was sure it was him that she'd seen. According to her memory, he had looked tired. She'd just finished a shift at that time and was on her way back to her home in the nearby small town of Aurora. She told Fredrick that she had seen the boy getting into a truck driven by an old farmer. She'd thought it was odd at the time.

Armed with that information, Fredrick was certain that he was closing in on Sparky's location. He relaxed in his booth and ordered a late breakfast. He had scarcely finished ordering when his cell phone rang. The name *Lys Grist* appeared on his screen. She was the private investigator he'd been told about and whose information he'd entered into his phone, just in case. He hesitated a moment before answering. As he thought about it, he figured he ought to at least consider talking to her. He had no intention of letting her interfere on his case, but he did answer the call.

"Detective Belina, my name is Lys Grist," the voice on the phone said.

"Yes," he answered. "Before you tell me what you need, let me advise you that I may not be able to help you for a day or so as I am just finishing up a case."

"I'm sorry. I should have introduced myself as *Detective* Grist. Like you, I am a private investigator," she said. "And I think we are working on the same case."

"You think so?" he said.

"Yes, I think that you and I are both working on a case involving the family of Donald Graves."

"What makes you think that?" he asked. He didn't like that she'd recognized his involvement. Nobody but Kal, his father now, and that young officer, were supposed to know what he was doing.

"You've talked to some of the same people I have along I-70," she said. "One of them gave me your card and told me you were asking about Sparky Graves."

No point trying to fool her now, Fredrick thought. But it would be best if he shut this down right now. He was close to finding Sparky, and he didn't need anyone else honing in on the progress he'd made. "I don't need any help, lady. I about have the case solved. But thanks for calling."

"Not so fast, Detective," Lys said, with what sounded to Fredrick like some urgency. "I'm not sure who hired you, but since you are looking for Sparky, I can tell you that you are too late. I already found him. You won't need to look further."

That deflated Fredrick. That knot-headed kid who had hired him might want some of his money back. *Like that was going to happen.* For a minute, he didn't respond to the detective on the phone. When he finally did, it was with a determination to find out Sparky's location and hurriedly report it to Kal. Then his money would be secure. "Where is Sparky?" he asked. "All I need to do is report his location to my client, and then I am finished with this job."

"I don't know who your client is," Lys began, but Fredrick cut her off.

"I am not going to tell you that," he said. "You know better than to ask. Just tell me where he is and we'll both have happy clients."

"Listen, Detective, I did not ask you who your client is, but I'm pretty sure it's either Donald Graves or his son Kal," she said. "And based on some information I gained in Goodland, I'm putting my money on Kal."

"I'm not saying who it is," he reiterated with a growl.

"Which tells me I'm right," Lys said with so much confidence in her voice that it made Fredrick's temper rise.

"Lady, I don't think we have anything else to discuss unless you want to tell me where Sparky is," he barked.

"Actually, we do need to talk," Lys said. "Because I have some information that you don't know you need, information that could save your life."

Fredrick snorted. "Are you trying to scare me? I don't scare easily."

"You'd better be scared," she said, her voice sharp with anger and concern. "Kal Graves is a cold-blooded killer, Detective Belina. Once you tell him or his father where Sparky is—if you are able to figure it out, which I seriously doubt you can do—I should warn you that he's not going to find you of any further use to him. And since he paid you with money he stole from his father, he's going to want it back. And he'll take it any way he can."

"Lady, you have it all wrong. Sparky is the killer," Fredrick argued.

"No, he is not! Kal is the one who killed Mrs. Graves, and two eyewitnesses have been located and can back up this theory," Lys said loudly. "Use your head, Detective. Kal is on the run somewhere. And I have a feeling that he's keeping track of where you are and following you. He can't be allowed to find Sparky."

Suddenly, Fredrick Belina felt his brain grind into gear. It registered that his earlier concerns about Kal were well founded, and assuming he could trust Grist's information, he had better find a way to shake the kid, and fast.

"Okay," he said to the woman on the phone, "Let's say I believe you now. The question is what I should do."

"That's simple. Where are you?"

"I'm in a restaurant just off I-70 at Salina, Utah," he said as his waitress brought his meal.

"Here's what you need to do; get in your vehicle and drive east as fast as you dare. I'm in Utah now and getting close to Green River. Another PI, a close friend of mine, is a ways behind me, and he plans to meet me there. The two of us can either meet you in Green River or somewhere along the way if Detective Hagen gets to Green River before you do, and we can continue west together."

"Detective Hagen? Brad Hagen?" Detective Belina asked. "He's your friend? I know who he is. I've never met him, but he has a good reputation. Former FBI special agent if I recall correctly."

"That's him," she responded.

"Okay, let me just finish my meal, and I'll head your way," he promised.

"Keep an eye out for Kal Graves. If he's following you, he could be close," Lys warned. "He's dangerous. He's smart and he is very tricky."

Fredrick ate his breakfast so rapidly that he scarcely tasted it. He was not a man who ever felt much in the way of fear, but a shiver of apprehension ran up his spine as he paid his bill. He walked directly to his car and got in.

"Where is Sparky?" a voice from his backseat asked even as something hard poked the back of his neck.

"Kal?" Fredrick asked in alarm.

"Just answer the question."

"I don't know yet. I told you I was getting close." This situation was suddenly very serious, more serious than Fredrick could have anticipated.

"How close?" Kal asked.

Fredrick realized that if Kal found his brother, another tragedy would occur. He had little conscience when it came to cutting corners in his work, but he couldn't let a murder happen if he could prevent it. He decided to partly lie and partly tell the truth in an effort to save his own life as well as Sparky's. "He didn't come this far, Kal. He's in Green River. I just confirmed that. I was planning to head back that way right now. Why don't you get in your car and follow me?"

"You lie," Kal said. "You are working for me. Tell me where he is, and then you can go home. Your job will be finished at that point."

"I'll take you to him now," Detective Belina said as he felt fear beyond any he had ever experienced. Sweat poured into his eyes. The pressure against his neck eased. He glanced toward his jockey box where he had a loaded pistol stored.

"I have your gun," Kal said with an evil laugh just before a blinding pain struck the back of Fredrick's head and he fell forward onto the steering wheel as blackness enfolded him.

***

Lys was not driving over the speed limit, as she knew that she would arrive in Green River far earlier than Brad. She was a good driver and a careful one. However, she knew that other drivers were not all careful. She was always watchful for anyone else on the road who might present a potential problem for her. Defensive driving, the experts called it.

She was driving in the inside lane of the two and slowed down as she saw just such a situation developing on the opposite side of the freeway. A speeding box truck was coming up very rapidly behind a large flatbed semi loaded with lumber.

She instinctively began to slow down while she observed the speeding box truck as it drove into the inside lane. She looked for a way to create more space between her and the trucks. She was blocked by a semi-truck with three trailers in the lane next to her. Another vehicle, a small truck, was not very far behind her and gaining rapidly, so she couldn't slam on her brakes like instinct told her to do without getting rear-ended.

Before the box truck had completed its pass, it suddenly swerved into the semi very near its front. The box truck was thrown violently toward her side of the freeway. It began to roll end over end while the semi jackknifed, striking other cars. She tried to take evasive action, but the semi next to her blocked any escape; Lys had nowhere to go. Frantically, she slammed on her brakes, but the small, speeding truck behind her smashed into the rear of her vehicle, and she and the box truck were suddenly on a collision course, and there was nothing she could do about it.

The box truck flipped over the median and was flying right into her path even as the small truck that had struck her from the rear continued to propel her forward. Helpless fear clutched her even as she thought about Sparky and how she would never be able to help him now. The box truck filled her windshield, and a fraction of a second later, she realized it was going to land right on top of her car and most likely kill her. "Brad!" she cried as blinding pain filled her head and her entire body, and then she was submerged in blackness.

CHAPTER EIGHTEEN

BRAD HAGEN SLOWED DOWN BEHIND a line of cars that were stalled on the freeway. Experience told him that there was very likely a wreck up ahead. At the same time, he noted the absence of vehicles on the eastbound side of the freeway. Whatever was causing the delay must be a very bad wreck. The last thing he needed was to be held up for very long. He and Lys needed to be heading west and he feared that they had very little time to spare. His gut told him that Sparky Graves was in serious danger and probably didn't even know it.

Unless the danger has already reached him. Brad seriously believed that Kal Graves was a dangerous young man, a psychopath. The thought made him sick. If he had not already found Sparky, Brad had little doubt that Kal would attempt to destroy his little brother as soon as he did.

He sat tapping his steering wheel as he waited impatiently, stuck in this infuriating traffic. As if he didn't have enough to worry about, he got a call from Sergeant Abel Bone. "Detective, I just confirmed that one of Donald Graves's employees is missing a pistol. It was taken from his car very recently. He finally reported it to us, but he claims he did so only because he is worried about who might have taken it. When asked if he'd told Donald about it, he said he had but that Donald just waved it off, that it had nothing to do with his family and certainly not his precious Kal. You and I know better. Donald's employee, after much pressure, finally admitted to me that he suspected Kal had taken it. So, as we feared, Kal is most likely armed with a 9mm pistol."

"That's serious," Brad said as his gut tightened.

"Donald still won't listen to anything I try to tell him," Sergeant Bone concluded. "He says that Kal would never do such a thing. When I asked him where Kal got the money to hire his own investigator, he blew up at me. But he did not give me an answer. He just repeated that Kal was the good son and

Sparky was the bad one. If he would get off the bottle and come to his senses, he would probably be able to help us."

Brad sighed. "It's hopeless, I'm afraid. Abel, have you or anyone at the department heard from Officer Snepper?"

"No, but we have put out the description of his personal vehicle. We have also learned that a vehicle was stolen from a motel about a hundred miles west of here," Abel revealed. "I can't help but wonder if Kal was the thief and if he's driving it. We have both vehicles being searched for. Let me give you the description of them; Snepper's is a full-size silver Toyota pickup. The stolen vehicle is a green Ford pickup. It's an F150."

"Thanks. If you hear anything more, let me know," Brad said. Then he spent a few minutes bringing the sergeant up-to-date on what was going on with him and Lys and the concerns they had about her client and Sparky.

"Did she tell you who the client is?" Sergeant Bone asked.

"Not yet, but she is planning to tell me that and where Sparky Graves is hiding out when we meet in Green River, Utah. She's probably there by now and wondering where I am. I'm stuck in traffic," Brad explained. "The entire freeway must be closed for some reason. There's no traffic on the eastbound side, and I haven't moved for a long time. I'll call Lys as soon as I get off the phone with you."

Brad did that, but the phone went to voice mail. Maybe she had finally gotten an answer from her client, he thought hopefully. If so, she would probably be calling shortly. But Lys did not call. A half hour later, as traffic began to move ever so slowly, she still had not called. And when he again tried to call her, her phone once more went to voice mail. He began to worry about her.

It was a half hour later when he finally reached the scene of a horrendous multi-vehicle crash that involved both sides of the freeway. One lane of traffic in each direction was now being funneled through. The officers who were directing the traffic would not let anyone stop, but the line was moving through the single opening on his side of the freeway at a snail's pace. That gave Brad a chance to rubberneck. His heart nearly stopped when he spotted the remains of a black Chevy Tahoe in the midst of the wreckage. *Surely it's not Lys's,* he thought.

After all, there were a lot of black Chevy Tahoes on the road. It might not be hers. Yet it also might. The thought hurt him deeply. He was worried about Sparky Graves, but now he was just as worried about Lys Grist.

Over the months they'd known one another, they had talked about their lives in a way that he never had done before with anyone except his ex-wife. Lys had told him things about herself that she said she'd never shared with anyone else. They had made a connection, and over the months, that connection had grown into a deep, romantic friendship.

Brad noted that there were no ambulances around the crash scene even though there was a multitude of other emergency vehicles. That meant, he supposed, that all injured parties, and any fatalities, had already been removed. He began to pick up speed as he moved beyond the wreck, but he was torn. If Lys was waiting for him in Green River, it would only delay him if he pulled over and walked back to the wreck. On the other hand, if he did not find out for certain if the black Tahoe was Lys's, he would go crazy with worry.

Never one to choose crazy, he pulled off the freeway and got out of his black sedan and began walking toward the accident scene. Brad was a person whose physical bearing and forceful personality always allowed him to command attention when he needed to. He needed to now.

An officer spotted him as he approached the accident and waved him away. He ignored him and walked faster. He had his PI identification in his hand and shoved it toward the agitated officer as soon as he was close enough. "I'm Detective Brad Hagen," he said. "Trooper Wasik, I am involved in a life-and-death investigation, and I need some information badly."

The officer, a young member of the Utah Highway Patrol, reacted exactly as Brad had hoped when he used the man's name. Of course, he had quickly read it from the name plate on his brown uniform shirt. "As you can see, this is a nasty wreck. What can I help you with? You'll need to make it quick," Trooper Wasik said.

Brad, who was an expert at summing things up, gave Wasik a quick overview of the Sparky Graves case. "Another investigator was to meet me in Green River, and together we were going to head for this boy's location. I have been trying to call her to explain why I am delayed, but I am getting no response from her. She was driving a Black Chevy Tahoe and was westbound like I am."

At the mention of the Tahoe, Trooper Wasik glanced in the direction of the black hunk of mangled metal. "I think that's a Tahoe," he said. "A woman was driving it. I don't have her name. Sorry. That's all I know."

Brad's demeanor slipped. He feared the worst. But he had to ask one more question of the trooper. "Trooper Wasik, did the woman die in the crash?" He was unable to keep his voice from cracking. He desperately needed Lys to be okay. Sparky Graves also desperately needed Lys to be okay.

He felt a measure of relief when Trooper Wasik said, "She was alive but not conscious. She had to be extricated from the Tahoe. Whether she survived the helicopter ride to the hospital in Moab, I couldn't tell you. A couple of other people, including a young man in the small truck behind her, were killed. There were a lot of other serious injuries, as you can imagine."

He could only imagine too well. "Thank you, Trooper. I guess I'll drive to the hospital. I hope it's not her, but if it is, I pray that she's alive. You've been a big help," Brad told him, his voice filled with anguish.

"Moab is south on highway 191. You turn before you get to Green River. Good luck, sir," Trooper Wasik said.

Once again, Brad thanked him. As he started away, he looked back toward the Tahoe, which was partly in the inside westbound lane and partly in the median. He thought about walking over and seeing the license plate, but that probably wouldn't help him, as he did not know Lys's plate number, only that it was a Utah plate. Anyway, he didn't want to test the young trooper's patience by running between the cars that were anxiously trying to get past the wreckage. So he headed back to his vehicle.

As an FBI special agent, Brad Hagen had been involved in many tragic situations, and he had always handled them well. But this was different. This was personal. He found himself trembling as he started his car and began to pull back onto the freeway.

Brad didn't fear a speeding ticket with so many officers tied up back at the crash site, so he pushed down the gas pedal on his big Ford and raced toward the turnoff to Moab. He had to slow down on US 191 as it was a somewhat narrow, two-lane road. He did push it as fast as he dared, however. Every few minutes, he tried calling Lys on his phone even though his instincts told him that she wouldn't answer.

Brad was still about ten miles from the hospital according to his car's GPS when he again got a call from Sgt. Abel Bone. Abel asked him if he had connected with Detective Grist yet. "No, and I fear the worst," Brad said, fighting to keep his voice even. He then explained the wrecked Tahoe.

"Oh no!" Abel exclaimed. "I will pray for her. I hope you find that she's okay."

"So do I," Brad agreed as he found himself losing the fight to keep his emotions in check. This was so unlike him. But then Lys was so unlike anyone else in his life. She had become a large part of his life over the past few months.

"Let me tell you why I called," Abel said. "The stolen Ford pickup has been found deserted in a rest area a short distance off I-70 about halfway through Colorado. So if it was Kal Graves that stole it, he has found another ride. We have no way of knowing what he might be driving now."

"That's not good news," Brad said as he finally gained control of his emotions. "I sure hope that Lys is conscious and can tell me where to find her client and where Sparky is hiding out. I hate to think what will happen if Kal finds him first."

"Yeah," Abel said with a sigh. "Oh, by the way, we have been trying to reach Officer Snepper on his cell phone. He's not answering. So who knows what he's up to now."

"Sergeant, I wonder," Brad began as a rather distressing thought crossed his mind. "Could Snepper and Kal have connected somewhere? Could the two of them be working together?"

"I suppose that's possible," Brad responded.

By the time the conversation with Abel Bone was over, Brad was pulling into Moab. He found the hospital, parked, and ran inside, his heart pounding unmercifully in his chest.

***

Officer Lawrence Snepper was aware of unfamiliar things around him and felt like he was lying in a bed. But how could that be? He could hear pulsating and humming sounds nearby. He tried to move his arm, only to discover that it was attached to something that restricted movement. He forced his eyes open and moved them back and forth. Ever so slowly, his mind began to register that he was in a hospital bed.

A door opened and a moment later, a nurse peered down at him. She asked him how he was feeling. He told her that he was hurting really badly. He asked her where he was, and she told him that he was in a hospital, that he was lucky to be alive. Then she asked his name.

Puzzled, he said in a halting, pain-wracked voice, "I'm Officer Lawrence Snepper. Didn't you check my ID?"

"You didn't have any ID on you when you were brought into the emergency room," she said. "You didn't have any keys or a cell phone. So I need to know who you are, and then maybe someone can figure out what happened to you."

"I told you my name. What's yours?" Snepper asked as his mind and vision began to clear.

"I am Alexis Markel," she said with a smile. A very nice smile, Snepper noted. She had medium-length blonde hair and bright-green eyes.

"So how long have I been here?" he asked as his memory began to return.

"This is the second day," Alexis said.

"You mean I've been unconscious that long?" he asked, startled by that fact.

"I'm afraid so," she responded as she began to check his vital signs.

For a couple of minutes, neither of them spoke, but Lawrence Snepper was remembering, and the face of Kal Graves came into his mind. "How did I get here?"

"I wasn't on duty, but I'm told that someone found you lying in a pool of your own blood at the side of a road a short distance from I-70. You were unconscious. They called 911, and an ambulance responded and brought you here," she explained.

"I am beginning to recall," he said, after another long period of silence. "I think Kal Graves, who I was trying to help, shot me."

"I don't know who shot you, but you were shot. Twice, I'm afraid. I've been told to notify the police as soon as you regained consciousness, so they could speak with you," she said. "I'll go do that now. You try to rest."

With that, Alexis left Officer Snepper alone with his thoughts and closed the door behind her. Snepper lay there, hurting but also gradually beginning to burn with anger as he slowly recalled more clearly what had happened to him.

Kal Graves had called him and told him he wanted to work with him in finding his killer brother, Sparky. Snepper had decided that might be a good idea, so the two of them connected at a rest area in eastern Colorado. Once they were together, Kal had told the officer that he had been hitchhiking and was hoping that, by working together, he wouldn't have to beg for rides anymore. He told Snepper that he was glad the two of them would be working together now, since none of the other officers were willing to do what it would take to locate his brother and bring him to justice.

Kal had thrown a duffle bag in Snepper's Toyota pickup and jumped in beside him. They'd headed west on the freeway. Snepper had been feeling pretty smug as Kal told him about hiring a PI by the name of Fredrick Belina and that he thought Belina had a good idea where Sparky was. They'd traveled maybe a hundred miles farther west when Kal had suddenly said, "Can you pull off the freeway at the next exit? I'm feeling car sick, and I think I might need to throw up."

Officer Snepper had done as Kal had asked him to. When they had driven just a short distance up a side road, Kal had said, "Stop now. I'm going to heave."

Snepper had slammed on the brakes, and Kal had opened the door on his side and leaped out, slamming the door shut. A minute or so had passed. The officer didn't hear anything over the music playing on the truck radio. Suddenly, there had been a tap on his window. Kal was standing there with an anguished look on his face. Snepper had rolled his window down and said, "Are you okay now, Kal?"

At that point, the young man had said, "Can you get out and help me? I'm awful sick."

Totally unsuspecting of anything, Lawrence Snepper had opened his door and stepped out of his truck only to find himself facing Kal Graves with a pistol pointed directly at his face. Kal's look of anguish had vanished. The look it had been replaced with, coupled with the gun held firmly in the young man's hand, had scared Snepper badly.

"Walk away," Kal had said. "I've decided I don't need your help but I am going to need your truck. The last thing I need is the help of a cop."

"Hey, I was trying to help you. What are you doing?"

Kal had hesitated briefly, but then he said, "If you want to live, get walking. I'm taking the truck." Snepper had walked, and then Kal had fired at his back. Snepper went down. Struggling, he turned from his back to his side, terrified at the sudden turn of events. A moment later, Kal's glowering face had appeared above him. He didn't say another word, but he pointed at Snepper's head and fired again. That was the last thing Snepper remembered until he woke up in this hospital bed.

Realizing now that Kal Graves had shot him was a shock. All this time he had believed that Kal was telling the truth about Sparky being a killer. He now realized that the killer was Kal, not his brother Sparky. Kal had left him for dead. He was indeed lucky to be alive.

With a shudder, he also realized that Sparky Graves could be in serious danger. For it wasn't hard, at this point, to assume that Kal had no intention of ever letting Sparky return to Goodland alive. Snepper admitted to himself that he'd acted foolishly, and he desperately wanted to make things right with his department, if that could even be done.

There was a telephone on a nearby nightstand, but he couldn't reach it. What could he do? Someone needed to know what Kal was up to. He searched for and found the call button and pressed it. A moment later, Nurse Markel rushed in. "What's the matter?" she asked.

"I've got to call my department. They need to know I've been shot and who shot me. He is going to kill his little brother if he can't be stopped," Snepper said urgently.

"There will be an officer here in a few minutes. Can't it wait until you talk to him?" Alexis asked.

"No, this can't wait. Please, help me make a call."

"Okay, I'll grab the phone here. Tell me the number and I'll dial it."

A minute later, Sergeant Abel Bone answered the call.

CHAPTER NINETEEN

KAL HAD THOUGHT THAT DETECTIVE Belina was withholding information from him, and the idea had outraged him. After knocking the detective out, he'd left Officer Snepper's pickup in the parking area and had driven Belina's car away from the restaurant with the unconscious investigator slumped over in the passenger side. He'd gone south of I-70 to a deserted area. Now he waited for the detective to wake up.

It wasn't long before Belina groaned. Kal had handcuffed him with a pair of handcuffs he'd found in the jockey box. He'd also used Belina's own belt to bind his feet. Then he'd put the seatbelt on and pulled it tight. Now he watched Belina as he slowly regained consciousness.

It was Belina who spoke first, even as he struggled in vain against his restraints. "Kal, you are making a terrible mistake. I don't know where Sparky is. I told you that I was getting close, and I am. But I don't know exactly where he's at."

Belina's voice was slurred, and Kal grinned to himself as he saw pain in his victim's eyes. He enjoyed what he was doing. But now he had to get the detective to tell him the truth. He was sure the guy knew exactly where Sparky was hiding. "Detective Belina, you better believe me when I tell you that I'm serious. Tell me where Sparky is, or I will make you pay with your life."

"I don't know," Belina said. "I tell you, I need a little more time to find him. I'm close, believe me."

"No more time," Kal hissed, and he reached across the seat and backhanded Belina in the face. Blood poured from his mouth.

"I don't know where he is. You've got to believe me."

"You are lying. I hired you to do a job. You're not doing it if you don't come clean with me. Now you need to tell me exactly where my brother is so I can take him back to Goodland," Kal said.

"You and I both know that you don't intend to do that," Belina said. "You will do to him exactly what you did to your mother."

"So you figured it out, did you?" Kal laughed. "But what happens to Sparky is not your problem. You need to think about your own life. Unless you want to die, you better start to talk and it better be the truth," Kal said as he drew back a fist and punched Fredrick in the side of the head.

For a moment, he thought the detective had lost consciousness again, but after a moment, Belina shook his head and mumbled, "I'll tell you what I know. That's the best I can do. Then you need to let me go. I'll be finished and go home. You'll be on your own then."

"Now we're getting somewhere," the violent young man said. "Keep talking or I'll start breaking your fingers." Kal had read about the pain that such an act would inflict, and he actually looked forward to doing that to this man.

"Sparky is somewhere near here, in this part of Utah. By the way, where are we?" Fredrick asked.

"Not far from where I found you," Kal said.

"Okay, this is what I know. I talked to a girl, a waitress at Denny's. She saw Sparky get in an old pickup truck with an elderly man. He had grain sacks in the back of the truck. The girl said he had to be a farmer and that he had to live somewhere near here."

"What else did she say?" Kal asked.

"That's all," Belina said.

Kal glared at him for a moment. He was afraid that was all the detective knew, but he intended to be sure. Five minutes later, Detective Fredrick Belina passed out from the pain Kal had inflicted, but he hadn't told him anything else. Angry beyond reason, Kal dragged the unconscious man from the vehicle and into the brush near the dirt road. He looked at Belina for a moment, and then he said, "So this is how it ends? Fine. I'll find Sparky myself then."

He pulled out the investigator's wallet, extracted several hundred-dollar bills, dropped the wallet on the ground, and walked back to the car. With a plan in mind, he calmly drove back toward the Denny's. He was the investigator now; he would find Sparky. And when he did . . .

***

Brad had finally been allowed into the intensive care unit and was now seated beside the bed of his colleague and best friend, Lys Grist. She was in critical condition, and he had been told that she may not survive even though the doctors had operated on her for several hours. Her face was practically unrecognizable, and she was hooked up to so many machines he could hardly count them. Nurse Tracy Anderson, who appeared to be around forty, constantly monitored Lys's condition.

"I can't say she won't live, Detective," Tracy said, "but I have seldom seen anyone who is this badly injured survive. If they do, they are usually left in a vegetative state. I'm sorry, but I don't want to give you false hope."

"I understand," he said, even as he felt his heart tearing apart. He had looked forward to a bright future with Lys. Now he was afraid that had been taken from him by the cruel hand of fate.

Brad, normally a man of action and decisive decision making, found himself feeling helpless. A woman he had grown to adore over the past few months lay dying before him. The teenage boy they were both trying to save could well be facing death himself if Brad didn't figure out a way to find him soon. He hoped it was not already too late.

He shook off his helplessness. He *could* do something. He *had* to do something. Lys would expect him to. There was nothing he could do for Lys, now, but pray. Either she lived or she died. That was in God's hands. He prayed that she would live and that he would yet be able to get to know her better. If he could locate her cell phone and her purse, he might be able to find the name and phone number of her client.

He pulled out a business card, handed it to Nurse Anderson, and said, "Please, call me if there is any change. A boy's life hangs in the balance, and I need to go now."

Assuming the wrecked Tahoe would be taken to Green River, he pointed his Ford north and pushed the pedal to the floor. He had scarcely left the Moab city limits when a call came in on his synched cell phone. He pushed a button on his steering wheel and said, "Hello, this is Brad Hagen."

"Brad, Abel Bone here. Things have taken a turn for the worse, I'm afraid. Where are you at?"

"I'm just leaving Moab. Detective Grist is in a coma and may not survive. I'm going to Green River to see if I can find her cell phone or her purse or both in her wrecked Tahoe," Brad responded.

"Are you thinking you may be able to discover who her client is if you can find them?" Abel asked.

"All I can do is try."

"I have no other ideas," Abel said. "But let me tell you what I just learned. I got a call from Officer Snepper."

"Has he come to his senses?" Brad interrupted hopefully.

"I guess you could say that. He somehow connected with Kal Graves the day before yesterday. He said he offered to help Kal, which the young man agreed to. Of course, Kal had other plans. What he really wanted was Snepper's truck. He shot Snepper and left him for dead on a county road in central Colorado."

Brad blew out a breath. "I take it he's okay now and that was why he was able to call you?"

"He's gravely injured. It appears that he was shot in the back, and then Kal shot at his head. Fortunately for Snepper, the bullet didn't hit anything critical in his head. In fact, it barely penetrated before coming out again. He was in a coma until an hour or so ago, but he seems to have retained his memory."

"That's good to hear," Brad said. "Does he have any idea where Kal is headed and if he knows where Sparky is?"

"Not exactly," Abel responded. "However, he told me the name of a private investigator that Kal supposedly hired. The guy is from here in Kansas. Fredrick Belina. Does his name mean anything to you?"

Brad groaned. "I'm afraid so. Belina is a bit of a maverick and not the smartest guy around. I've crossed paths with him three or four times, and he has failed to impress me on any of those occasions."

"I think we need to find him," Abel said. "Kal told Snepper that Belina was closing in on Sparky. He needs to be warned not to trust Kal or give him any information. I was going to call him, but it might be best if you do, Brad. He might listen to you better than he would to me."

"I can do that. You don't happen to have his number do you?"

"No. I can get it, but I wanted to call you before I did anything else after talking to Snepper."

"I have a bit of a drive ahead of me. I can find the number and call him if you want me to, Sergeant."

"Thanks. Let me know what happens. I'm going to chase down Donald Graves and see if I can get him to listen to sense now. First, however, I intend to find out whatever I can from the officer that was going to interview Snepper at the hospital in Colorado."

"I'll let you know what I learn from Detective Belina," Brad said, and then the call ended.

It didn't take but a minute for Brad to get a phone number for Belina's office. He tried the number, and like he hoped, it forwarded to the PI's cell phone. It went to voice mail. He waited a few minutes and tried again with the same result. Finally, he called Sergeant Bone back and informed him of the results of his efforts. "I'll keep trying his phone," Brad told the sergeant.

"I guess that's the best we can do. Let me give you an update from my end," Abel said. "I found Donald at his shop after talking to the officer handling Snepper's case. At first, he didn't want to talk to me, but when I told him what I had learned, that Snepper was in serious condition and that a warrant had been issued by Colorado authorities for Kal for attempted murder, he finally let me into his office."

"Did he believe what you told him?" Brad asked skeptically.

"Not really. He was still belligerent, reeked of alcohol, and said that he doubted it was Kal who shot Snepper. He kept insisting that Sparky was the dangerous one, not Kal. I stopped arguing with him at that point. Instead I called the Colorado officer I had talked to, and he spoke with Donald," Abel reported. "Donald still refused to believe Kal could or would do such a thing. He berated the officer for jumping to conclusions."

"So Donald is still refusing to look at the truth?" Brad asked.

"The officer in Colorado went back to the hospital, and he allowed Snepper to speak with Donald. Snepper didn't beat around the bush. He told Donald what had happened and how Kal had told him that he would take care of Sparky himself. Donald went very quiet after that and finally asked me if I thought Kal had hurt his younger children. I assured him that he had not, that you had located them and they were fine. He wanted to see them, but I told him they were in protective custody and that, for now, it was going to stay that way. He wasn't happy with me. But then I've gotten kind of used to that."

"We tried to tell him all that before," Brad said. "So has he finally come around to the truth and is he willing to accept it?"

"Believe it or not, he's still hanging on to his belief that Kal is a good boy. He just can't seem to admit that he's been wrong all this time. He's a stubborn man. At any rate, I was wondering if you would mind calling the woman who is taking care of Donald's younger children. What I would like is for her to call me and then to let one or both of the children speak with Donald. He's at home now, and I told him that I would see what I could work out," Abel said.

"Sure, I think that would be okay, but I am not at all comfortable telling Donald where they are or where they can be reached," Brad said. "Until Kal is caught and Donald accepts the truth about him, we just can't take any chances."

"I agree," Abel said. So they set up a call to allow that to happen, but only with Abel monitoring the call very closely.

Brad tried Belina's phone again but once more failed to reach him. A few minutes later, he pulled into a wrecking yard in Green River where Lys's Tahoe had been towed. He explained who he was and was given permission to take a look. As he viewed the wreckage, he wondered how she had survived the crash. Of course, he knew that her survival might not last. He prayed, however, that it would.

With the aid of a mechanic from the garage, he sifted through the ruins of Lys's vehicle. By some miracle, he found her phone. But it was a useless miracle, for it had been badly crushed. There was no way he was going to be able to find anything on it. He also found her purse.

Somehow, the contents were not spilled from the purse. He made a cursory search, hoping to find an address or an appointment book. He did see a wallet which he left closed. Unlike a lot of women's purses that he'd seen in the course of his years of investigation, Lys's had been organized, very indicative of her personality. He felt guilty looking in it and closed it. Too painful. *Maybe later,* he thought.

He felt a pang in his chest. The purse was a heavy one with a very strong latch. If her phone had been in her purse, it may have survived the crash.

Brad was indecisive for a minute, but then he forced himself to make a decision. He turned to the man from the garage and told him that he would have to take the purse so he could give it to her in the hospital in Moab. He referred to Lys as his partner, which was very close to the truth, as he spoke in a confident, commanding tone. To his relief, the man agreed as long as he gave him a receipt. That done, he left, taking the crushed phone and the purse with him.

Back in his car, he sat for a moment wondering what course of action to take. There were not a lot of choices. He could drive west and stop at various places where Sparky, Kal, or Detective Belina may have stopped, or he could go back to Moab. His heart pulled him to Moab. If and when Lys awoke, he wanted to be there. At this point, that was the only way he knew how to obtain information regarding her client.

Being the practical man that he was, however, he called the hospital in Moab first. He was eventually connected to the very nurse in the intensive care unit who had been taking care of Lys earlier.

As soon as Brad identified himself, the nurse said, "Oh, Detective Hagen, I am so sorry but—"

He ended the call and leaned down onto his steering wheel. He did not cry, but he wanted to. He knew what the nurse was about to say before he'd ended the call. Lys had passed away. The very thought depressed him like he had never been depressed before. How this woman had gotten such a hold on him would forever be a mystery to him, but he would long cherish her memory.

Knowing that Lys was dead, he decided the best course was to go ahead and proceed west. His heart was hurting, but he had a duty to perform if he possibly could. There was no doubt that Lys would want him to do that. Sparky Graves, if he was still alive, needed Brad to find him. He shook off the depression over the death of Lys Grist the best he could and headed onto the westbound freeway. Serious grieving would have to wait.

A few minutes later, his phone rang. It was Sergeant Bone again. "Brad, I think we finally convinced Donald that it is his eldest son, not Sparky, who is the evil killer in his family."

"So he talked to his kids?" Brad asked.

"He did. Brad, he cried and broke down, went clear to pieces after hearing what they had to say. He's in the hospital now under sedation."

"What did the kids say to him?"

"Mrs. Boyer—she told me her name—got both of the children on the phone together. It was hard to tell which was which as they talked. They sound a lot alike," Abel explained. "At any rate, they told their father that they didn't want to come home, that Kal would kill them like he did their mother. Donald, still stubborn in the face of all the evidence, tried to tell them that it was Sparky who had done that, but both children spoke at once and said, practically screaming, 'No, Dad. It was Kal! We saw him do it.'"

"Was that what turned him around?" Brad asked.

"Pretty much. The children did go on to explain that Kal had hurt them and told them they had to tell their dad that they'd wrecked on the bike even though they hadn't. They went on to tell him that Sparky was always protecting them from Kal. They got pretty explicit as they poured their little hearts out to their father," Abel said. "It was gut-wrenching to watch Donald. He finally told them that he would never let Kal hurt them and that he would try to find Sparky and bring him home."

"It's too bad he's been so stubborn about Kal," Brad said. "A lot of heartache could have been prevented if he would have listened to reason in the first place."

"I agree," Abel said. "It was right after the phone call that Donald fell to pieces. He had a total meltdown and, like I said, had to be taken to the hospital and sedated. So, tell me, did you find anything of value in Detective Grist's Tahoe?"

Brad, carefully controlling his fractured emotions, told him what he had found. "I have the purse and what's left of her phone. I was going to take them to Moab and leave them for her there, but . . . well . . . she won't be needing them again."

"Brad, are you telling me she didn't make it?" Able asked.

Just then, he got another incoming call. It was the hospital. He was torn. "I guess I'd better take this," he said to Abel. "It's the hospital again. They probably don't know who to contact about her body, where to have it taken. I'll need to see if I can locate her family."

"Take the call. And Brad, I'm terribly sorry," the sergeant said.

Brad answered the call from the hospital. It was Nurse Tracy Anderson calling him back. He braced himself for her to finish what she had started to say to him earlier about Lys not making it. "I'm sorry that we got cut off earlier," Tracy said. "Those crazy cell phones drop calls at the most inconvenient times."

Brad didn't say anything. He was not about to admit that he had intentionally ended the call. It was so unlike him to do something like that, but he had, and now he was not only brokenhearted but embarrassed. He braced himself to hear the fateful words spoken.

"Anyway, I was calling to update you. It's not a lot, but your partner moved her fingers and toes. She also opened her eyes briefly, but she has not regained consciousness," Tracy said. "But I wanted you to know. It gives us a glimmer of hope here."

Brad was stunned beyond words. *Lys is alive!* She might still have a chance. He had to go to her.

"Are you there, Detective?" Tracy asked. "I hope we haven't been cut off again."

Brad found his voice between his tears. "No, I'm here. I'm finished in Green River and am returning to Moab. I'll be there as soon as I can."

"All right, Detective. But you be sure to drive carefully. There is no need to hurry now," Tracy said.

"I hear you," he agreed. Tracy was wrong; there was a need to hurry. If, and when, Lys woke up, he needed to be able to ask her where Sparky was and prayed that she would, after all the trauma, still remember. It was his best, possibly *only* chance at finding the young man.

He took the very next exit and headed east. Try as he might, his speed kept creeping up. Each time he slowed down and let the cruise control take over to keep his speed down, he would just find his foot again pressing on the accelerator. Lys had to make it. She had to wake up. She had to tell him how to find Sparky Graves.

***

Donald Graves was resting quite peacefully when Sergeant Abel Bone entered his hospital room again. Abel stood and watched him for a minute. He wanted to speak with him again, to assure him that everything that could be done to help him and his family was being done. As he stood there watching the poor guy, Donald's eyes opened. "Sergeant, that you?" Donald asked.

"Yes, Donald. Are you feeling any better?" Abel asked.

"I am. I'm sorry I was so difficult and drunk so much. I had no idea that Kal had fooled my wife and me so badly all these years," he said. "I still have a hard time understanding it."

"Do you believe now that Sparky is innocent?" Abel asked.

"Yes, and I am so sorry for the way I despised him. But I know that Johnny and Courtney were telling me the truth. I just can't believe Kal could do such horrible things. I always thought he was the good son. But now as I think about it, I believe my dear Sydney suspected all along that it was Kal who was behind all the trouble. I guess Kal must have figured that out. Sparky never did come back, did he? The kids left on their own like they told me."

"No, he did not," Abel agreed. "The children ran away because they feared Kal, and they knew you would believe him over them. They are lucky they weren't hurt by someone besides Kal. That's a dangerous world out there. I believe God watched over them for you."

"Oh how I wish I could go back and do it all over again," Donald said with a catch in his voice. "God will never forgive me. I have been such a blind, drunken fool." He began to cry.

Abel let him. Finally, after he had gained control again, the sergeant told him that they needed to talk now. "I need you to tell me everything you can about both Sparky and Kal. Are you up to talking for a few minutes?"

"I'm okay now. Can we leave here and go talk at your office or at my house?" Donald asked.

Abel's phone rang. "Sure, I think we can do that, but I need to take this call first."

Abel shook his head a few minutes later as he arranged to have Donald released. The call had been from Detective Brad Hagen. It turned out that Lys Grist was still alive after all and that was giving Brad some hope. He prayed that she would be okay.

They went to the police station as soon as Donald was discharged, and there Abel questioned and listened for a couple of hours. At the end of the session, he was no closer to figuring out where Sparky might have gone, or Kal either, for that matter.

CHAPTER TWENTY

"THIS PHONE IS FINALLY WORKING," Sparky said enthusiastically. "The rice thing worked. It dried it out. Why don't we call Detective Grist and see what she's learned?"

"Sure, or we can use the landline," Alfred said.

"I'll use this one." Sparky made the call and then handed the phone to Alfred. "It's ringing, you talk to her."

Sparky watched Alfred as he waited. Finally, he handed the phone back to Sparky and said, "She's not answering."

Sparky checked his phone and found that there had been several calls from Lys's cell phone. "Lys has been trying to call me. I'll bet she's tried your phone and the landline too."

"That worries me," Alfred said. "I wonder what's going on with her."

Sparky thought for a moment. He was also worrying. "I think I should leave. What if Kal knows where I am?"

"If it's anything like that, Lys would keep trying to reach us," Alfred said, but the tone of his voice was not convincing to Sparky.

Another thought occurred to Sparky, and that one made him shiver. "Alfred, what if Kal has done something to Lys? Maybe she *can't* call us now."

"Oh, surely that's not the case. Lys is a smart woman. She would never allow Kal to get the best of her," Alfred argued.

"We don't know that for sure. I should leave. I'm putting you in danger," Sparky said. "If you want me to, I'll come back when I am no longer in danger."

"Please stay here with me, Sparky. I need your help. Besides, where would you go?" Alfred asked.

Alfred needed him. No one had ever said that to Sparky before. His resolve weakened. "I don't know where I would go," he said. "I guess that I would do what I did before."

"Please, don't do that," Alfred said.

Sparky was torn. He'd come to love his elderly benefactor. "Okay, maybe, if you want me to, I'll stay here for a while longer."

"How long is a while longer?" Alfred asked.

"I don't know. Maybe until we hear from Lys. Or maybe she will tell me I need to go. I'm confused, Alfred." He didn't want to go. The thought of trying to travel by sneaking rides did not appeal to him at all. He felt like he'd finally found a home where he was loved and trusted. He thrust the idea of leaving out of his mind. "Okay, I won't go for now," he said after the two of them had been silent a minute or two. "What would you like me to do?"

"I'd like you to stay," Alfred said.

"I mean, what work should I do now?" Sparky asked. "I'm staying for now, but I want to get to work. And Alfred, we need to be watchful. Who knows what Kal might be up to."

"How about if both of us get on the four-wheelers and check the whole farm out? Let's make sure the beavers aren't damming the stream again. And we should make sure the pastures are all okay and not overgrazed. Then, maybe we should clean some pens. That's dirty work and hard, but I've put it off too long. When we get back, we can start with the old boar pig's pen. Sherman can be mean, so we'll need to be careful."

Sparky didn't care how hard the work was. He just wanted to get at it and try to forget Kal and his past. To live in the here and now. He secretly wished that Kay Dell was going to be here. He enjoyed her company.

As if reading his mind, Alfred said, "I did catch one phone call in the house a little while ago. Kay Dell wanted to know if she could come today. I told her she could." He looked at his watch. "She should be here by the time we finish checking things out."

Sparky grinned. "She'll be just in time to help clean old Sherman's pen."

Both fellows chuckled and headed for the four-wheelers.

***

Kimberlee Owings kept thinking about the private detective she'd spoken to as she waited tables at Denny's in Salina, and about the young man he was searching for. It was hard for her to imagine why someone would ever want to run away from home. She had a wonderful family and was always glad to see them when she arrived home from her shifts at Denny's each day.

She hoped the detective could find the boy and get him to return to his family. Detective Belina hadn't told her anything about the kid except that his name was Sparky. He may have mentioned the last name, but if he had, she couldn't recall it. She came out of her reverie when a Sevier County deputy sheriff that she saw quite often entered the restaurant. He was a young guy, cute in his uniform, and always nice to her. In fact, he flirted with her some, and she enjoyed it.

His name was Hy Jones and he was single. He always made sure to speak with her even if he wasn't at a table she was waiting on.

He saw her as she stepped away from a table where she had just placed a cup of coffee for a trucker. Hy walked straight to her, smiling, making her tingle. "Hi, Hy," she said with a slight giggle.

"Hello, Kimberlee," he said. "Have you got a second? I need to talk to you."

"Sure," she said, hoping that maybe at last he was going to ask her out. He'd hinted at it before.

He signaled for her to follow him to an empty part of the restaurant and then spoke to her in a soft voice. His face had become very serious, and she let her hopes rise. However, she was disappointed when he said, "There's a pickup parked outside with Kansas license plates. We've been looking for it. It was reported stolen in Colorado by an officer from Kansas who was shot by the guy that stole it."

The tingle she'd been feeling changed to a shiver of fear. "Stolen," she said. "Is the guy in here?" She looked about as she spoke.

"Could be," he said. "The engine is still a little warm, so it was driven not too long ago."

She folded her arms across her stomach in an attempt to calm the chill she was feeling. "Scary," she admitted.

"Let me tell you what he looks like. I don't have a picture, just a name and a description. His name is Kal Graves and—"

Kimberlee interrupted him as a memory came to her. "That's the last name of the guy a private detective was looking for. I was just thinking about him. The detective called him Sparky, and I couldn't remember the last name until you said it just now. Could it be the same guy?"

Hy's face lost some color. "No. Sparky Graves is his brother. His picture has been on the news a lot lately. He was accused of killing his mother, but it turns out Kal is the killer. Sparky is in danger if Kal Graves finds him. We've got to find Kal and arrest him."

Kimberlee felt her knees go weak, and she put a hand against the wall to support herself. "Hy, I told that detective that I had seen Sparky."

"Are you sure you saw him?" the deputy asked.

"Yes, I am. Almost three weeks ago, he got in an old pickup with an elderly farmer just up the road toward the freeway. But the detective told me Sparky was dangerous," she said.

"He's not. Let's get back to that in a minute. First, let's figure out, if we can, whether or not Kal Graves is in here or if he has been," Hy said. "Kal is about five eight and slender. His hair is dark brown and touches his collar and covers his ears. His eyes are dark brown. Does that sound familiar to you at all?"

"No, I haven't seen him. I'm sure," she said with relief.

"Good. I'll check with some of the other people in here to make sure, but please, Kimberlee, if you see him, call 911. If you even see someone you think might be him, call 911, and be really careful," Hy said, causing her to again feel chills.

Kimberlee went back to work, but she was nervous. She watched as Deputy Jones talked to other people in the room. She was just coming out of the kitchen area with a plate of food for a customer when Hy approached her again. "Looks like you were right," he said. "But be alert since we haven't had any reports of any other cars being stolen. He could still be in the area. I'll talk to you later."

"Okay, Hy. I hope you guys catch him soon," she said, her voice weak. He smiled at her, and she turned and headed for her customer's booth.

***

Brad walked into the intensive care unit, straight to where Lys lay, still in a coma and still hooked to a lot of machines. Her nurse, Tracy Anderson, was leaning over her. She straightened up when she saw Brad and smiled. "She's doing better, Detective," she said. "But she's still in critical condition."

"Is it okay if I sit here with her?" Brad asked as he gazed at the badly damaged face of his best friend.

"Of course you can. We have not heard from any of her family," Tracy responded. "Do you have a way to contact anyone?"

Brad shook his head. "I don't know of any family. She's never mentioned any to me in the months since I met her. Maybe while I'm sitting here with her, I can get on my phone and do some searching."

"Please let us know if you find any family. Is that her purse you have there?" she asked when Brad laid the bag on the stand beside the bed.

"It is," he said. "I found it in the wreckage of her vehicle. I need to look through it. Maybe there will be something in there about her family."

"I hope so," Tracy said. "I need to step out for a moment, but I will be close by if you think she needs me."

"Thanks, Nurse Anderson," he said.

After she had left, he stepped near Lys's bed and gazed down at her for a long time. His heart was aching for her while, at the same time, he was worrying about Sparky Graves. He was so torn. Should he stay here with Lys and hope she woke up and could tell him where the young man was hiding? Or should he leave and try to find some clues along I-70 that might help him?

For now, he was going to stay here. He simply could not tear himself away. He finally took a seat near Lys's bed and pulled her purse onto his lap. Pushing aside the feeling of invasion, he opened it for the second time. There was an undamaged small thirty-eight caliber revolver in a specially designed pocket that was easy to access. He left it in its pocket and began to remove other items. In a wallet, he found her driver's license, her PI credentials, a couple of credit cards, a debit card, and some cash. He put everything back the way he found it and explored some more. He felt a prickling when he pulled out a tiny address book from a small pocket inside the purse. Most people kept things like addresses and phone numbers on their phones these days, but perhaps she might be different.

The little book did not contain a lot, but there were several names and phone numbers. He pulled out his cell phone, intent on making some calls. He punched in the very first number in the book, Anderson. There was an address listed for an apartment in Salt Lake City. This entry was the only name starting with A in the book. Brad recognized the name—he had met her when he'd visited Lys in Salt Lake. She was a close friend of Lys's but not a relative.

There was no answer and he went on to the next name which was the only entry in the B section, a Joe Barnacle who had an Ogden address. Before punching in the number, Brad skimmed through the rest of the book. He shook his head at the small number of names—only twenty-five. Most of the pages contained no names at all. To his dismay, that included the G page. There was no one in her book with the last name Grist. That was disturbing to Brad, but he had expected it. They'd come to know each other so well that if she had any family, she would surely have told him. He knew that her parents had died years ago and that she had never been married.

He went back to the B pages and dialed the number listed for Joe Barnacle, another of her PI associates. A deep voice answered on the first ring. "This is Joe Barnacle of Barnacle and Holman Investigations."

"I'm Brad Hagen, a private investigator from Kansas. I'm calling in regards to a colleague of ours by the name of Lys Grist."

"Lys," the deep voice said with pleasure. "She's a great investigator. She and I have worked together on a number of cases. What are you wondering about her? I haven't seen her in five or six months."

"She has told me about you and your partner Blair Holman and speaks highly of your professional abilities. Your name is in a small address book I found in her purse. She has been seriously injured, and I'm trying to locate any family she might have."

"Injured!" Joe exclaimed. "What happened and where is she?"

"She's in a hospital in Moab, Utah. She was in a very serious wreck on I-70," Brad said. "I'm sitting here with her hoping she soon comes out of the coma she's in."

"Were you working with her on an investigation?" Joe asked.

"I was, and she has some information in her head that I need if I am going to be able to save a young man's life," Brad said. At Joe's urging, he went on to give him a brief overview of the case.

"Sounds like a serious matter," Joe said when he had finished. "I hope it works out. And please, let me know how Lys is. That woman is a class act. It breaks my heart to hear about her like this. I'll need to call my San Francisco associate and let him know. Oh, you asked about family. To my knowledge, she has none. I think her parents died years ago."

Brad shook his head. Then he had an idea. "Hey, Joe, before I let you go, maybe you could help me with something."

"Sure, what do you need?"

"There are not a lot of names in Lys's book. Would you mind if I read them to you and see if you recognize any of them?"

"Sure, let's have them," Joe agreed.

Five minutes later, Brad ended the call with Joe Barnacle and thought about what he'd learned; Over half of the names were ones that Joe had recognized as private investigators, including Joe's San Francisco partner. Ten names were left. One of them was the Anderson lady whom he'd met. He tried her number again, but it went to voice mail. He left a message and went on to the next name. He ended up leaving six messages and speaking with four people. Those four were women and were all friends of Lys's in both the Salt Lake area and in Ogden. She had, he was quite certain, mentioned each of them to him over the months of their friendship.

All of them were horrified to hear of Lys's accident and made Brad promise to let them know if anything changed in the next few hours. They all took his number down and promised to keep in touch until Lys was out of danger. Three of them told him they were going to drive to Moab as soon as they could get away. Every one of them cried and expressed their love for their friend. Well, he thought, Lys might not have family but she had some really good friends. Nurse

Tracy Anderson was in and out several times while Brad made his calls. Finally, when he was finished, she pointed to the many instruments Lys was attached to. "I like what I'm seeing here, Brad. She's improving."

He couldn't determine anything from the instruments, but Tracy's words were very encouraging. A doctor came in a little later and added to his hopeful feelings. Lys, however, still remained in the coma.

He explained to Nurse Anderson that Lys had no family but three very good friends were coming to see her. "When one of them gets here, I'll leave and get back to work on our investigation," he said, glancing at Lys as he did so.

CHAPTER TWENTY-ONE

HER SHIFT AT DENNY'S WAS almost at an end. Kimberlee was exhausted and anxious to go home. There was a sudden rush of customers, making her finish a little late. When she finally headed for her car, she was surprised to see a couple of police cars parked beside the Toyota pickup that Hy had told her belonged to an injured officer and had been stolen by Kal Graves.

Kimberlee attributed part of her exhaustion to the worry she had been experiencing over the young killer who might still be in the area. She looked about her as she hurriedly walked to her car. She glanced back at where the two officers were standing beside the stolen silver Toyota pickup. Deputy Hy Jones spotted her, called her name, and hurried toward her.

She had already unlocked her car when he got there. They both smiled at each other.

"How come that stolen truck is still here?" Kimberlee asked. "I thought it would have been gone a long time ago."

"I was about to have it towed when I was told that some investigators from Colorado were coming. They want to take it back there so they can examine it for evidence," Hy explained. He shrugged. "That's fine with us. That means we don't have to take care of it."

"Have you been here all this time?" she asked.

"Yep," he said. "I was told not to leave until the other officers got here. I'm bored stiff."

"I'm sorry. That doesn't sound like fun," she said. Then, thinking again of Kal Graves, she asked, "So have you guys caught the guy that left it here?"

He shook his head. "I'm afraid not. Kimberlee, be really careful going home."

"I will," she promised, though, honestly, she wasn't sure how to do that besides watching for someone that looked like the guy Hy had described to her earlier. She shivered.

Hy noticed. "Hey, tell you what, Kimberlee. If you'll give me your number, I'll give you mine. Call me as soon as you get home, so I won't have to worry about you. Tell me again where you live."

"Aurora. It's not far," she said.

"How long does it take you to get home?" he asked.

She told him, and then he said, "If I don't hear from you by the time you should be home, I'm going to call you. So let's exchange numbers."

***

Kal was fuming. He couldn't believe the cops had already found the truck he'd stolen from Officer Snepper, who he was sure was dead. He had planned on going into the Denny's where a waitress had told Belina that Sparky had caught a ride with an old man and headed west.

He watched the pretty girl with short brown hair come out of the café and walk to her car. That gave him an idea. Who knew? She could be the girl he needed to talk to. If not, she could surely tell him who else worked there that he should talk to. He bristled when one of the cops hurried over to her car and began talking to her, standing very close. When he saw them pull out their phones and type in them, he assumed they must be friends.

He waited in Belina's car, drumming his fingers on the steering wheel, hoping the officer would go back to Snepper's truck and that she would leave. He would follow her until she got to where she was going, and then he would have a little chat with her. The sun was starting to get low, and he hoped she'd drive out before dark. It was easier to get people to talk if it was light.

***

Kimberlee smiled as she pulled out of the parking area. The last thing Hy had said to her before he walked back to join the other officer was, "Hey, now that I've got your number, maybe I can call you sometime. I mean, you know . . ." His face went red and he turned and walked away. *Did* she know? She hoped so. If he called her and asked her out, she would say yes in a heartbeat.

She had not been on the freeway more than a couple of minutes when she noticed a car in the rearview mirror not very far behind her. That car was blue like the one she'd noticed parked a short distance from Denny's. She'd been looking around, making sure she didn't see anyone who looked like Kal Graves. The car had been far enough away at the time that, with the lowering sun reflecting off the windshield, she hadn't been able to tell if anyone was in it.

She sped up to see if it sped up too. It did.

Now she was nervous. She slowed down, and to her dismay, so did the blue car. She slowed down even more, hoping it would pass her. It slowed too. She sped up, going faster and faster, until she was going over ninety. The blue car stayed right behind her. She was petrified.

What should she do? Then she remembered that she now had Hy's phone number on her phone. She slowed a little, reached over to her purse, and pulled out her cell phone. She knew she wasn't supposed to use the phone while driving, but she wasn't supposed to speed either. If a cop stopped her, she figured that would be okay. She might get a ticket, but at least she would be safe.

She managed to find Hy's number and call it without running off the road. It rang. She willed Hy to answer. She was afraid it would go to voice mail before he answered it. She was relieved when he finally said, "Hi, Kimberlee. Sorry it took me a minute to answer. The cops from Colorado are here. Is everything okay?"

"No, it isn't!" she cried. "Some guy is following me!"

"Are you sure?" he asked.

"Yes, I'm sure," she said and briefly explained her situation.

"Slow down, but don't stop. I'm coming. I'll try to catch up with you before you go too much farther. Whatever you do, don't stop for the guy," Hy said.

"I won't," she promised.

"Okay, I'm going to hang up so I can drive fast. I'm coming, Kimberlee. I won't let anyone hurt you."

She did as he'd told her to and slowed down to fifty. She didn't dare go slower than that. The blue car was still behind her, and it was gradually getting closer. Suddenly, she got a look at the driver in her rearview mirror: a young guy with brown hair growing over his ears. *Kal Graves!*

Panicked, she shoved the gas pedal to the floor. It took her a moment to realize that if she did that, Hy would never be able to catch up. So she forced herself to slow down again. Suddenly a loud bang sounded from beneath the front of her car. It began to shake terribly and pull to the right. She'd blown a tire. Oh how she wished she'd replaced her badly worn tires like she'd been thinking of doing.

She had to keep going, even if she was driving on the rim. If she didn't stop, the guy in the blue car wouldn't either. Soon she was down to twenty miles per hour and the sounds coming from beneath her car were terrible. It was all she could do to keep steering. The car pulled hard to the right. She was concentrating so hard on keeping control of the car that she didn't notice the blue car begin to pass her.

When she noticed it, it was right beside her, and the driver was pointing to the front of her car and signaling her to pull over. She ignored him, and then to her horror, he pulled in front of her and slowed down. She tried to go around him, but he simply pulled that way, slowing more, until finally, he had forced her to stop.

She was shaking with fear as he got out of his car and approached hers. The guy—definitely Kal Graves—had a wicked grin on his face. She thought she was going to pass out. When he reached her window, he signaled for her to roll it down. She was not about to do that, and when that message became clear to him, the grin left his face, and in its place was a look of fierce anger like she had never seen.

He reached behind his back, and a second later, she was looking at the barrel of a large handgun. She screamed.

"Roll down your window," he shouted.

She did not. Surely someone would stop to help her. He shook the gun at her, and then there was a loud blast as he fired. The glass flew all over her and the interior of her car.

He reached through the window and calmly unlocked the door. "I just wanted to talk to you, but you have made it hard. You are coming with me now," he said, and Kimberlee passed out, slumping onto her steering wheel.

***

Deputy Hy Jones was quickly approaching a pair of cars that had pulled off to the side of the road. His siren was blaring, and his lights were flashing. He sped around a car that was slowing down in response to his lights.

He could see someone pulling a girl out of the rear parked car by her hair. Hy was approaching so fast that he was unable to come to a complete stop until he was right alongside the cars.

He recognized both Kimberlee and her car just as the young man dropped her head, whirled around, and fired a gun. The bullet whizzed by Hy's head as glass shattered. A second bullet flew as he exited his patrol car on the driver's side. He felt a hard tug in his right shoulder but gave it no more than a passing thought. His own gun was in his left hand, his dominant hand. He dropped to the ground and peered under the car as another bullet flew by him.

Cars were stopping all around him.

Suddenly, the shooter sprang to his feet, ran for the blue car, and jumped in. By the time Hy was able to get to his feet and fire a round, the car was already moving. He'd missed it completely.

He didn't try again, for he was more concerned about the girl lying on the pavement between his patrol vehicle and her car. She was bleeding from a number of cuts to her face and arms, but when he knelt beside her, he could see her chest moving up and down. She was alive and breathing!

A number of people swarmed to give assistance. Someone approached him and shouted that he was shot and bleeding badly. Indeed, with a great rush, the pain hit him suddenly. He felt himself passing out, and as his service revolver dropped from his hand, he mumbled, "Make sure she's okay."

***

Kal sped away. If that cop hadn't come along when he did, Kal would have gotten the girl in his car and left with her. He cursed, then a short while later, he slowed down as cop cars passed him going east, their lights flashing. No one paid any attention to him. So at the Richfield exit, he pulled off the freeway and parked behind an Arby's fast-food restaurant.

For a moment, he simply sat and caught his breath. He cursed himself for not finishing off the waitress before he left. She might remember him, which meant cops would be after him. But for now, he felt safe enough to saunter around to the front door of Arby's and enter.

He ordered and then took a seat in a booth next to a bunch of girls who were giggling and carrying on. He was trying to ignore them, but then their conversation caught his interest.

"For reals. I saw the old guy that Kay Dell is working with on the farm a few miles from Monroe. The old guy's name is Alfred Briggs."

"Come on, Nova, you didn't," another girl, Susie Leacham said. "Anyway, why do you care? She can do what she wants."

"She's so stuck up—thinks she's better than me. It makes me mad. And yes, Susie, I did. I followed Kay Dell, and it took me right to the old guy's place."

"Really? What did she do?" Susie asked, clearly bored of the subject.

"You won't believe this, but there was another guy there. I didn't get a good look at him, but he seemed young, tall, and really well built. I knew she was up to something she wasn't telling us about, and she definitely never told us about this guy."

"What did he look like?" Susie asked, her interest picking up again. Kay Dell never talked much about boys, so it surprised her.

"He was cute, that's for sure. His hair is blond, I think, but I'm not sure because he had a hat on."

"We gotta go out there and meet him. Do you have any idea who he is? Could he be the old guy's grandson?"

Kal was elated. Could it possibly be Sparky who they were talking about? He continued to listen, and he clenched his fist in delight when one of the other girls told the one called Susie that the guy couldn't be a grandson because Mr. Briggs never had children. That clinched it. All he had to do now was find out where that farm was, then he'd take care of Sparky once and for all.

This was his chance to accomplish what he had to do to protect himself. Kal watched the girls for a moment. He found them looking his way and smiling. He knew what he had to do next, so he got up, carried his meal over, and took a vacant chair at the girls' table. "Hey, ladies, mind if I join you?" he asked, trying to sound seductive.

"Sure," Nova, the one he needed to get close to, said. "Where you from?"

"Colorado," he lied. "I'm looking for my brother."

"What's his name?" Susie asked, just curious but not really caring.

"Sparky," was all Kal said in response.

"Oh. Do you think he's around here somewhere?" Nova asked, batting her eyes at him from across the table.

"I think so, but I'm not sure. He's blond, a little over six feet tall. He's well built."

The girls glanced at each other, clearly thinking of the guy they'd just been discussing. Finally, Nova said, "There is a guy living outside of Monroe, where we all live. He's working on a farm. But I don't know his name."

"Probably not him," Kal said, "but just in case, I'd like to know how to get to the farm you mentioned." He gave a short chuckle. "I can't see Sparky working on a farm. That's not his thing."

"Why isn't he still at home with your family?" Nova inquired.

"It's a long story, but mostly it's because he and our dad had a really bad disagreement, and Sparky was so upset, he left home. Mom got a letter from him, and it was posted in someplace called Richfield, Utah, so they sent me to see if I could find him and talk him into coming home."

"I hope you can find him," Susie said, and the other girls murmured their agreement. "By the way, what's your name?"

"I'm Johnny," he said, using his little brother's name, the first name that came to mind. He hadn't anticipated having to give anyone his name.

"Well, Johnny, I know where he's working," Nova said.

"Really? That's great. Would you mind showing me?"

"Sure, I could do that, but what's in it for me?" she asked, batting her eyelashes. The other girls giggled.

"Well, let's see," Kal said as he leaned back and smiled his best seductive smile. "I'll bet you and I could work something out. Maybe I could even spend a little time with you before I see if that's my brother out there. I promise it would be fun."

"So you plan to surprise me?" Nova asked, grinning from ear to ear.

"Something like that," Kal said. "My car's in the parking lot. Maybe, if you don't mind, you could ride with me when we all finish eating, and you could show me where he is. Then we could go do something together for a while a little later this evening."

"Sure, that would be great," Nova said as she winked at the other girls. "I'd like that."

"I bet you would," Susie said, a hint of disgust tinged with jealousy in her voice.

"Sorry, but I'm the only one who knows where the stranger lives."

"Sure you're sorry," Susie said, but she was smiling now. "Hey, Johnny, I have an idea. Maybe when you find Sparky, you could let me meet him."

"It's a deal," Kal said, and he began to eat. He couldn't believe his luck. He and this Nova girl would have a good time, but Susie would never get to meet Sparky, because Sparky was going to die. He just hoped that the guy at the farm was, in fact, his brother, because Kal needed to finish this and then do whatever he had to do to keep the cops from finding him.

**

Amberly Powell, the first of Lys's friends, showed up while Brad was still sitting hopefully beside her bed. He visited with Amberly for a little while. She seemed like a really nice person. He asked her if she was going to be staying very long with Lys, and she told him she was planning to stay as long as it took for her friend to come out of the coma.

"In that case," Brad said, "I think I need to get back to looking for the young man Lys and I were hoping to find. However, I have a huge favor to ask of you."

Amberly agreed.

"When she wakes up, will you tell her that I'm still looking for Sparky? And if she can, I would like her to tell you where Sparky is, if she knows, and who her client is. I just hope her memory is okay. From my experience, people who have suffered brain trauma like Lys has may lose their short-term memory. I sure hope she can remember. A young man's life depends on it."

Amberly asked if he could tell her anything more about the case, so he gave her a brief sketch.

"Now remember," Brad continued, "if she can give you any information, call me right away. It is very, very important that you do. And one other thing, let Lys know that I'll be back as soon as I can."

Within a few minutes, he was on the road, heading back to I-70. He planned to go west once he reached it, but what he would do after that, he was not at all sure. Perhaps he could simply begin to inquire at every stop about Kal, Sparky, and Belina.

He had not gone more than a few miles west on the interstate before he received a call from Sergeant Abel Bone.

"Snepper's truck has been located. It was abandoned at a Denny's restaurant just off the freeway in a place called Salina. I've looked at a map. You're headed the right way."

Brad sped up. "I'll get there as soon as I can," he said urgently. "This may be just the break I need."

CHAPTER TWENTY-TWO

"DO YOU WANT TO STOP here and go talk to your brother?" Nova asked after taking Johnny down the lane toward the farm where she thought the brother he called *Sparky* might be living.

"No, let's go back to town. It's getting dark now, and I promised you a good time, and I always do what I promise," Johnny said with a lecherous grin.

"Okay, I'd like that," Nova said, returning the grin. She had originally made the devious decision to find a way to meet the boy that worked on the old man's farm, if for no other reason than to get one over on Kay Dell. But now that she'd met the guy who was probably his brother, she was going to take every advantage of his promises. He was cute, and she shivered with delight at the prospect of spending some really fun time with him.

Johnny turned the car around in the lane just a short distance from the yard and drove back to Monroe. Nova had slid close to him, and he put an arm around her, pulling her even closer. He'd told her he had plans. *Big plans.* He explained that he was not going to reveal them to her until he was ready to carry them out, and that would not be until well after dark.

She was so excited when he told her that. She reached up and kissed him on the cheek. He chuckled. "You and I are going to have fun tonight," he said. "But I do have a favor to ask of you. My brother knows this car. I want to make our meeting special, which means I want to surprise him. So I don't want him to see me or the car if he happens to come into town this evening."

Nova snuggled closer. "What's the favor?"

"I need to borrow a car from someone. And I want to hide this one until after he and I have got together," he said.

Nova thought about that for a moment. "We have a big garage. You can park it in there. And then you can take my car, as long as I have it back by tomorrow sometime."

"You are too sweet," Johnny said. "You and I will have a great time tonight, and we'll use your car while mine is in your family's garage."

A few minutes later, they pulled up in front of Nova's parents' large house. "Why don't you wait here while I go tell my mom what we're going to do?"

"She won't try to stop you from letting me park in the garage, will she?" Johnny asked.

"Of course not, Johnny. My parents are great. They let me do whatever I want," she responded. "In fact, you don't need to wait here, if you don't want to. You can come in and meet Mom."

"No, that's okay, babe," he said sweetly.

"All right," she said as she savored the way this cute guy called her *babe*.

As expected, her mother was fine with whatever Nova wanted. So she backed her red Corvette out of the garage, and Johnny pulled his in where it had been. She dangled the keys out to him.

"This is a cool car, babe. Are you sure you want to let me take it?"

"Of course I am, you silly boy. My parents gave it to me when I turned sixteen a few months ago," she said as she gazed at his handsome face. She was starstruck.

"My brother will be so surprised. He'll definitely want to go home when he sees me in such a sweet car," Johnny said. "Of course, he'll be disappointed when he finds out that all I have is that old blue clunker of a Monte Carlo. But by then, he'll have realized that he should never have left home, and he'll be glad to return in my old car."

"You are such a great brother," Nova said. "I sure hope that really is Sparky who is living out there at that old man's farm."

"I hope so too," Johnny said. "Hey, I need to go back into . . . what's the name of the town where we met?"

"Richfield," she said.

"Yeah, Richfield," he said. "Anyway, I need to go there and buy a couple of things for my brother. I'll take them to him when I go to meet him tomorrow in your pretty red car."

"You aren't going until tomorrow?" she asked.

"That's right," he said, as he reached out and pulled her to him. To her delight, Johnny kissed her long and hard. "There'll be more of that tonight. I feel like fortune led me to you. I've never met anyone as pretty and sweet as you are."

As he drove off in her car, promising to return later, she watched him go. She shivered with pleasure. Then she thought about Kay Dell, and she laughed.

Nova wouldn't have to try to steal Kay Dell's friend away like she'd planned to. She was certain that Johnny would take him back to wherever they were from. And then, she was equally sure, Johnny would come back to her. She couldn't believe how lucky she was. She was getting one over on Kay Dell while getting a great guy all for herself.

***

Brad pulled into the parking lot at the Salina Denny's at dusk. As he'd expected, Officer Snepper's Toyota pickup was gone. The first thing he did was enter the café and ask the people working there what they knew about the guy who drove the Toyota there. All he got were blank stares and shrugged shoulders. Apparently, nobody knew anything.

He was hungry, so he sat at a table and ordered some dinner. While he was waiting for his food to arrive, he called the Sevier County Sheriff's Department. He was told that the officer who had responded to the call on the pickup was in the hospital, that he'd been shot while trying to rescue a waitress from Denny's who was on her way home. When Brad explained that he was almost certain he knew who the shooter was, he was told that he would be allowed to speak with Deputy Jones at the hospital.

When the waitress brought his dinner, he was anxious to head to Richfield to the hospital where both the deputy and the waitress had been taken. Kal was totally out of control. He knew what Kal would do if Brad didn't get to Sparky first. He just hoped Kal hadn't yet been able to pinpoint Sparky's location.

When the waitress, a young lady in her mid-twenties, put his food before him, he asked her about Kimberlee Owings. The girl, whose name tag identified her as Keri, began to cry. "She got shot at today and so did Deputy Jones," she said through her tears. "That's all any of us know. We have no idea how bad she's hurt or him either."

"Did Kimberlee say anything to you or anyone else here about a young fellow by the name of Sparky?" he asked.

"Not to me, and no one else has mentioned it. Is that someone she knows?" Keri asked as she wiped away her tears.

"I don't know. Listen, I'm in a bit of a hurry now. I need to get to the hospital in Richfield as soon as I can. Could you get me a box, and I'll take this food with me?"

"Sure," she said. "Here, let me take it back to the kitchen, and I'll get it boxed for you." She returned a couple minutes later, handed him the box, and gave him some plastic utensils. He handed her a twenty-dollar bill.

"Keep whatever is over the cost of my meal as your tip, Keri. Thanks so much for your help."

It was awkward, but he was able to shovel his food down as he drove rapidly on the freeway to Richfield. By the time he took the exit his GPS told him to take, he was finished. At the hospital, he leaped from his car and ran inside. He found an officer outside the door to Deputy Jones's room. He introduced himself and was told that he was expected and to go right in.

Deputy Jones was awake but clearly in pain when Brad entered his room. "Deputy Jones, my name is Brad Hagen. I'm a private investigator from Kansas. I've been trying to locate the man who shot you," he said. "I need all the help from you that I can get."

"How do you know who shot me?" Hy asked. "Was it that guy everyone is looking for? Kal Graves?"

"Yes. I've been after him for some time. I'm working with an officer from Goodland, Kansas, over the disappearance of a young man, a teenage boy actually, from Goodland," Brad said. "His name is Sparky Graves."

"Yeah, I've heard the story. Kal killed his mother." Hy's eyes lit up anxiously.

"You're right. Sparky will surely be murdered if Kal finds him. I believe Sparky is somewhere close by," Brad told him.

Jones agreed and explained that he and another officer had been looking for Kal when Kimberlee called for help, saying she was being followed and that she was sure it was Kal. The deputy went on to explain everything he knew.

Brad, in turn, gave the officer a brief account of what had happened. "So I need you to tell me anything you can remember about him. And also, the girl he injured. I need to know about her, and I will also need to talk to her if she is able. I understand she is also here in this hospital."

Deputy Jones described the young guy who had shot him. "I'm pretty sure it was Kal Graves," he said again.

Brad had no doubt. "What was the shooter driving?"

"It was blue, but I'm honestly not sure of the make. It wasn't new. I know that," Hy responded. "The shooting started, and I didn't have time to worry about what he was driving."

"That's understandable," Brad said. "What about other people? There must have been witnesses."

"Other officers, of course, handled the investigation. They told me a little while ago that everyone there was so focused on the shooting that no one could recall anything more about the car than what I've told you."

"Okay, so we only know it was blue and not very new," Brad summed up. He talked with the officer a moment longer and then went to the room of the injured waitress, Kimberlee Owings. As soon as Brad saw Kimberlee, he knew she was not as seriously injured as the deputy. Her face had been cut in a lot of places, and she had hit the pavement very hard when Kal had pulled her from the car. She was, with effort, able to speak. She recounted for Brad what she knew, starting with her having been approached by the private detective, Fredrick Belina.

"Tell me, Kimberlee, if you can, everything you told Detective Belina," he said.

She then explained how she saw a young fellow over two weeks ago who fit the description of Sparky Graves. He had been getting in an old pickup driven by an elderly man not far from the westbound I-70 on-ramp. "I told him that, but that's all I really knew. He seemed to think it was probably Sparky," she said. "And I think the old man was a farmer, so he had to have been from around here somewhere."

"I assume this is a largely agricultural area," Brad said, and she agreed. He could see that she was tiring but he pushed on. "No one seems to be sure what the guy that shot at you was driving."

"I'm not good with car makes," Kimberlee said unhelpfully. "I know it was blue and a bit older."

"What about the truck the old man was driving? Can you tell me anything about it?" Brad asked.

"It was old, and I mean *really* old," she said, and for the first time since he had entered her room, she managed a thin smile. "I don't know what color it was. It could have been blue or gray or green. I don't know."

"I take it you didn't get the make?" he asked.

Kimberlee suddenly grimaced with pain. "That guy banged my head really badly when he dragged me from the car."

Brad patted one hand. "Kimberlee, thanks for your help. I'm sorry this happened to you."

She nodded, and a tear rolled down one cheek. His heart went out to her. Kimberlee was another innocent victim of Kal's viciousness. She was also a lucky one. She owed Deputy Jones for saving her.

When Brad left the hospital, he wasn't sure what to do. The only thing he was sure of after speaking with Deputy Jones and Kimberlee was that Sparky had gone west with an elderly farmer in a very old pickup and that Kal had also gone west driving a blue older-model car after shooting the deputy. That was not a lot to go on. However, he was convinced that the farmer was most likely from this area. Whether Sparky stayed with him or went somewhere else was anybody's guess at this point. But Lys knew. If only she could tell him . . .

Brad had just climbed into his vehicle when he got another call. It was the local dispatcher telling him that he needed to go back in the hospital at once, that Deputy Hy Jones needed to talk to him.

He hurried back inside and found the deputy on the phone. Despite the obvious pain that the young officer was in, he clearly had something to say. "What's up, Deputy?" Brad asked.

"The sheriff, my boss, called to tell me that there is a dead body, a man, in a remote area south of the Salina exit off I-70. The couple who found him described him when they called 911. The description matches the one Kimberlee gave me of the PI she talked to."

"That would be Fredrick Belina," Brad said. "Do they have officers at the scene yet?"

"No, but someone is on the way now. The sheriff called me to see if the description meant anything to me. I wish I could get out of here and go," Hy said.

"Tell me where to go and I will head that way now," Brad told him.

"I thought you'd want to. If it is that other PI, then the car Kal was driving was probably that guy's car."

"I'll get someone looking into what Belina drives as I'm driving out to where the dead man was found. Tell me where to go," Brad said, anxious to be on his way.

A couple of minutes later, he was back in his car. As soon as he was on his way, he called Sergeant Abel Bone. "Any luck?" Bone asked as soon as he answered.

"Not a lot," Brad said, "but it looks like there may be another victim of Kal Graves's ruthlessness." Then he said, "Kal could be driving Belina's car. I was wondering if you might be able to find out what he drives and then let me know. Kal was driving a blue car, not very new. That's all the witnesses here can tell me."

"I'll get right on it," Abel promised.

By the time Brad arrived at the scene of the murder it was quite dark, and there were a couple of sheriff vehicles there. He bounded from his black sedan. The deputies had already been told he was coming, so he had no trouble getting to see the body. As Hy had told him, the body fit the description given by Kimberlee. As with Officer Snepper when Kal had left him for dead in Colorado, all of the identification had been taken. But Brad was pretty sure it was Belina.

He told the deputies there that he couldn't stay, that he needed to get back on the search for the killer, who was almost certainly Kal Graves. He was about halfway back to I-70, driving way too fast, when Abel called him back. "Belina is not answering his cell phone, which we expected of course, if the dead man is him."

"It's almost certainly him," Brad told him. "But Kal stripped him of his ID."

"Okay, so here's what I've learned about his car. It's a blue 2007 Chevy Monte Carlo," Abel said and then gave Brad the Kansas license plate number. "I'll get it out to officers west of here."

"I'll call the Sheriff here in Sevier County, Utah, and have them get it broadcast locally. Maybe we'll get lucky now," Brad said.

"So do you think Sparky is somewhere near where you are now?" Abel asked.

"I do," Brad agreed. "But all I have to go on is that the farmer is probably from the area, and it's a pretty big place, lots of farms. I've got to find that one farmer. If only Lys would wake up and could tell me who her client is."

"Are you thinking her client might be that old farmer?" Abel asked.

"That's exactly what I'm thinking," Brad said. "Hey, I have another call coming in. I'd better take it. I'll get back to you."

Brad answered the call.

"Detective Hagen, this is Nurse Tracy Anderson. Lys Grist woke up a few minutes ago."

CHAPTER TWENTY-THREE

"Can she speak?" Brad asked urgently.

"A little. She's not very easy to understand," Tracy explained. "But she keeps saying something like *rigs*. Or there could be a *b* on it, so . . . *briggs*? Could be a name, I suppose. She seems quite urgent about it. She also said something about some place, some location, maybe a town. All I can tell is that it starts with an m, I think. Her speaking is very slurred."

"Great. Tell Lys I'll follow up on it, and as soon as I can, I'll get back there to see her," he said as he found himself full of emotion and gratitude. He was also filled with a sense of extreme urgency. He feared that Sparky's life was hanging in the balance and that he had to act quickly.

The first thing Brad did, even as he drove back toward the freeway from the scene of Detective Belina's murder, was to call the sheriff's office in Richfield. He asked if there was a town nearby that started with an *m*. They had an answer for him immediately: Monroe.

He entered Monroe into his GPS and sped in that direction, worried that it was so dark. If Kal had discovered Sparky's location, surely he would strike in darkness.

Brad prayed as he drove. Deep down, he knew that he needed help and so did Sparky. He did believe in God, and that was whose help he desperately sought.

He kept thinking about the word Tracy said Lys was trying to say. *Rigs* or something like that with a *b*. He consulted Siri about any names like that in the area and was rewarded with the name *Alfred Briggs*. Siri even gave him a phone number. Encouraged, Brad called that number, but there was no answer. He searched for an address, and once he found one, he headed there immediately. It was his best bet.

After driving for a few more miles, he called the hospital in Moab. He was in luck. Tracy Anderson was still on duty. He wondered if she was ever off duty. In response, she explained that another nurse had called in sick, and she was pulling a double shift. Still, she seemed happy about it, as she had taken such an interest in Lys.

"Tracy, how is Lys doing?" he asked.

"About the same," she responded. "But I'm pretty sure she is saying *Briggs*. She's said it several times."

"Good. Can you ask her a question for me?" he asked.

"I can do that. She's sleeping at the moment, but I suspect she'll be waking up again before long. That seems to be the pattern she's developed."

"This is very, very important. I need to know if her client's name is Alfred Briggs. Is there any chance you can wake her and ask that question?"

"I'll try. Let me call you back."

So he waited, drove rapidly, and finally got a call back from Tracy.

"Any luck?" he asked her.

"Yes. She still isn't able to speak well, but when I asked her about Alfred Briggs, she squeezed my hand and her eyes lit up. So then I asked her if Sparky was with Mr. Briggs, and I got the same response. I hope that helps."

"More than you can possibly imagine," he responded. "Thank you. Let her know if you can that I'm acting on what she's told you. And call again if you learn more."

Just as he was approaching the first Richfield exit, he got another call. It was Deputy Hy Jones, who told him that the car belonging to their murder victim had been located in the town of Monroe.

"Did they release you from the hospital? Are you back on duty and working?" Brad asked in surprise. "You can't be doing that with a bullet wound like you have."

"Oh no. I am still in the hospital, but the sheriff here in Richfield is shorthanded, so with his permission, I'm helping any way I can from here in the hospital," Jones responded. "I can use my phone, so that's what I'm doing. I was asked to call you."

"Okay, so where is Detective Belina's car?" Brad asked.

"It's in a garage belonging to a family by the name of Heylep in Monroe. Further," Hy said, "the daughter, age sixteen, left earlier with a young man who fits the description of Kal Graves. Her name is Nova."

"What are they driving?" Brad asked as he pressed harder on the gas pedal of his black sedan.

"A brand-new red Corvette that her parents gave her for her birthday when she turned sixteen."

"Do the Heyleps understand that Nova is in the company of a stone-cold killer?" Brad asked.

"Apparently they had no idea when they let her go with him, but they know now. A deputy told them that just moments ago."

"What was their reaction?" Brad asked.

"Sheer panic," Hy responded. "They've been calling her cell phone for the past few minutes and are getting no answer."

Sheer panic is the right reaction, Brad thought. "That girl's life is in danger," he told Deputy Jones. "She needs to be located immediately."

"We know that," Hy agreed. "We're already starting an all-out search for her and her car."

"I'll be watching as well, but right now, my first priority is to get to Alfred Briggs's farm outside of Monroe. I've got to get there before Kal does. Keep me informed of any further developments," Brad said. "And I'll do the same for you."

***

Kal grinned with self-satisfaction as he worked his way through the fields beyond the house where he was sure Sparky was hiding out. It had taken a while to get here, and it was very late, and he knew he still had a bit of a walk ahead of him. He'd hidden the car he'd stolen after disposing of the red Corvette and the girl who owned it. He'd hated to part with such a nice car, but it had to be. He had decided not to drive right into the farmyard. If he was going to surprise the two of them and give them no time to react, he couldn't show any sign of his arrival. At this point, he wasn't taking any chances that might spoil his dream of success. He'd already taken too many, he admitted to himself. He intended to do what he came for and get away clean after he was finished.

There was still a niggling doubt about whether the kid was actually Sparky. But at this point, he was committed. He had to proceed as if he were, in fact, Sparky. Whoever it was, his fate was sealed. And if he wasn't Sparky, Kal would lay low for a bit and then start looking for him again. His little brother had to be silenced.

He had plenty of time to think as he made his way slowly in the darkness toward the old farmhouse. His mind drifted to his younger siblings. Surely ones so young couldn't survive out in the world on their own. However, on the off chance that they did get found and returned to his father, he would have to take care of them too. They had seen too much, and at this point, he feared even his father may begin to believe them, but that was for another day. Right now, Sparky was his problem.

***

Despite the lateness of the hour, word spread fast throughout the community about the disappearance of Nova Heylep. Susie Leacham, a close friend of Nova's, called Kay Dell. She was crying and could hardly talk. Kay Dell tried to calm her down by saying, "Hey, Susie, whatever it is, if you need my help for some reason, please talk slowly so I can understand you. I can't understand what you're saying."

It took a minute, but Susie finally got control of herself and said, "It's Nova. She's missing."

"Missing?" Kay Dell asked. "What do you mean she's missing? Didn't some of you guys go to Richfield this afternoon? And didn't she go with you? Did she take her car?"

"Yes, she did go with us, but she left her car home. We were in my Mom's van," Susie said as she again began to babble.

"So did she come back here with you?" Kay Dell asked.

"No . . ." More sobs, then, "She left with some boy we met at Arby's," Susie said. "He was a cute guy and seemed really nice. And you know Nova. She flirts with any cute boy she sees."

Slowly, Kay Dell managed to drag the entire story out of Susie, from Nova leaving with the guy in a blue car and then letting him put that car in her garage to leaving with him in her Corvette a couple of hours later. When Mrs. Heylep had heard on the news that a blue car was being hunted in connection to an attempted abduction of a waitress from the Denny's in Salina and the shooting of a deputy sheriff, she'd panicked. She'd tried to call Nova, but Nova didn't answer her phone. Then she'd called the cops and told them about the blue car that had been left in their garage. "That's why everyone is so worried," Susie concluded. "Nova always answers her phone."

For Nova to go off like that with some guy late at night she'd never met didn't surprise Kay Dell, but it did worry her when she heard about the shooting on the freeway.

"You don't seem all that worried, Kay Dell. We thought you'd want to help. We've got to find her and get her to leave that guy."

"Wait, Susie, what else have you heard? Mom and I and my siblings just got back from Richfield an hour or so ago ourselves. We didn't have the radio on in the car, and we haven't listened to the news on the TV either. But yes, I'm terribly worried."

"Okay, so it seems that the guy we met at the Arby's is wanted for murder. They're saying that he not only shot the cop and injured the waitress, but he is wanted for killing his mother, almost killing another cop, one in Colorado, and for killing a private detective earlier today!" Susie revealed dramatically as Kay Dell's mother stepped beside her, a worried expression on her face. "And now they think he's looking for his brother from Kansas. And Nova . . . poor Nova, she's with this guy. I hope he hasn't hurt her too."

Or worse, Kay Dell thought as she was suddenly sick to her stomach. *Kal is here in Monroe! He's after Sparky.* Brother Briggs was also in danger. She had to do something. "I've gotta go, Susie," she said urgently.

"Aren't you going to help us?" Susie demanded.

"Yes, but in my own way," she said and ended the call.

"Kay Dell, what in the world is going on?" her mother asked her. "You look like you've just had the scare of a lifetime."

"Mom, Sparky's brother is here. He's in Monroe. He killed a guy today and nearly killed some other people," she cried. "He's probably killed Nova Heylep, and now I'm sure he's after Sparky."

"Kay Dell, slow down. What exactly has happened?"

"Mom, I need to go to the farmhouse and warn Sparky and Alfred that his brother is here in Monroe," she said. "They both need to get away from there and hide until the cops catch him."

Her mother's face turned to the color of putty. She sank back into a chair. She was suddenly shaking. "You know that your father isn't here. You can't go out there alone, Kay Dell. It would be too dangerous. And I can't leave the little ones."

"Mom, Alfred Briggs and Sparky could be killed!" she said with desperate intensity. "I need to warn them."

"Call them on the phone," her mother suggested.

Kay Dell felt foolish. Of course she should call them. She took a deep breath and retrieved her cell phone from the table where she'd dropped it after talking to Susie. Five minutes later, she spoke to her mom again. "They aren't answering. Now I'm really scared for them. We've got to go out there. Kal may have already been there, but if not, I've got to warn them."

Her mother started to shake her head. "I guess you're right, but first we've got to call the sheriff's office. If they can get there first, then we won't go."

After hanging up, Kay Dell's mother said, "A lot of officers are looking for Kal, and they will make sure someone checks out the farm as soon as they can, but they said it will be quite a while. So I guess if anyone is going to warn them, it will have to be us, but that scares me. Let's go now, but I'm taking one of your father's pistols. We'll see if the neighbors will watch the boys while we do that. But first, we'll pray together, and when we get out there, we'll be really careful. We can't take any chances. I just wish the cops were closer."

With that, they hurried to contact their neighbors and jumped in the car as soon as they could.

"Mom, have you ever even shot that gun before?" Kate asked as her mother laid the pistol on the seat between them a few minutes later. "Is it even loaded?"

"Yes, Kay Dell, I have shot it quite a few times, but mostly before you were born. Your father and I used to go out and shoot quite often," she said. "And it is loaded. But don't get me wrong; I don't intend to use it unless it becomes absolutely necessary. I'm sure that won't be the case or we wouldn't even be going. Now you watch for Nova's red car. I'll pay attention to my driving."

Kay Dell would never admit it to her mother, but she was scared. Nothing had ever scared her so badly in her life. Ironically, she was not afraid for herself but for two guys she scarcely knew but had come to like and respect a great deal.

She kept trying to call, but there were still no answers on Alfred Briggs's house phone or Sparky's cell phone. She knew it was working now, or at least it had been, because he'd called and thanked her for the tip on using rice to dry it out. She finally quit trying the phones and watched for Nova's red Corvette.

***

Sparky couldn't believe he'd lost his cell phone. After having nearly drowned it and then saved it with rice, he thought that was that. But not so. It wasn't until he got back to the house that he realized it wasn't in his pocket. He and Alfred had been all over the farm on the four-wheelers and had done a variety of work. Not once did he hear it ring, but that was to be expected, because the only people who had his number were Lys Grist, Alfred, and Kay Dell's family.

Sparky and Alfred had been looking for it with flashlights for the past two hours. They had painstakingly retraced the route they had taken, and they'd searched carefully at every spot they remembered having stopped and worked. Searching with flashlights was slow and tedious work and far from effective with all the tall grass and other growth where they had been. And to make it even worse, they had traipsed through a couple of fields, cutting out some thistles late that afternoon. It could have fallen anywhere. Even worse, one of the animals might have stepped on it.

Finally, the two of them walked slowly back to their four-wheelers. "I'm sorry, Alfred," Sparky said. "I should have been more careful. They're expensive. I've got to find it."

"Not tonight, my boy. It's very late. We'd better get back to the house. I don't know about you, but I'm hungry as a horse. We missed suppertime, you know," Alfred said as he shut the gate they'd just walked through.

"I don't know how hungry a horse gets, but I could use some food too," Sparky said as he considered the old farmer fondly. He'd never known anyone so kind in his life. "Alfred, after we get the chores done in the morning, I'll look for it again, if that's okay."

"That's fine, Sparky. Let's get on these old four-wheelers and go home now."

***

Kal saw lights bouncing along a bumpy road in the distance. He was tired, so he leaned against a fence post and watched as the lights moved in the direction of the house where he suspected Sparky was hiding out. They went out of sight, and then a minute later, he saw them again. He didn't know how far away from the house he was now, but he was sure he could get there in less than a half hour if he hurried. He rubbed his hands together, pushed away from the post, and climbed the fence.

Kal cursed when he felt a barb from the wire of the fence rip a large hole in his pants. Worse, he felt it tear a gash in his leg as well. Blood ran down his leg. He finally got across the fence only to stumble and fall. One knee hit something hard on the ground, shooting pain all the way up and down his leg. "Sparky, I will get you for this," he said as he pulled himself to his feet.

His anger grew as he found that it was now hard to walk, and he had wanted to hurry. Without a flashlight, it had been tough going so far, but he'd taken his time and done just fine until now. He blamed his bad luck on his brother, and forced himself to limp along. His hatred for Sparky pushed him on, despite the pain. Kal would get him in a little while, and then his revenge would be complete.

CHAPTER TWENTY-FOUR

"There's a car coming up behind us," Elena said to Kay Dell.

Kay Dell looked back. "Mom, it's coming fast." She felt a twist of fear in her stomach. "It could be Kal. Speed up. We can't let him beat us to the farmhouse."

"Kay Dell," Elena said with a trembling voice. "I don't think this was such a good idea. And I can't drive faster or we might wreck. The road's a little rough here."

"Well, at least he can't pass us because this road is narrow," Kay Dell said, trying to feel some satisfaction at the thought but failing miserably. "I'll say a prayer, Mom."

"That's a good idea," her mother agreed.

Never in her life had Kay Dell prayed with such intensity and fervor. After saying *amen*, she felt better.

"Thanks, sweetheart. That was a wonderful prayer."

They could both see that the car behind them had nearly caught up to them, but neither said a word about it. Elena kept driving and Kay Dell kept watching behind them. Finally, she said, "Mom, it's too big for a Corvette. And I'm pretty sure it's either black or dark blue."

Her mother dashed her hopes of someone friendly being in that car when she said, "Kay Dell, we need to keep in mind that Kal might have stolen another car. He might not be in Nova's anymore. We shouldn't have come, but it's too late now."

***

Brad Hagen needed to get past the car in front of him and then drive as fast as he could to the Briggs farm. But the lane was quite narrow and passing could be dangerous.

He flashed his lights impatiently. The other car sped up for a moment but then slowed again. He flashed them again. If it would just pull tight to the right of the road, he could get past. The other car just kept going, so he tried his horn. That seemed to get better results, as the other car slowed and began to pull over. But it was not yet far enough to the side to let him pass, and it suddenly stopped. The interior lights came on, and he saw two women frantically scrambling to exit the car on the passenger side.

Two women. He had no idea what they were doing out on this country lane at this time of night, but they were driving toward trouble if they didn't turn back. His first thought was that they were two teenage girls. Maybe two teenage girls out looking for their friend, Nova Heylep. He had to stop them.

***

Elena and Kay Dell managed to get out of the car, and Elena was able to hold onto the gun as they did. They dove into the long grass and brush on the side of the road, just as they had planned when the car started flashing its lights at them. Kay Dell was terrified, but she led the way, crawling away from the road. She bumped into a fence. Her heart sank.

Then a man's voice, a deep voice, called out, "Girls, stop. I'm on your side. You were driving into a dangerous situation. You need to go home and let me go help Sparky and Alfred."

Elena was now beside Kay Dell. The two clung to each other. The man called out again. "My name is Detective Brad Hagen. I'm trying to get to Sparky before his brother Kal does. Please, come back, move your car over, and I'll go past. I'm armed and know how to handle situations like this."

"You won't hurt us?" Elena called out.

"Of course not. Who are you ladies?"

Elena whispered to Kay Dell. "I think your prayers are being answered. Let's stand up." Then louder, she said, "I have a gun. Don't shoot. We are friends of Mr. Briggs and Sparky. We were going to warn them that Kal is in the area."

Then they stood, and the man moved toward them. "I'd better take it from here, ladies," he said softly when the two of them struggled through brush and grass and stepped onto the road. "Now if you will pull your car over as far as you can, I'll go on by and hopefully get to Sparky and Mr. Briggs before Kal does. Unfortunately, there are no deputies who can get there for a while."

"We knew that. That's why we came," Kay Dell announced firmly. "I'm going with you."

"No, let him go," Elena said. "He's a professional. Your dad will wonder why I ever let you talk me into coming out here."

"I'm their friend," Kay Dell said. "Sparky and Alfred both trust me. I have to know they're okay."

"No time to waste," Brad said urgently.

"Mom, you can go home. I'll ride with the detective."

"If you're going with him, then I'll have to go too," Elena said.

Brad didn't feel like he had time to argue with them. "Pull your car as far off as you can, and then you two get in with me. And bring your gun, ma'am."

A few moments later, the three of them were on their way.

***

Brad couldn't help but admire the spunk of this young lady seated next to him. "How did you come to know Sparky?" he asked her.

"I just started to help him and Alfred on the farm. They tried to make me and my dad think that Sparky wasn't really Sparky. But I figured it out, and finally Sparky admitted it to me," she said. "He trusted me. And I trusted him. And we both trusted Alfred. So we told him, and I don't keep things from my parents, so we told them too. But no one else knew until Alfred hired Lys Grist to prove that Sparky wasn't in Kansas when his mother was killed. Sparky was pretty sure it was Kal who did that."

Brad nodded in the dimness of the car's interior. "He was right. That's all been proven now, but as you probably know, Kal is coming after Sparky. I just pray we aren't too late."

"We're almost there," Kay Dell said.

"All right, I think we'd best walk from here," Brad said as he pulled over and shut his car off. Stay right behind me, and if I say get down, you two do it. You got it?"

They both agreed to that.

"Okay, I'm getting out now. You do the same. Have your gun with you, Mrs. Finch. You do know how to use it, don't you?"

"I do," Elena said firmly.

"Okay, let's get out. And don't worry about lights coming on in the car when we open the doors. I have them set so they won't do that," he said, and he opened the door. A moment later, the three of them started along the road, staying close to one edge and walking single file. Brad had a flashlight in his hand, but he would not use it unless he absolutely had to. He didn't want to alert Kal to their presence if he was somewhere nearby.

**

Sparky the dog growled and scratched at the door. It was a menacing, angry growl. "Sparky, let him out," Alfred said from where he stood looking in the refrigerator.

"Could there be someone out there?" Sparky asked.

"I suppose that's a possibility, but if there is, he'll let us know. He won't go too far." Alfred seemed quite sure about it, so Sparky opened the door, and the canine Sparky bounded out. At the edge of the covered back porch, the dog stopped, and once again, he emitted a deep-throated growl. Sparky shivered involuntarily and closed the door.

"Lock it, Sparky," Alfred said after closing the refrigerator door. "Then go lock the front door as well."

Sparky did as he was asked. When he reentered the kitchen a minute later, he was surprised to see Alfred coming in from the hallway leading to the bedroom, a shotgun in each hand and a couple of boxes of shotgun shells tucked under his upper arm. Sparky felt fear shoot through him.

"What are those for?" he asked.

Alfred smiled, attempting, it appeared, to look unworried. The smile didn't work. It only made Sparky worry more. Then Alfred said, "Sparky, have you ever shot a shotgun?"

"Yeah, a few times," he said.

"Good. This one is a twelve gauge," he said and held it out to Sparky. "Take it. I'll take the sixteen gauge, cause it doesn't kick as much when it's fired."

Alfred placed the gun on the table after Sparky had taken the bigger shotgun. Then he handed a box of twelve-gauge shells to Sparky and said, "Load it. I'll load the other one." With that accomplished, Alfred said, "Okay, let's turn the lights off and just sit here in the dark and listen to what the dog has to say."

A moment later, all the lights were out and the two sat side by side in the kitchen on two hard-backed chairs. "It's probably nothing, Sparky," Alfred said, his voice quite soft now. "It could be a coyote. But we'll just wait here and listen for a while."

The silence was eerie. Sparky shivered again. He kept a tight hold on the shotgun. He prayed he wouldn't have to use it. Sparky the dog growled again, more menacing than before.

"Definitely something out there that dog don't like," Alfred whispered. "But like I said, he's staying close to the house."

Sparky made no response. His heart was hammering away in his chest so hard it felt like it was trying to get out. Alfred seemed very calm, but Sparky knew the old man felt like there was something dangerous out there, dangerous to the two of them, not to the dog. He listened silently.

***

Kay Dell, her mother, and the PI were approaching Alfred Briggs's farmyard on foot. They walked as silently as they could. After a moment, Brad stuck out his arm, and the three of them stopped. They could see the house now, a large shadowy figure in the distance. "No lights on in there," the PI whispered.

"I heard a door open and close a little while ago," Kay Dell said.

"I did too," Brad confirmed.

"Do you think it was someone going into the house or leaving it?" Elena whispered.

"Could have been either," the PI responded. "Let's slowly move a little closer. Stay close to me." A short distance later, he again put out his hand. "Listen."

Kay Dell strained her ears. "Is that Sparky growling?"

"No, it sounds like a dog to me," Brad responded.

"That's what I meant," Kay Dell whispered. "Alfred's dog's name is Sparky."

"Strange coincidence," Brad whispered, and then the three of them lapsed into silence again. He signaled them to move forward but stopped them once more a moment later. He signaled for them to drop to their knees as he did the same.

A moment later, they could hear the growling again. Kay Dell, knowing the layout of the house, was sure that Sparky the dog must be on the back porch. She shivered. "He knows me," she whispered so softly she hoped Brad could hear. "He wouldn't growl at me."

Brad patted her arm in response. And they all listened again.

***

The blood was still running down Kal's leg. The barbs on the fence must have cut him worse than he'd thought at first. He took a chance, ducking to the ground, sticking his gun in a pocket, and then he shined his light on his injured leg. He gasped. It was really bad. His whole pant leg was soaked, and the deep, long wound just kept bleeding. But there was nothing he could do about it now. It made him angrier than ever at Sparky. The injury meant he would need to move a little faster.

He had seen the lights go off in the house a little while ago. That meant the two of them had gone to bed. He hoped they'd be asleep by the time he got to the house and entered it.

After he was finished with Sparky and the old man, he'd find something in the house to bandage his leg. He was pretty sure he could find some pants to change into. Sparky was bigger than him, but the old man might be smaller. Surely there would be something he could wear. Then he'd head back to his latest stolen car. Once Sparky and the old man were no longer alive, he wouldn't need to be so careful about his small flashlight. He'd use it to make his retreat. It would be faster that way, and he wouldn't get hurt on the fence again.

He put his light away, pulled the pistol out, and got to his feet. He moved forward as quickly as he could. Another fence was in his way—one built of logs. At least this fence wouldn't rip his pants and tear into his leg. He started to clamber over it, heading in a straight line toward the dark house.

Then he hesitated. He was sure he heard a dog growl. That could be a problem. He could shoot it easily enough, but then it might alert Sparky and the old man in the house. After he got across this fence, he'd look around for a big stick. He could just club the dog. In fact, he would quite enjoy that.

***

Sherman, Alfred's very large boar hog, was nestled in one corner of his pen. He was really quite comfortable. But like always, he never slept soundly. Something scraping on his fence first alerted him that he had company, then, a small moment later, the smell of fresh blood hit his nostrils. Always hungry, Sherman sniffed the air as he poked his ears forward. For a short time, he just waited, listening and smelling. He was not afraid. Nothing in his life's experience had ever caused him to feel fear. He was curious though, so after a little while, he rose slowly to his feet and stood there a moment longer. Finally, he stepped out of his comfortable bed and took a couple of tentative steps toward the tempting odor.

The people in his life always fed him well. But he was a pig, after all, and pigs were perpetually hungry. No matter how much he was fed, he could always eat more. That was the nature of his species. He waited, sensing both by sound and smell that the blood was getting closer. He opened and closed his massive jaws in anticipation. He rolled his head back and forth. He was armed, although his tusks were simply part of him, a part he could use if he needed to. They were razor sharp, and even though he didn't think much about it, he just knew by nature that he could hurt anything with them if he needed to.

Sherman recognized the less pungent but very distinct odor of a human. It wasn't as sharp as the smell of blood, but he still recognized it. He also knew that smell was not the humans who fed him. That, to his pig brain, meant that whatever was in his pen shouldn't be. So not only was his sense of hunger alerted, but so was his sense of self-preservation. It was attack time. Whatever human was in his pen was about to get a huge surprise.

***

Kal sensed movement a short way in front of him, but he had barely started to lift his gun when he felt like a tank had hit him. He fell backwards and started firing, not knowing for sure what he was firing at or if he was even close to hitting it. The one thought he had before he felt his flesh being torn was that it must surely be a big dog. And since it was, surely his bullets had hit it.

***

Brad Hagen reacted instantly when shots rang out. "Stay here," he ordered Kay Dell and Elena. "Get down and stay there."

Kay Dell's heart hammered. She wanted to go with Brad, but could tell from the command in his voice that he meant what he said. So she and her mother huddled low to the ground and close together in the darkness at the edge of the road.

Brad left in a crouching run. In a moment, he was but a shadow, and then he disappeared. Kay Dell had never been so scared in her life. The fear still wasn't for her, it was for Sparky Graves and Alfred Briggs, her newest friends, and yet in a way, her best friends.

Tears washed down her face. Her mother's arm went around her, and together they sobbed, and they waited. And they prayed.

CHAPTER TWENTY-FIVE

"What in the world is going on?" Alfred asked as he jumped to his feet. "I hope nobody shot Sparky."

Alfred grabbed the flashlight that he'd laid on the table earlier. "Unlock the door," he said. Sparky did as he was asked and then followed him out onto the porch, letting the door swing shut behind them. A terrible scream filled the air. It was followed by more screams and the frantic barking of Sparky the dog. When the old man racked a shell into the chamber of the sixteen-gauge shotgun, Sparky racked one into the twelve gauge. Adrenaline rushed through his body, and yet he had to hurry to keep up with his elderly friend. He couldn't imagine anyone of his age and in his arthritic condition moving so rapidly.

They hurried together toward where the shots had come from. They hadn't gone far when they heard running steps behind them. Panicked, Sparky spun around. A voice he had never heard in his life shouted, "Sparky, Alfred, stay here. I'm with Lys. I'll get Kal." He'd fired the words rapidly and hadn't even slowed down, but Sparky understood them.

When the stranger mentioned Lys, Sparky suddenly felt safe. The same must have been true for Alfred, because he lowered his shotgun, and the two of them watched in amazement as the stranger darted past, running crouched, a pistol held in front of him. The screaming continued for a little longer. Then it ceased. Alfred started to move forward, and almost in a daze, Sparky followed him.

Sparky the dog suddenly appeared in the beam of Alfred's flashlight, his eyes shining like little candles. Then he was jumping around them like he'd just found a long-lost friend and like nothing had happened. Yet Sparky knew that something had happened. He just didn't know what it was.

"Is that you, Sparky and Alfred?" the stranger's voice called as they approached the corrals.

"Yep, sure is," Alfred called back.

"Call 911, will you please?" the stranger asked.

"We don't have our phones," Alfred replied as a flashlight shined a short way ahead of them.

"I can run to the house," Sparky volunteered.

"What happened? Do we need an ambulance?" Alfred asked, wheezing now from his sudden and unusual exertion.

"Yes, and a veterinarian and the local cops," the man said as he walked through a corral gate and right up to them. "I'm Detective Brad Hagen," he said. "And I know who you are."

At that moment, a voice called out loudly, "Sparky, Alfred, are you guys okay?"

"I thought you were told to stay there," Brad said, but the harshness in his voice was offset by a soft chuckle a moment later. "Do either of you have your phone with you?" he asked. "I dropped mine somewhere in the corral, I think."

"I have mine," Kay Dell said as she and her mother ran up to the three men. "Are you all okay? We heard shots. We were scared to death."

"It's okay, Kay Dell," Sparky said.

"Call 911. We need an ambulance and the cops at once," Brad said urgently before they could respond to Sparky. "And I need to run to my car and get a first aid kit."

"I have one in the house," Alfred said. "I'll go get it."

Kay Dell made the call to 911 while Alfred went after the first aid kit.

"What happened?" Kay Dell's mother asked. "Who was shooting?"

Just then Sparky noticed a pistol in Mrs. Finch's hand. It was now hanging at her side, but he was surprised.

"I don't know," Sparky said.

"We also need a veterinarian," Brad said. "Alfred has a badly injured animal, and I suspect that it might be a valuable one."

Sparky's head was spinning. He couldn't believe Kay Dell and her mother were here. And this detective . . . He hadn't finished his thought when Alfred came hurrying back with a large first aid kit. As he handed it to the detective, he asked, "Where is Lys Grist? You said you were with her."

"She's a very close friend of mine and we've been working together," he said, but Sparky couldn't help but notice the tone of sadness that had suddenly come into his voice. "She's been injured. I'll tell you about it later. Right now, I need to administer some first aid. Alfred, you need to call your vet."

"Okay, but what's wrong with Sherman?" Alfred asked, urgency in his voice.

"Your boar?" Kay Dell asked, alarm in her voice as well. "What happened? I need to tell the 911 dispatcher."

"I'm sorry, Alfred," Brad said, talking over his shoulder, "but he's been shot. I think he can be saved though. Sparky, come with me. I'll need you to hold a flashlight."

Alfred started to climb over the log fence. "I've got to get to Sherman," he said urgently.

"Whoa, hold up there," Brad said as he reached out and stopped Alfred at the edge of the boar pen. "Sparky, hurry. The rest of you, stay back."

"Was it Kal?" Sparky asked as he vaulted into the boar pen. "Did he shoot Sherman? Did he get away? We've got to stop him."

Before Brad could answer, Sparky's flashlight shone on a body on the newly cleaned pen floor, not far from the prone, unmoving boar. Sparky leaped forward. "It is Kal!" he said in shock as Brad knelt and opened the first aid kit.

"Shine the light in here, so I can find what I need."

Reality suddenly hit Sparky. "Did the pig . . ." He couldn't finish the sentence.

"Kal's badly hurt. I need to see if I can help him," Brad said as he pulled a large bandage from the kit.

Kal moaned. Sparky leaned down over him. "Kal, it's Sparky. We will help you. Hang in there."

A second flashlight joined Sparky's light. "Let me help," Alfred said.

He shined his light only briefly on his boar before bringing it back to Kal. "I need to get his shirt cut off," Brad said. "Alfred, do you have a knife?"

The old man handed him a large and very sharp pocket knife. Sparky knelt near his brother's head. "Kal, can you hear me?" he asked as Brad began to cut the shirt away.

"I . . . should . . . a . . . killed you," Kal said, his speech ragged and full of hatred. "You . . . ruined my . . . life."

"You killed Mom," Sparky said. "Why did you do that?"

Kal's voice became stronger. "She decided she believed you." He took a ragged breath, then went on. "I couldn't let her make Dad believe you too."

"Why do you hate me?" Sparky asked, his voice choked with emotion.

"You should never have . . ." Kal began to gurgle. He coughed. Sparky waited while Brad did what he could for what Sparky could see were terrible wounds.

"What should I not have done?" Sparky asked.

Kal coughed again and spit blood from his mouth. "Never been my brother. You didn't belong. You ruined my life."

"I'm sorry. I had no control over that," Sparky said.

"You were always causing me trouble. I should have killed you a long time ago," Kal said, his speech ragged. "I hate you."

"I don't hate you," Sparky said. "You're my brother."

"No, we . . . are . . . not . . . brothers. I will . . . get . . . you . . . yet!"

"Kal, we can work this out," Sparky said as tears filled his eyes, and he knelt down next to Kal. He meant what he said. Despite the enmity he'd felt for his brother before, he felt only sadness now.

"Oh sure!" Kal coughed, and there was a gurgling sound in his throat. "I killed Mom." More coughing and gurgling. "Thanks to you . . . I'll go . . . to . . . prison. But I will get you!" The coughing became worse. So did the gurgling. Kal moved one hand. "I'll strangle . . . you."

"Lie still. This man is trying to help you," Sparky said, knowing Kal couldn't hurt him now, even though he clearly wanted to.

He waited, expecting Kal to say something else, but he didn't. Brad touched his neck. Then he stood up and stepped back. "He's dead, Sparky. I'm sorry. There's nothing anyone could have done to save him."

"He's dead?" Sparky asked, a catch in his voice. "But he was talking to me." Sparky couldn't believe how much Kal hated him. It made him sad. He'd never wanted Kal to hate him.

"Yes, he's dead," Brad said firmly. "Now, why don't you and Alfred join the others and all of you go back to the house?"

Sirens could be heard in the distance. Alfred was still in the boar's pen, leaning against the corral fence. "Are you okay?" Sparky asked him with concern.

"I'm winded," he said. "Please help me over the fence and to the house. I need to lie down. I've overdone it tonight."

Sparky was alarmed. He helped his friend over the fence, then took his arm and started toward the house with him. Kay Dell and her mother joined them.

"Stay with Sherman," Alfred said sharply to Sparky. "These girls can help me to the house."

"He's right," Brad said in an abrupt about-face. "Let's see if we can do anything for the boar."

The two of them climbed back over the fence. Sparky tried not to look at the brother he'd never hated but who had hated him more than he'd understood before he finally left home. "Sherman tore Kal to pieces, didn't he?" he said as he and Brad moved toward the injured pig.

"Well, not as much as he might have done if Kal hadn't gotten a lucky shot in that stopped the old boar."

"It's good Alfred and I cleaned this pen," Sparky said. He saw a cell phone on the ground near the fence and picked it up. "There was a foot of muck in here before we did. Here, is this yours?" he asked the detective.

"It sure is. I was afraid it was done for. Thanks, Sparky," he said.

***

The veterinarian had assured Alfred that Sherman would live and soon be as good as new. Now Alfred was asleep, being totally exhausted from his strenuous and mentally trying evening.

After Kal's bloody, lacerated body had been removed, Sparky and Kay Dell shifted their attention to the missing girl, Nova. Brad had already left to search for her. He had found the car that had been stolen, driven to an area near Alfred's farm, and then parked on the edge of a dirt road.

Before leaving to assist the local sheriff's department in the search for Nova, Detective Hagen had taken time to briefly update Sparky on Lys Grist's accident and current condition. Finally, after helping Sparky find something to eat, Kay Dell and her mother had gone home. However, both Kay Dell and Sparky promised to call the other if they learned anything about Nova, regardless of the time of day or night they heard it.

Sparky had not gone to bed but was dozing fitfully in Alfred's favorite chair, waiting for Brad to return. It was four in the morning when Brad rang the doorbell, waking both Sparky the dog and Sparky the boy. Sparky the boy let him in. "Has anyone found Nova or her car?" Sparky asked anxiously.

"Yes, and Nova is alive, though that clearly had not been Kal's intention when he ran her Corvette into Fish Lake near where the car he stole and drove here was taken from," Brad said. "Nova is a very lucky, albeit foolish, girl. The car did not sink all the way, and Nova was able to keep breathing until a deputy and I found the car. She's in the hospital now, and the car has been towed to a garage."

After Brad left to find a hotel room, Sparky woke Kay Dell up by calling her cell phone from Alfred's landline. They spoke for only a short time, but before ending the call, Kay Dell said, "Sparky, I'm coming out to the farm in a few hours to help you. I think Alfred is going to need to rest all day. And I will help you search for your cell phone."

The two teenagers made sure Alfred had a good breakfast a few hours later and left him to rest before they went out and did the morning chores. Kay Dell actually helped milk the cow for the first time. Sparky, although he was not great at it yet, did manage to do okay. Between the two of them, they got a pretty nice pail of milk.

Later, they took both four-wheelers and began a daylight search for the missing cell phone. The one thing that Kay Dell insisted that they do, that Sparky and Alfred had not done, was have a prayer. Sparky wasn't sure how much good that would do, but within less than an hour, Kay Dell spotted the phone, undamaged and ready to use again.

She did not say, "I told you praying would help us," to Sparky, but her smile and the look she gave him as she held it up to show him conveyed that message. And it touched his heart.

Brad showed up shortly after that and reported that Lys Grist was doing much better and that Nova had been released from the hospital. "I spoke with Sergeant Abel Bone a little while ago and updated him on what has happened. I gave him your cell phone number and Alfred's home phone number. I see you found your phone, so you might expect a call in a little while."

"Kay Dell found it," Sparky said even as he thought about the prayer she had offered. "Who will be calling? Sergeant Bone?"

"He may, but he was going to give the number to your father. I also gave the number to the lady who is taking care of Johnny and Courtney. They will also be calling," Brad said.

"I'm glad the kids are going to call. I miss them. My dad, on the other hand . . . I don't think I have anything to say to him," he said.

Kay Dell touched him lightly on the arm. He looked at her, and she said, "No one could blame you for being mad, but if he calls, you might want to give him a chance."

He shook his head. "I'll have to think about that."

She nodded and smiled but said nothing more.

Johnny and Courtney called, and Sparky had a good talk with them. He assured them that Kal would no longer be a threat to them. When asked where Kal was, Sparky simply said, "Kal got killed in an accident." He didn't expound and they didn't ask. Maybe someday they would learn the whole truth, but now was not that time, if that time ever came.

That evening, Kay Dell had gone home again, Brad had headed for Moab to see Lys Grist, and Alfred was sitting in his favorite chair dozing when Sparky's cell phone rang. He recognized his father's cell phone number. He let it ring several times, not sure he was ready to speak with him yet, if ever. But Kay Dell's sweet voice entered his head, urging him to try.

He wasn't sure he could forgive him, but he was able to force himself to answer the call. "Hi, Dad," he said, fighting to keep the bitterness that he felt from his voice.

"Sparky, I'm so sorry," his father said, and then he could not go on. Sparky simply held the phone and waited, listening to his father cry. Finally, his father seemed to get some control back, and Sparky found that he had a small spark of desire to mend his relationship with his father.

"I guess you know about what happened to Kal," Sparky said.

"I do. Sparky, I had no idea he was so evil. All along, I thought it was you. I'm ready for you to come back now so we can start over," Donald said.

"Dad, I'm going to try to put all of this behind me, but it will take time. As for coming home, that's not going to happen. I am both needed and loved where I am now, and I intend to stay," he said.

"No, Sparky, you belong here with me and Courtney and Johnny," his dad said, the emotion in his voice enough to bring tears to Sparky's eyes. But he knew he had to be firm. Alfred needed him. And there was Kay Dell . . .

"Dad, I have a better idea. Why don't you bring the kids here for a visit? I want us to still be a family, but I could never live at home again. The memories there are too bitter. You have no idea what Kal put me through," he said. "Please, promise me that you will come here. I want to see you and to see Johnny and Courtney, but this is my home now. I am not leaving here. Will you come?"

The shoe was on the other foot now. It was up to his father to decide if he still wanted to be Sparky's dad. For a long time, there was only silence on the line. But finally, Donald Graves said, "You have my word, Sparky. As soon as they are back home, we will come visit you. I'm so very, very sorry."

Sparky had not been aware that Alfred was awake until he ended the call and the old farmer said, "Was that your father, Sparky?"

"Yes," he responded.

"Did he ask you to come home?"

"Yes."

"When are you leaving?"

"I'm not. Dad and the kids are going to come visit me here. This is where I belong now. If you will have me, that is," Sparky said.

"Of course I will, Sparky." Tears suddenly streamed down his friend's weathered face. "You are the son I never had. I love you, Sparky."

"And I love you, Alfred. Thanks for saving me."

"From what?" Alfred asked.

"I don't know. We will never know what might have happened to me if you hadn't picked me up along the road that day. One thing is for sure: you saved me, Alfred. And I can never repay you for what you have done for me."

"You already have, my boy," the old farmer, Sparky's friend, responded. "You already have."

CHAPTER TWENTY-SIX

SIX YEARS LATER

IT WAS A SAD DAY in Monroe, Utah. In a few minutes, Alfred Briggs would be buried. Sparky and Kay Dell Graves were walking hand in hand, following the casket to the hole it was to be lowered into.

"Alfred changed our lives, Sparky," Kay Dell said with a sniffle. "If not for him, I wouldn't have you."

"If not for you, I wouldn't be able to dedicate his grave. I love you, Kay Dell. And I thank you for being patient with me while I was struggling about the Church."

"You found it, Sparky. And we found each other." She patted her growing stomach. "And in a few months, there will be three of us," she said with a smile.

Sparky gripped her hand tighter. "We have some struggles ahead of us, Kay Dell. I just hope that farm Alfred gave us will be big enough to support a family. I don't want to live anywhere else."

"Neither do I," Kay Dell assured him. "We'll make it work. We both love the farm and our animals and each other and the Church. Together, we will make it work."

"I'll sure miss Alfred, though," Sparky said with a catch in his voice. "His spot with us on the bench at church will seem mighty empty."

Kay Dell smiled. "This little guy will soon fill it," she said as she brought Sparky's hand to her abdomen. "He'll surely fill it."

ABOUT THE AUTHOR

CLAIR M. POULSON WAS BORN and raised in Duchesne, Utah. His father was a rancher and farmer, his mother, a librarian. Clair has always been an avid reader, having found his love for books as a very young boy.

He has served for more than forty years in the criminal justice system. He spent twenty years in law enforcement, ending his police career with eight years as the Duchesne County Sheriff. For the past twenty-plus years, Clair has worked as a justice court judge for Duchesne County. He is also a veteran of the U.S. Army, where he was a military policeman. In law enforcement, he has been personally involved in the investigation of murders and other violent crimes. Clair has also served on various boards and councils during his professional career, including the Justice Court Board of Judges, the Utah Commission on Criminal and Juvenile Justice, the Utah Judicial Council, the Utah Peace Officer Standards and Training Council, an FBI advisory board, and others.

In addition to his criminal justice work, Clair has farmed and ranched all his life. He has raised many kinds of animals, but his greatest interests are horses and cattle. He's also involved in the grocery store business with his oldest son and other family members.

Clair has served in many capacities in The Church of Jesus Christ of Latter-day Saints, including full-time missionary (California Mission), bishop, counselor to two bishops, Young Men president, high councilor, stake mission president, Scoutmaster, high priest group leader, and Gospel Doctrine teacher. He currently serves as a ward missionary.

Clair is married to Ruth, and they have five children, all of whom are married: Alan (Vicena) Poulson, Kelly Ann (Wade) Hatch, Amanda (Ben) Semadeni, Wade (Brooke) Poulson, and Mary (Tyler) Hicken.

They also have twenty-six wonderful grandchildren and two great-granddaughters.

Clair and Ruth met while both were students at Snow College and were married in the Manti Utah Temple.

Clair has always loved telling his children, and later his grandchildren, made-up stories. His vast experience in life and his love of literature have contributed to both his telling stories to his children and his writing of adventure and suspense novels.

Clair has published forty novels. He would love to hear from his fans, who can contact him by going to his website, clairmpoulson.com.